SECRET
TURNING

A Collection of Short Stories
about Life in an American Orthodox Parish

STEPHEN SINIARI

LIBRARY OF
CONGRESS
SURPLUS
DUPLICATE

ANCIENT FAITH PUBLISHING   CHESTERTON, INDIANA

Secret Turning ©2022 Stephen Siniari

All rights reserved. No part of this publication may be reproduced by any means, electronic, mechanical, photocopying, recording, scanning, or otherwise, without the prior written permission of the Publisher.

Published by:
   Ancient Faith Publishing
   A Division of Ancient Faith Ministries
   P.O. Box 748
   Chesterton, IN 46304

ISBN: 978-1-955890-17-5

Library of Congress Control Number: 2022932615

Printed in the United States of America

To

My Margot, Alexander, and Elizabeth
And to
The orphan children of Byzantium
Piteous in procession
Ragtag pilgrims of the Absolute
Scattered like star-shaped shards
Over the long veil of night
Sparks persistent
From the once luminous mosaic icon
Of life in the Garden
Stubbornly brilliant fragments
Longing for a Paradise
Long ago shattered
By selfishness, savagery, and death
The dogged Church of the Orthodox
Living inside her woundedness
Limping daily down the centuries
Looking to the Kingdom which is to come
Remembering her future
Given to her in the past
Resolute in her present
Forsaking every earthly care
Taking up her cross daily
In the face of all despair

Gathering together
The splinters of His Cross
Strewn along the narrow Way
Her steadfast heart
Clothed in the light of His Transfiguration
The Bride
Alive in the eschaton
Singing the Thrice Holy Hymn
Following the Christ of God
Like a Bridegroom in procession

Foreword

————•————

THE STORIES OF FR. STEPHEN SINIARI are different. But it is not easy to pin down just where this difference lies. This is, perhaps, because the difference lies deep.

They are, at first glance, stories like any other stories. Stories, tales, or what we post-moderns, given as we are to the impersonal, like to call narratives. They are what the Ancient Greeks simply called *mythoi*.

But they are not "just stories." They seem to somehow be true. And this is not because they represent fictionalized renderings of things that actually happened, people whom Fr. Stephen used to know. Doubtless to varying degrees they probably did, and perhaps in some cases most likely are. But be that as it may, that is not the most important kind of truth that is at work here.

Perhaps what we find in them is something like the kind of truth that we can recognize from the so-called "New Journalism," associated with Tom Wolfe and Joan Didion, both recently reposed, in which outwardly unimportant and often somewhat subjective impressions and observations are noted, strung together like colorful Christmas lights, and juxtaposed in an apparently casual way to form what gradually emerges as an overall greater truth—but one that cannot be formulated within a more linear, discursive narrative. And in this way, journalism can be made to surprise the reader with more than first meets the eye. Yes, but Fr. Stephen's stories are not documentary truths that are then crafted to make them seem like stories. Rather, they are truly stories. They abundantly possess all the integrity that genuine stories must have. While in some very important sense, they are nevertheless true.

Perhaps a better analogy might be drawn from a midnight walk that took place long ago on the campus of Oxford University. It included J.R.R. Tolkien and C. S. Lewis, and it was the occasion that finally convinced the skeptical Lewis to convert to Christianity. For being himself a literary scholar, Lewis knew that the great story of a high god who enters the world, suffers and dies and returns to life once again in order to save his people, closely resembles a central narrative of many religious traditions in the ancient world. And surely, he had long believed, this must mean that Christianity was "just a story." One among others. A most beautiful story to be sure, the most beautiful story to have been handed down from antiquity, indeed the most beautiful story in the world, but still just a story. Yet Tolkien that night, under the streetlights and walking amidst the falling leaves of autumn, managed to persuade Lewis that there could be such a thing as a "true myth"—that is, a story that had all the power and deep resonance of myth, yet that was at the same time a true story, relating something that actually had happened. Could it be, Lewis began to wonder, hoping against hope, that the most beautiful story of all, the myth that all the other salvation myths actually appeared to herald and anticipate, was itself actually true? Yes, he concluded, and he went on to become one of the twentieth century's greatest Christian apologists.

But perhaps the notion of "true myth" is not quite right. Perhaps "mythic truth" might have been an even better phrase? That's what I was thinking tonight, as I took my evening walk beneath the streetlights of a different century, a later season, and a different town, and saw all the colorful Christmas lights that had been put up everywhere, up one street and down the next street, from one side to the other. For in a secular time when the media seem to think that Christmas is about Frosty and Rudolf, ordinary people still string lights all around, on trees and bushes and lampposts, outlining houses and fences and garages. Even now, they still sense, however inchoately, that in this darkest time of the year, and even in these dark times we endure, we can still celebrate a new light that has come into the world. A barren tree is strung with glowing and sparkling lights. Color now shines abroad everywhere. Every bush is now burning. And every shepherd can hear angels singing, if only he will listen.

And all this because long ago, a baby was born to a traveling couple lacking even a real roof to cover their heads or proper walls to shield their little baby from the cold. It happened in a faraway land that even at the time seemed rather obscure and marginal and unimportant. One more baby came into the world. One more truth among others. Yet with that birth, the world was changed, the very cosmos became radically different, everyday stories now mattered because with this everyday event, God Himself had now entered the world, had truly become Emmanuel, God-with-us. The Light of Christ was now shining and glimmering all around us. The ordinary was now brightly colored. Not just kings and sages and prophets, once the only people who really mattered, but ordinary people now mattered very much, now were eminently worthy of our attention. How colorful everyday people had become, because they were now each and every one many-hued points of light, each uniquely, peerlessly mirroring the Light that has now come into the world to be with us, and to address us. Cosmology became cosmogony, a new world began, and the birth of a baby radiated unfathomable energies. Truth had become mythic, and now every other temporary event is saturated with the light of eternity—for those with eyes to see. For we are told that not just distinguished professors of astronomy from Persia, but also ordinary shepherds from the neighborhood, agrarian folk who moments before had been busy taking care of their livestock, all had eyes to see—unlike the innkeeper, who had he been able to see more clearly and more deeply would have surely given up his own sleeping quarters without hesitation. And happily for us, Fr. Stephen also has eyes to see the eternal at work in everyday events, along with the art of finding words to give it utterance. Every bush is burning, every person in these stories is aglow with light, even when in their interaction with one another, none of them are quite able to entirely see it. And who of us is able to fully grasp the eternity unfolding itself before our eyes, the mythic dimensions of the most everyday things that truly do happen?

For traditional Christianity, which we fondly call Orthodoxy, has never understood the truth as merely propositional. Indeed, our great statement of faith, finally formulated in Ancient Nikea, City of Victory, has long been called not the X-Numbered Set of Propositions, but the Symbol of Faith. And a symbol is what brings together into one, what connects and binds the temporal with the eternal, not through a series of propositions or statements, but by means of a disclosure, a manifestation—it is what helps us see. And our Lord Himself, born on earth in an uncouth cave, taught not in propositions but in strange stories that he called parables. Difficult and sometimes troubling stories that called for eyes to see and ears to hear.

Like the New Journalists, Fr. Stephen juxtaposes seemingly everyday events to present a larger truth, in this case the truth of village life unfolding in a big city. For it was in the life of the village, centered around the parish church, that Christianity grew and took shape in Europe and much of the Old World. The Church permeated every aspect of life, and it is vital for us to be reassured that this is still possible, that it is still taking place. But there is more. These stories of village life unfolding amidst the mean streets of a big city do far more than show us how Christian community can thrive even in urban America. They show us how everyday events can breathe the air of eternity, glow with the Light of Christ like the primordial light shining from that storied feed-trough in ancient Palestine. And they show us this not by recounting how other people happen to have discovered certain religious truths, but by involving us in the disclosure of those very truths themselves in the midst of our reading, while inviting us to see them unfolding in our own lives and neighborhoods. If, that is, we have ears to hear, and eyes to see.

Bruce Seraphim Foltz
Emeritus Professor of Philosophy, Eckerd College
The Synaxis of the Theotokos, December 26, 2021

Contents

Secret Turning

I. Just Saying

RED-HEADED TISSY and Dayna with the dark brown hair had known each other from second grade. They'd grown up together, from dolls to bikes to boys. Been bridesmaids at each other's weddings. Godmothers to each other's kids.

Fought with the old ladies in the Teuta Ladies Baking Society at church over whether to get new vestments for the old priest, Naum, or use the money from their bake sale to buy a DVD player for the Sunday school kids.

Both went back to work when their kids went off to college. Both liked to do yoga stretches in front of the TV and take walks together. Just two friends strolling the river-walk. They'd done it many times.

Tissy said to Dayna, "Something's bothering you."

Maybe it was the cloudy day. April along the Schuylkill could do that to you.

Dayna knew her friend could tell. She tried not to cry when she said, "My Elizabeth's gonna be a nun. She's gonna leave me and go to some monastery out in the western part of the state."

They stopped in front of the last house on Boat House Row,

the Sedgeley Club, the one with the lighthouse on Turtle Rock. They held hands and cried.

"My little girl," Dayna said. "It's the name of our church that did it."

Tissy said, "What?"

"Our church. She ended up with that boy, remember, the Muslim kid, Emir?"

Tissy said, "He was a nice kid, but . . ."

"She became Muslim," Dayna said. "She never told us. She never even told me and Joe. They were reading some Persian poet at the college. Anyhow . . ." Dayna wiped her eyes with her sleeve, put her hand through Tissy's elbow, took a folded napkin from Tissy's pocket, raised both their arms together to blow her nose, and started them walking again.

"So the boy got her to convert?" Tissy said. "And don't put that napkin back."

"No. He wasn't even religious, so he said. He thought our Lizzy was . . . I guess he thought she was going too far . . . He told her she was losing her head over some poet, getting carried away. And at that point, from what I know, that's when she dumped him."

"He was a nice kid." Tissy shrugged and made the *go figure* face.

"Anyhow, she had some dream, about Saint Alexander, from our church . . . And that started the whole nun thing."

"The Whirling Dervish." It was like Tissy was hearing it for the first time. She said, "What is a dervish, anyway? Can a Christian be a dervish?"

Dayna was shaking her head. Trying not to, wanting to say, *I heard of the church of Saint Mary of the Mongols, in Constantinople* . . . but knowing if she said it out loud she was gonna start crying again.

Tissy pushed another napkin her way.

Dayna refused it.

"Well, what'd you expect?" Tissy said. "You're the one took her to church all the time. Talking that religious talk every chance you got. Keeping your house like it was some kind of church. Icons everywhere, and incense and everything. Making your kids keep the fasts from when they were little. It was like they grew up living in a church . . .

"I mean, Dee, you're acting like it's some kinda surprise. And after what you did. The time I saw you in the hotel. Not to bring up a sore point. But a little hypocritical, wouldn't you say? I mean, Lizzy find out eventually, did she? Or'd your dumb ass feel the need to confess and tell her about you and that guy?"

Dayna froze. "What did you say?"

Tissy said, "I'm just sayin' . . ."

Dayna slapped her friend Tissy, hard across the face.

Both felt the heat.

Neither really understanding where it was coming from or why they were taking it out on each other.

One walking off hurting one way, the other standing there hurting another.

Tissy could see *Fishtown String Band* on the back of Dayna's jacket, fading like daylight down the lane of riverside trees, dissolving into dusk like mummers strutting south on Two Street at the close of the parade on New Year's Day.

Soldered to her spot by a slap, her eyes never leaving her friend, melded in place, red-headed Tissy, putting an unbelieving hand to her face, soaking up the heat from her cheek, whispering to herself, "Dee . . . I was just sayin' . . ."

II. An Innate Longing

ALEXANDER WAS A YOUNG MAN from Thessaloniki. His religious parents thought sending him almost three hundred miles away to the Aegean seaport town of Smyrna would lessen the chances of his being influenced by Islam in the Sanjak of Salanik—what the Muslim conquerors called Thessaloniki, a pivotal administrative center in that particular wedge of the Ottoman Empire.

Alexander's Orthodox parents were right to worry. They knew their kid.

From his earliest years, Mom and Pop knew Alexander to have a heightened sensitivity to the passage of time, to the fragility of life. It frightened them sometimes, their boy's fierce insistence on honesty and truthfulness.

The kid would never be satisfied with a life that had no significance beyond the temporal.

"Animals know that other thing," Alexander once told someone. "And you know they know it. You know they love you without them ever saying a word."

He was blessed and cursed, his parents said, with an innate longing, a compulsion almost, to dig for a deeper meaning in being alive.

He had some crazy idea that it was his calling to fight off

despair and darkness, and struggle for what he could only describe as light.

They did their best, his parents, even took him to the priest. But adults often underestimate a child's wonder and try to set in its place some baby explanation, a counterfeit of a truth the child already naturally possesses, already experiences, already sees.

In Smyrna, things were no different for Alexander.

There was something so familiar about the bearded old man in the long white robe repeating a short prayer, calling on the name of God, the man with the beads through his fingers. What was it about this man that made Alexander unable to resist following him?

III. Ain't Judging

IT WAS UNINTENTIONAL. They looked across the room and saw each other. A minute later Dayna got up to go to the Ladies. Tissy excused herself from her table and went too.

Dayna checked all the stalls. They were the only ones in there, looking at each other in the full wall mirror.

Dayna said, "I'm not with my husband."

"None of my business," Tissy said.

Dayna looked sick. She said, "You?"

"It's a training seminar, for work," Tissy said.

Dayna had spotted redheaded Tissy at the long table across the hotel restaurant with all the people from her office.

Tissy had seen her friend Dayna too, the long-legged brunette in the short skirt at a table for two in the corner.

Joe, Dayna's husband, was a nice guy from the neighborhood. Worked on the putty factory loading dock with all the other guys from the church. A little pudgy now. Maybe not the Joe she'd married. Beer every night on the couch'll do that to you.

The guy Dayna was holding hands and making eyes with across the hotel table was no Joe. That was for sure. Tall. Fit. Well dressed. Full head of wavy blond hair. Then again, Dayna'd kept herself pretty good too. No denying that. Girl was still a looker.

After church that Sunday Dayna pulled Tissy aside. She said to her redheaded friend, "It was a one-time thing. Seeing you, Tiss, was like a warning, a wakeup call. I thought about the kids. I told him I couldn't do it anymore."

Tissy told her friend, "Dee, I ain't judging ya."

Dayna said, "I know. I know you're not. You're not like that. If anybody had to see . . ." Dayna couldn't look Tissy in the eye. She tried to focus on Tissy's freckles.

Now, walking away, pissed, under the trees down the Parkway, away from the river, away from her Tissy, away from her best friend, Dayna suddenly stopped . . .

And Tissy almost ran up her back.

Both smiling and hugging and crying. Dayna said, "You bitch."

Tissy, smiling and crying at the same time, said, "Ah, that's my Dayna."

They held hands and walked toward the car. Tissy said, "Whaddaya know about this dervish guy?"

IV. A Secret Turning

ALEXANDER FOLLOWED THE OLD MAN through the streets of Smyrna, listening as he talked about love and service, about deserting the illusions of ego and coming to know God.

The old man said, "Remember, the deep root of your being is the presence of the only Being. Give your life to the One who already owns your breath and your movements."

Alexander said, "Pir Baba is a wise man."

The old man, Pir Baba, slapped Alexander and said, "So says Rumi."

His eyes never leaving the Sufi master, soldered by a slap, melded in place, Alexander, an unbelieving hand to his face, soaking up the heat on his cheek, followed the old man to the Tekke, the dervish lodge, whispering to himself, "Perhaps my foolishness will save me yet."

For Alexander, the path to the mystical life of Sufi asceticism started that day when he took an oath—called a *bai'at*, a word meaning "transaction"—an oath of allegiance to the old man who would become his teacher, the day Pir Baba first called him Iskandar.

Iskandar swore allegiance to the old man, Pir Baba, who was called Musa Shaikh. Iskandar repented of his sins, and the old man pronounced him *murid*, one who is committed.

Iskandar's *batin*, his life of ascetic struggle, began that day to turn in him, and to turn him in earnest toward the light.

A secret turning in us
Makes the universe turn
Head unaware of feet

And feet of head
Neither cares
They keep turning

So says Rumi, the great poet of Persia.

Sama means "listening."

Dhikr means "remembering."

Of all the dervishes in the *tekke*, the dervish lodge—those singing, those playing instruments, those reciting prayers and poetry—of all of them, it was the young man Iskandar, the convert from Thessaloniki, who was most lost within the *sama*, the spinning dervish ceremony of liturgical dance.

His tall camel-hair skufia hat, Master Musa told him, "represents the tombstone of our ego."

His wide, white skirt, billowing like a sail on the Aegean, Musa said, "represents our ego's shroud.

"When we remove our black cloak," Pir Babba Musa said, "we are spiritually born again to the truth of our being.

"When we begin the sama dance," Musa the old man instructed, "when we hold our arms crosswise, the dervish represents the number one and testifies to God's unity.

"And, while we whirl, our arms are wide open. The right arm to the sky, ready to receive God's blessing. Our left hand, upon which our eyes concentrate, is turned toward the earth.

"The *semazen*," Musa said, "sama, singer, from Arabic. And *zan*, the one who does, from Persian, is meditation put into physical form. It conveys God's gifts to those who are present and witnessing the sama dance."

Musa Shaikh began revolving from right to left, saying, "The gifts of God revolve around the heart, and we who practice sama embrace all people with love. Human beings have been created by God with love, in order to love."

Iskandar the whirling dervish seemed lost in ecstasy when Musa recited, "All loves are a bridge to divine love. Yet those who have not had a taste of it do not know! So says Rumi."

Iskandar was aiming to reach the light of perfection. He cried to God that he might abandon his egocentric existence and personal desires by hearing the mystic music of heaven with more than his ears, by focusing on God with more than his mind, spinning his body in circles as a symbol of the planets orbiting the sun.

Morning to evening he recited the prayers, coupled with the dancing and whirling, begging that he might be gifted, just for a moment, with a vision of the love of the Creator with more than his eyes.

And, as it happens to many people, Iskandar, the seeker after truth, came to know the truth of being in the suffering of others, a suffering that an honest man can't help but see as being a part of the truth of his own being, a suffering he must willingly embrace.

The suffering of people all around him who were forced to pay a yearly stupidity tax and receive a ceremonial slap with the tail of a horse because they were not enlightened enough to surrender to Allah.

People beaten and required to walk in the street where the toilets were emptied. People deprived of property and education with no standing or recourse in the courts of sharia law. People stoned and beheaded because they confessed Jesus as the Christ of God.

Was it doubly hard for Iskandar to see their suffering because they were people who had chosen not to abandon Christ but to remain Orthodox Christians?

V. Easy to Say

DAYNA SAID TO TISSY, "I don't have a problem with monastics. With people dedicating their life to the Kingdom of God, trying to make sense of this world by turning away from it, but I said to my Lizzy, what about *be fruitful and multiply?*"

Tissy said, "Yeah. Where's she think monks and nuns come from?"

Tissy was trying to get Dayna to smile. And she did.

But then Tissy said, "But what about when Jesus said, 'Not everybody can accept being a monk, but only those it's been given to.' I guess there're people born with it, people made that way by things other folks did to them, and people who make themselves monks and nuns for the sake of the Kingdom. Didn't He say, 'Let the one who can accept it, accept it?'"

"Easy to say," Dayna said. "But hard to accept, T, when it's your kid."

Tissy said, "I hear ya."

VI. Remembering

MASTER MUSA STOOD in the position of honor in the corner of the dancing place, and the dervishes passed by him three times. Each time they exchanged greetings until the circling movement of the dance began.

When it was noticed that Iskandar had become too enraptured, another Sufi, who was in charge of the orderly performance, gently touched his robe in order to curb his movement.

The one who had been Iskandar whirled to a halt.

Something was happening.

His feet were not able to stay in one place. It seemed as if the floor of the lodge were the deck of a ship caught in a storm of secret turning.

He was remembering something, remembering something from the past as a memory of the future. It was as if he could sense something or someone who was remembering him.

He thought of a story he'd heard:

A Bektashi dervish was traveling as a passenger in a rowboat going from Eminönü to Üsküdar in Istanbul when a storm blew up. The boatman tried to reassure the dervish by saying, "Fear not—God is great!" The Bektashi dervish replied, "Yes, God is great, but the boat is small."

Suddenly, the life of a religious mendicant, one who chose or accepted material poverty, began to seem to Iskandar a very small boat indeed.

He stood in wonder.

Dervishes, he understood, tried to approach God by a virtuous life and individual experience, not by scholarship. And like many dervish ascetics, he had taken a vow of poverty and begging in order to learn humility—not begging for his own good or gain but to give the collected money to other poor people.

Days, he begged, and in the evening he earned money cleaning fish in the market. He had been obedient to Musa in the *tariqa*, the place where the lessons were offered. Where the path was laid out that might lead one to the ultimate truth, the path desired by every mystic.

But now

As he stood melded in place

Realizing he was alone in a vortex of individuals
The circular motion of the others
As they continued to whirl
Formed a cavity
In the center of his being
That seemed to draw
The light away
In a whirlpool of chaos
And that which
He had thought
To be light
Began suddenly to mock him
And blackness descended
Like a starless sky
Over the tombs of those
Bound alone in their grave clothes
Descended over the tombs of the deceived
The black matter so intense
It smothered the shrouded Alexander
Like the lid of a coffin
Blinded by the lie
That life could be
A voyage without others
No longer able to see
Anything beyond
The confines of his isolated being

He lifted his head and removed the camel-hair hat. "Mulla," he said, "I was an Orthodox Christian, and because of my foolishness, I denied my faith and became a Muslim. I have realized my former faith was light, which I lost, while your faith, as I have come to know it, is darkness."

Iskandar had seen the cruel treatment of those who were not Muslim. The same torture he had seen, he knew he would soon endure.

"So I come before you to confess," Alexander said. "I have made a mistake by denying the light and accepting darkness. I was born an Orthodox Christian. I want to die an Orthodox Christian."

Those present thought they were listening to a madman. One by one, beginning with the mulla, they began to plead with him, in all kindness, to come to his senses. How could he, a dervish, shame his religion?

"Behold, Mulla," Alexander said, "you have heard my decision. Now do to me whatever you wish. For I am ready to endure every torture, even spill my blood, for the love of my Jesus Christ, whom I wrongly denied."

Alexander, who was aiming to reach the light of perfection, had cried to God that he might abandon his egocentric existence and personal desires and hear the mystic music of heaven with more than his ears, by focusing on God with more than his mind, by spinning his body in circles as a symbol of the planets orbiting the sun.

Morning to evening he had recited the prayers, coupled with the dancing and whirling, begging that he might be gifted, just for a moment, with a vision of the love of the Creator with more than his eyes.

And, as it happens to many people, Alexander came to know the truth of being in the suffering of others, a suffering that an honest man can't help but see and embrace as a being who is a part of a community of beings, a part of the truth of his own being.

Alexander was arrested on the most serious charge—that of having made a profession of faith in Islam and now deciding to retract it.

They had given him the chance to return to Islam or face torture and execution.

Everyone knew Islamic law forbade forced conversions. Still, at certain times, in certain circumstances and places, even people who profess love give in to their frustration.

Even people claiming to seek after the truth become persecutors of the worst sort. And where in history is a religious group free from this infestation of evil?

VII. Religious Types

DAYNA MET WITH TISSY later in the evening. "Joe and I been talking."

"What'd Joe say?" Tissy asked.

"He said at least we'd have somebody up at the monastery now praying for us."

Made Tissy laugh.

Dayna said, "You gonna go and visit her with me when I go?"

Tiss said, "Long as I don't have ta wear one a them robes."

Dayna told Tissy, "I think about his parents . . . Saint Alexander."

They were both quiet for a while.

Then Tissy said, "You ask Prifti 'bout your Lizzy?" Meaning the priest.

Dayna nodded.

"What'd he say?"

"Naum was sad himself," Dayna said. "He has a kid. He asked me—well, no . . . What he did was, he told me, when he feels like his kid hurt him or let him down by some decision his kid made, or something the kid actually went and did, Naum asks himself, 'I ever let God down? I ever make a decision, even think about doing something, or do the thing I was thinking of doing . . . a thing or a thought that hurts God, makes God sad? What my kid's done to me? I've done to God.

"'And then I ask myself,' Naum said, 'how my thoughts and actions against God compare with what my kid decided, or did, that makes me sad—and how it may or may not have hurt me—and usually that's enough to make me put my hand over my mouth.'"

Dayna said, "Then Naum and I made the cross and just sat there and didn't say anything else."

Redheaded Tissy knew they were probably both saying some kind of prayer. Two religious types, what else would they be doing, sitting there quiet?

But redheaded Tissy didn't say so.

VIII. Holy Martyr Alexander, Pray for Us

MANY PEOPLE—Muslims, Orthodox Christians, Westerners, and Armenians—gathered for the execution of Alexander.

Alexander stood in the center.

The executioner flashed his sword in front of Alexander's eyes to frighten him.

But the martyr remained unaffected. "I will not exchange the light for darkness," he said. "I worship Father, Son, and Holy Spirit, the Trinity consubstantial and undivided." And he made the sign of the cross.

Alexander was ordered to kneel, at which point the order came for a stay of execution.

They waited for an hour, hoping the stay of execution would give him time to consider and change his mind.

Alexander prayed. But he did not change his mind.

So Alexander the Whirling Dervish from Thessaloniki sacrificed his life for the love of Jesus Christ, in the city of Smyrna, Asia Minor, on May 26, 1794.[*]

Holy Martyr Alexander, pray for us.

---

[*] Father Michael Vaporis first related the story of Saint Alexander more than thirty-five years ago during a breakfast visit at the author's home in Massachusetts.

Tea with Misto

ONE AFTERNOON IN SUMMER, Antigone, one hundred and three, decided to visit with her older cousin, one-hundred-and-five-year-old Olga, and one of the younger girls from the church, Nunna Durres.

Not even her children were sure if the date on Nunna Durres's old-country birth certificate, which would have made her ninety-three, was correct.

"Do you drive?" Kusheri Nastradin asked Antigone.

One hundred and three. She smiled. Antigone.

"You did," Nastradin said. "I remember seeing you coming to church with all the Sunday school kids in the back of your husband Misto's big blue Buick. You went house to house collecting them."

"I did," she said.

Kusheri said, "When did you get your license?"

She smiled.

Kusheri Nastradin had arranged to have his friend Jimmy Miller bring his limo, on his day off, and drive the girls to the Crystal Tea Room on the ninth floor of John Wanamaker's Department Store in downtown Philadelphia.

Hats and white gloves. One-hundred-and-five-year-old Olga, in her pearl Sunday dress. The one she was so proud of. The one she said made her feel young. The one she wanted to be buried in. The dress with the tiny red flowers and a matching pill-box hat . . . "I would look good for the Kentucky Derby."

Antigone? Her favorite color was green. Had been since she was a girl. Any shade of green, but most especially emerald green, the way her husband, Misto, described her eyes.

The same color as the U-neck, half-sleeve, calf length dress she wore, with the cinnamon trim and belt and the buckle shaped like twin shells.

To Kusheri Nastradin, whatever Antigone wore, or maybe it was the way she wore it, somehow brought to mind the traditional Albanian way of dressing.

The young Mrs. Durres, ninety-three, Daphnia's mother, had been a widow for more than forty years. And in all those years, no one had ever seen Nunna Durres in anything other than black. Even up to the day of her daughter's wedding. Black shoes. Black head covering. Black glasses. Black gloves and a black sweater she had knit. Even her *bastun*, her cane, the one she used to poke people with, was black.

So you can imagine the shock when Nunna Durres came out to Jimmy Miller's limo fresh from Besa's Beauty Salon, wearing the same outfit she'd worn to her daughter's wedding. Smiling like Queen Teuta in her silver-rimmed glasses. Wearing a dress the color of cantaloupe and honeydew with a watermelon-red pillbox hat dotted with black seeds in a summer melon pattern.

So proud, Nunna Durres. Fine white gloves. A new walnut

gold-knobbed cane gripped in her right hand. Her never-before-seen handbag. Fat and shiny as an overripe papaya.

Old man Shook, the proprietor of Shooky's Taproom, who knew a thing or two about the restaurant business, was jealous when he heard about the nunnas' expedition.

He told Kusheri Nastradin, "The Crystal Tea Room, my friend, is the largest dining room in Philadelphia. Probably in the world."

Kusheri was worried Jimmy might not find parking for the limo. "I don't want my nunnas to have to walk too far."

Shook told Kusheri, "Parking schmarking. That dining room is worth the walk. Just to see inside it. Serves over a thousand people at a time. They got breakfast like you wouldn't believe. Luncheon? Out of this world. And what're you going for, afternoon tea? Aye! Like heaven.

"The queen of England would curtsy," Shook said.

Kusheri said, "You know anything about what they got for parking?"

"Parking, again? The kitchen's ovens," old man Shook said, "can roast seventy turkeys at a time."

"But parking, Herr Shook," Kusheri said.

When Kusheri asked Prifti Naum about parking, Naum said, "Drop them at the door, there's a doorman at Wanamaker's to help them, and then have Jimmy drive the limo to our downtown church and park there. Be about a seven-block walk back for you and Jimmy."

Kusheri said, "Too far."

Naum said, "It's free."

Kusheri said, "Close enough."

Jimmy said he'd wait for the pick-up call in the limo.

Antigone and her husband, Misto, were a match marriage in the old country, promised by their fathers when they were infants.

When they married, she was thirteen, and he was fifteen.

The day of the wedding, the old men in the village told Misto he had to hit his wife. He had to make clear from the beginning his station and her place.

The families were listening outside the newlywed room the first night. They could hear everything.

"It was loud." Misto was one hundred and five when he told Naum.

When they emerged in the morning, the young Misto had two black eyes.

She had given as good as she got.

One-hundred-and-five-year-old Misto told Naum, "I never hit her again."

Naum said, "No wonder, Babagjysh, she would've killed you."

One-hundred-and-three-year-old Antigone sat crocheting.

Naum asked her, "Nunna, in all your years of marriage, did you ever consider divorce?"

Antigone listened, making loops in thread with an olive-wood crochet hook. A slender shaft interlocking stitches. Her crooked fingers working the hook as gracefully as a young bride, lithe and listening to the story she'd heard many times. The story about their first night.

The priest had asked, "Did you ever consider divorce, Nunna?"

"I considered murder." She didn't miss a stitch. Not a half. Not a double. Not a treble or a Granny Stripe stitch.

Her glasses were thick, but when she stopped crocheting to

examine Naum's reaction over the lenses, the priest could see why Misto loved the emerald mischief in her eyes.

Misto knew.

He knew his Antigone knew.

Every week after liturgy the old couple took home a portion of the *antidoron*, the blessed bread. Its name means "instead of the gift." In Albanian we call it *nafora*. Antigone and Misto kept a portion of the nafora and made it last throughout the week.

Every morning they went to their icon corner.

Every morning they prayed.

They started each day with a sip of holy water and a nibble of the nafora, the bread blessed by the priest at Sunday liturgy.

When they could no longer sleep in the same bed, twin beds were pushed close together, a little space between.

Misto and Antigone held hands all night across the space.

———

ON THE DAY ANTIGONE, Olga, and young Nunna Durres went to Wanamaker's Crystal Tea Room, the priest Naum visited with Antigone's husband, Misto.

They sat together under a makeshift awning in Misto's Orange Street backyard.

Misto plopped down in his favorite chair, what people used to call a beach chair or a lawn chair. Aluminum tube framing with green-and-white vinyl webbing sagged to just the right tensile stretch of bottom-hugging perfection.

The plastic armrests were worn so smooth, it made you want to do what old man Shook called, "Der Schlittschuhläufer-Walzer, the Skater's Waltz, by good old Émile Waldteufel.

Close your eyes and skate your fingers in figure eights around the well-worn armrests. Put your head back, close your eyes and hum the waltz . . ."

Once Misto got to doing that, there was no getting him out of his chair.

He motioned to the coral-colored two-seat rusty metal glider and said to Naum, "Sit."

Naum sat.

Propped against the back wall of the two-story brick row home sat a scrap-wood homemade bench. Long and low and bowed in the middle. Its weather-worn silhouette looked like it was crying for help. Straining with the last of its plywood fiber to support the bulky old Philco TV, rabbit ears and all, which Naum was pretty sure hadn't tasted electricity since the Fishtown Power Plant went online at the end of Lewis Street at the river in the 1920s and lit up the night with the white light sign you couldn't miss coming over the Ben Franklin from Jersey: *Philadelphia the Electric City.*

"Now, cornflakes?" Misto said.

"I like cornflakes."

"With tea?" Misto said.

"Sure," Naum said.

"Then go make it," Misto said. "And for me, and toast, please."

Naum stood. He'd been to the house many times before.

Misto said, "You get lost, we sending Çerçiz Topulli the hero to find you."

Naum said, "He get a new donkey?"

Misto told him, "Oh, so now you *batakçi*?" (trickster).

"Sorry, Babagjysh."

"I am no ancient. So make Babagjysh toast. Two pieces, *me pelte, rrush*, please."

"With grape jelly," Naum reminded himself.

Naum came back and set the TV tray between them.

Misto said, "You forget icon."

When Naum returned, he placed the icon on the tray.

They made the prayer.

Naum sat down and said, "I wanted to hear what you told Kusheri Nastradin about the saints."

Misto took a spoonful of cornflakes. He said, "Bananas?"

Naum pointed to the tray, bananas and a knife.

Misto said, "You think of everything. Tea?"

Naum said, "Yes."

Misto said, "Antigone make with lots of lemons."

Naum apologized for the one lemon slice floating in the tea.

Misto sliced the banana onto his cornflakes and poured the tea over the top. He said, "Okay. Nastradin tell about saints. And you believe? Okay. So now I tell?"

Naum said, "Yes."

Misto said, "It's true, what I'm say. No matter what Nastradin says . . . So, still you gonna hear?"

Naum knew it would be three times. He said, "Yes, please."

Misto said, "I only tell Nastradin because he trick me. You no gonna trick me too?"

Naum said, "Only if I have to."

"Ah . . ." Misto said, "I can no trick you."

Naum took a bite of toast, lifted the bowl of cornflakes off the table, and sat back.

Misto liked to tell the story, and Naum liked Misto.

He said, "When I was young man I escape from Turkish army."

"They conscripted you?"

"My father, good man, had enough to bribe *beys* (local officials) for my brothers, but no' for me. I was youngest. He give me pistol instead. But they catch me anyway and take me."

"Is it true you hid in the outhouse for an entire night while they searched your father's property?"

"*Po* (yes). Up to here. They look in, but no look down. Sure, laugh now, but no funny when brothers bring me out. Big smell."

"But eventually the Turks did find you and drag you away. They were gonna send you to fight in Africa, right?"

"Po. But I no go. I'm making plan to come back to my Antigone. But telling no one. No soldier. No friend. No one. They no' speaking our language, you understand? Speak me in Greek or Turk. *Kuptoni ju?*" (Understand?)

Naum nodded.

One-hundred-and-five-year-old Misto took a soft pebbled oblong folding leather wallet from his inside pocket and showed Naum the priest.

A sepia-tone young Misto
In Turkish uniform
A trim full beard
Proud in the fustanella
The pleated skirt draping just below the knee
A colorfully decorated mendani waistcoat
Detached sleeves folded over his shoulders
From the sleeveless heavy fermeli linen coat
His selachi belt cinched around his waist

Silver embroidered over the fustanella
A cross-body bandolier of bullets
Over his long thick hair
A fez-like cap
Opingari calfskin shoes
The kind with red woolen balls on the upturned tips
A long rifle angled across his chest
And a Suleyman bursa dagger like death in his belt

"One night I'm thinking my plan. With rifle. Sit by fire. Shen Gjergi dhe Shen Demetrios, *appear*—to me."

"Saint George and Saint Demetrios? Both at the same time?"

"Po. In Turk uniform, like officer."

"The saints? In uniform?"

"Sure, uniform. They soldiers. They say me, 'What you got in mind to do, do now.'

"But all around, Turcoman soldiers. Musselem. Guards. Officers looking. Tents twist top like cones. Rifles lean. Stacks. Like points on tent. And other tents too. Like square rooms. Flags above. Mules. Carts. Horses. Wagons. No end to see. Cannon and cook fires. Make the smoke, lots of smoke. And the fires light up enemy heads and deserter heads, heads cut off on tall spikes.

"How can I do this? Make escape like this?"

"What did you do?" Naum said.

"The saints appear again. This time, no got uniform, but like icons. So what they say this time, I do. 'What you have in mind to do, do. Do now. *Tani*! Now!' So I get up, put rifle in stack, and walking, walking, and no looking back. Just keep walking, walking. Not run. Saints say no run, no to run.

"Afraid? Sure, but I was so much missing mother and new wife, and wanting to go home, and more afraid to no do what saints tell me do.

"I don't care, *Urata*, I just trusting deh Got, and the saints. You understand, yes? And walk, walk, on muddy road. Not even knowing where Misto is going. Walk, walk, dark night, no look back. Dragging mud with balls on shoes."

In a strange land with no idea where to go, Misto walked toward the lights of a seaport town, where by chance in a small group, he heard his native language being spoken.

After helping him dispose of his uniform and finding him a suit of baggy clothes, the good Samaritans booked him on board the ship they were taking. He was hidden by villagers in the mountains on the Greek border, still miles from his home.

Ottoman sympathizers living in the village were constantly threatening to report the strange young Christian to the local bey, the overlord. But the bey already knew he was there.

Misto told Naum, "Any day, they could take my head."

Naum set his cornflakes to the side.

"For long time, Urata, I living, eat nothing but bread and soup kind ladies bring me. And berries. Each berry I pray, 'O God, have mercy on me, sinner.' All day, pray. Living with animals in cave in mountain. Praying, praying, all time, praying. They thinking I must be some kind monk, or holy man, with big beard now, but is only Misto."

He put his hands on his knees and laughed. "Me. Monk."

Misto told Naum the son of a nearby prominent Moslem family became ill with fever and an earache that caused him such pain, his family was sure the boy would die.

The bey sent for the holy man living on stale bread in a cave with animals.

"I no doctor. What I can do? Pray. Pray like my mother. '*O Zoti Jesu Krisht, shërues i shpirtit dhe i trupit*, healer of souls and bodies . . .'

"I do what I see her do, and grandmother. I make olive oil hot, no, no hot, warm. And stirring, stirring, with little *bosilok* (sweet basil) and ginger, grinding, grinding fine like powder, other things mother show, yarrow, zambak, make salt, little bit, wine, maybe vinegar, wine, no remember, squeezing onion, make liquid.

"Then Misto praying to deh Got to help this boy. To help Misto. Make cross, three times, over oil. They hold boy, screaming boy, pour in ear, three times, *Ati dhe Biri dhe Shpirti Shent . . .* (the Father and the Son and the Holy Spirit).

"He crying, but next day. Boom. All gone, earache. All better. After this, no report Misto, but big Lord Bey help Misto go home."

Stories and backyard sun have a way of making old men sleepy.

⊷━◆━⊶

JIMMY MILLER COULD BARELY SQUEEZE the limo down Orange Street. He told everybody, "Hold your breath."

Kusheri Nastradin said, "It's good we dropped Miss Olga and Nunna Durres first. We'd have to grease the curbs if they were still here."

Antigone said, "Good we no live around corner on Miller Street. Even more tighter."

The house was quiet when she went inside.

Antigone took off her hat. She put her gloves on the table next to the sofa. Walked through to the kitchen, green-eyed Antigone, and saw an empty bowl in the sink. "Ah, cornflakes. And toast. And tea." She could tell. "With bananas."

There they were in her yard. The two of them.

Dreaming of twisted-top tents made of Turkish delight.

Her Misto in his chair. And Prifti Naum stretched out on the coral-colored glider.

On the table was an untouched bowl of cornflakes and the icon of Saint George and Saint Demetrios.

Antigone knew her Misto had been telling his story.

She could hear him saying, "It's true, what I'm say."

She wondered if Prifti believed him. She wondered if anybody believed him.

You know what they say in the neighborhood about stories like that. Prob'ly. Prob'ly not.

But Antigone?

She knew boys were happiest when they were telling stories.

She kissed both on the head.

One hundred and three.

Antigone didn't need believing. Antigone knew.

Antigone knew.

Crazy Faith

⟶⬥⟵

NAUM'S FATHER CONFESSOR told him seven things.

"The enemy is becoming more visible all the time.

"A good deal of the irresolvable troubles you encounter will be from people who are not from your parish and who do not support the work of the gospel in the parish community in any material way, not so much as a *meshe*, but only come to take.

"There will be people coming into the faith who will wander from church to church, looking for the perfect priest and the perfect parish.

"The enemy will delude them into believing their issues are the spiritual struggles they've read about in ascetic literature.

"They will many times be well-read 'theologians,' not at all like what our Greek brethren call *Yia Yia theologians*. You know very well the ones I'm talking about—our good, spiritually perceptive, honest women, our grandmothers and mothers. They will *not* be like them.

"These poor people will think nothing of taking up all your time and depriving your faithful of their spiritual father.

"You will know them because they are people who will not accept it when you offer the Cross.

"Christians know, in life," Naum's confessor told him, "we will suffer with Christ."

Naum said, "I will know them by their fruits, Father?"

"No," his confessor said. "You'll know them by their crazy faith."

NALANI WAS OLD-TIME Philadelphia gentry with family homes downtown on Rittenhouse Square and up in Chestnut Hill. She had been attending on and off for several months. She was one of the few who never missed Orthros or Vespers.

She rode three-seat tandem with the charismatic slain-in-the-spirit Dolly and her husband, the icon expert, Doctor Rosko, translator of Greek patristic classics and professor of esoteric heremetic philosophy. All three having much to contribute at study groups.

Happy fellow travelers going church to church for weekday liturgy and meeting after in coffee shops to critique rubrics, celebrants, and westernized icons.

"Let's meet in Chestnut Hill at the end of the 23 line," Nalani told Naum. "I know a great little art-house coffee shop not far from my summer home right where the trolley turns around. It's called the Mocha Goat."

"And things are tight right now," Priftereshe Greta told him. "No extra money for the next month, the putty factory being closed, two-week mandatory vacation? You go easy on that car."

He called Madeline and told her he wouldn't be able to make his regular study group with the Teuta Ladies Baking Society.

He heard her pretend to cover the phone and tell the ladies, "The one who calls herself Nalani. Her. He's going to see. Again."

Whenever the priest asked Nalani her baptismal name, she always changed the subject, saying, "Someone has to be the first Orthodox Nalani, no?"

Carol said, "Yeah, her name's Elaine. In my consignment shop every other week. Her real name's on her checks."

Naum felt bad when Madeline said, "No problem, Father. Maybe next time."

He had a hell of a time bumping up Germantown Avenue over the cobblestoned trolley tracks in his lemon-cream '66 Impala beater. Every jolt caused a vibration that made him sure the next axle-cracker would be the one that snapped his lug nuts and made the wheels fall off.

When she entered the frame and stepped into the arched doorway of the Mocha Goat, the slim silhouette of tall Nalani toting a pooch in a baby pouch was projected like a negative image backlit in sunlight.

Naum the priest squatted behind a stubby-legged table on a low-slung sofa. When his old knees tottered, coagulated espresso ordered almost an hour before did the shimmy around the rim of the demitasse cups and pooled in the shallow conduits circling the bottom of the porcelain saucers.

She said, "Ah, you didn't have to stand for me."

He checked the front of his cassock for splatter.

Nalani looked at the puddled espresso and said, "Oh, Naum, you ordered for both of us? Aren't you sweet?"

She gestured to the drinks and said to the barista, "Come and take these away, sweetie, will you, please?"

The speakers were putting out a low-frequency mix of melodies and mantras. Nalani moved the white dog in the pouch to the beat. "Snatam Kau." She said. "You like?"

Naum smiled.

She asked if she was *very* late.

The barista interrupted. "Your usual, Nay-Nay?"

She said, "Yes. And for Girard. Thank you."

Nalani put Girard on a mat under her chair and told Naum he was a bichon frise. The stuffed-doll dog with the button-black stare.

The kid with the jet-blue hair, the piercings, and the purple forelock over one eye returned with panini sandwiches and coffee.

Nalani had ordered for all three of them.

"Bring napkins," she told the kid. "They never bring napkins."

The barista piled a stack of napkins on the table and slid a saucer underneath to Girard.

"Ah, nirvana on a plate," Nalani said. "Chao Tofu and Quorn Roast Turkey . . . The best vegan in the city." And she bent to break Girard's sandwich into bite-sized pieces.

Raisins. Some kind of onion-bialy roll with a skirt of green and purple-edged leaf Naum couldn't identify. Pesto spread with nut chunks. Funny-looking cheese. Specks in it.

The coffee cup was small. Small and geometrically hard to handle. Oddly warped handleless ceramic. Two hands to lift. Sitting on an oversized saucer. Just a sip and a sigh and Naum could see the mottled bottom.

Nalani said it was a liquid morsel.

Nalani smiled.

She had a beautiful mouth.

There was an earthy sensuality
About the woman
With the precisely
Messy hair
Words like *fecundity*
Hearty roots
And good stock
Reached across the table
In a subtle exhalation
As each breath
Caused the rise and fall
Of her dove-gray turtleneck
Legs stretched out
Crossed at the ankles
Fashion-forward
Hole-in-the-knee jeans
Paddock boots
Perfectly dappled in their broken-in prime

Attire so nonchalantly put together, Nalani would have fingered her one-loop gold earring and answered, "No, just something I threw on."

When Nalani booted up her 12.9-inch iPad, Naum asked for more coffee. She texted for three refills and said to Naum, "Freshly ground each time, by hand. So, while we're waiting . . . Let me enhance your visuals and color your senses."

One-minute Instagram videos—fifteen-second TikTok clips
Metempsychosis rebirthing
Channeling with crystals

Otzi the Iceman and his karmic body art

Astral-projecting the Tao in Christ

Environmental Eucharistic Ecology . . .

"They were all part of my God-intended pilgrimage from universal consciousness to Orthodox consciousness. Father Justin, who received me out in New Mexico, called it my Illumination.

"He'd seen my website and the list of all the Orthodox things I'd read and recommended to my online followers. I'm an *influencer*, Naum.

"He said the forty days of Great Lent would be more than enough time, and when I opened my eyes, I was in the ultimate state of Orthodox soteriological release.

"Frankly, Naum, I haven't felt so alive since I stood there barefoot on that Saltillo Mexican tile floor, free . . . Wearing nothing but a smile and that gauzy white Bottega Veneta sheer.

"Truthfully, as a priest of the mystic, I'd have you illumine me once a month if you'd do it. But what the Yogini channeled through me, when I was back East in the ashram, before my current illumination, well, no offense, but be better if we took the time to know each other a little first, wouldn't you say? After what that bastard tried to do to me, or tried to get me to do to him."

She took a moment to adjust the piercing in her nose. "I mean, right?"

Nalani had all the answers. She had all the questions.

She told Naum, "My partner keeps getting sick, despite my vitamin regime. And as for me, I have a great idea for a consignment shop, but she's of no help while she's sick, and I'm praying for the best thing to happen.

"And I'm having a hard time with the news these days, Naum. The fires in Australia. Millions of kangaroos and koala bears. Just hearing about it breaks my heart. That, and what's going on in the Middle East. And our repressive oligarchy here at home. It drains all my karmic energy and commits murder on my motivation. There are times when I really wonder how God can stand it when I know He sees it all."

When she noticed she was doing all the talking and Naum had gone quiet, she said, "And believe me, I understand your silence. And I can tell by your colors that you think it makes you appear very wise. But I can also feel your disruption. The aura around you is not a healthy emanation. At least not in your present specific. It isn't hard to see you're just getting by at Saint Alexander's . . .

"Well, I guess we'll all just have to hang in and maybe the rumor that the bishop is going to ordain Dionysios the Deacon . . . But that's not until summer. Long time away. But if we get to August and the karmic flame doesn't improve . . . Well, I'm no prophet, but we may have to rethink our commitment, Dolly, the professor, and me.

"Saint Alexander's is so different than the church we came from in New Mexico. It's not unfriendly, but it's not friendly either.

"My partner and I probably won't stay in Philadelphia anyway. She's dying to retire to Los Ranchos de Albuquerque. You'd love it. You could even bring your wife. I'd love to live there and help Father Justin with his healing ministry. But we'll see what happens."

When Naum said he was curious about how many funerals

she'd attended . . . The light in her clear gray eyes showed she was consciously channeling patience.

She said, "Enough."

Nalani channeled the same forbearance when Naum asked how much of the New Testament she'd read. She said, "Ah . . . Such a lovely simple priest from such a simply lovely little parish . . . in *Fishtown.*"

Nalani had the whitest teeth.

Her *It's okay, I know you can't help it if you're from* smile when she said, *Fishtown . . .*

The Hebrew tattoo in the web between her forefinger and thumb when she put her hand over his, the knotted red bracelet he'd never noticed on her left wrist.

"You know very well, Father Naum," his confessor told him, "our women, our grandmothers and mothers. *Nunna knowledge.* Women who for generations have lived and, by the grace of God, have kept the faith as it was first delivered. Let the new ones sent by God, men and women, stay by the old nunnas for at least two years."

Nalani put the iPad away and plied Naum with a table full of pamphlets on healthy living and vitamin supplements.

"I'm a certified natural healer, Naum. You knew that, right? And I can actually diagnose the deep disharmony you're carrying. By your breathing. Your chakra colors. The smell of your . . ."

The wind-chime ringtone started. The screen on her smartphone was no smaller than the screen on Naum's first TV.

She said, "I do have to take this, one of my patients, *my* flock, needs their mother."

Nalani said, "Oh, my dear Dolly," went outside, and disappeared behind the potted palms.

Naum didn't want to leave without saying goodbye but after half an hour, when the barista brought his credit card and had him sign . . . No free refills at the Mocha Goat, like at Betty's Café.

Later, when Naum gave her the bill, forty-eight dollars and sixty-eight cents, Priftereshe Greta explained, "You didn't have to leave another three dollars, darling. Look." She pointed to the receipt. "Twenty percent gratuity included."

———◆———

ON SUNDAY RABBI SAW NAUM locking up after liturgy. "Father," he said, "have a minute?"

Naum crossed the street to the temple.

His old friend told Naum, "So, I hear a couple of yours have become a couple of ours, sort of . . ."

Naum said, "Not the first time, Rabbi. Big conversion, Russia, the 1500s . . . Two Greek priests became Jewish and led hundreds with them."

"Not that," Rabbi said. "But you've maybe heard of Rav Yehuda Ashlag?"

It wasn't hard to tell when Naum was stumped on a crossword clue . . . Rabbi could see it.

"Well," Rabbi said, "then let me give you another clue. Madonna. Lindsay Lohan. Britney Spears. Roseanne Barr. Sandra Bernhard. Enough?"

Naum still didn't get it.

"Yehuda Ashlag, the early 1920s, one of the founders, the

Kabbalah thing. Right here in Philadelphia. Bigger than ever now with these New Agers.

"Maybe you've seen the young folks with the Hebrew-letter tattoos. The knotted red bracelets. Kabbalah, my good friend. They say it's a sect of Judaism. Purports to explain the relationship between the eternal, unchanging God and our mortal, finite world."

Rabbi Aaron said, "They think there's an alphanumeric code hidden in the Scripture that has a mystical interpretation, predict your future, even yours, Naum."

Naum said, "I coulda used that prediction yesterday."

"Well, Father," Rabbi said, "I got a call from Malka, one of our students downtown. Bright kid. Attended a session for a comparative religions class she's taking. They don't take notes anymore, these young ones, Naum. She videoed the whole thing. I can have her text you an Insta . . ."

Naum shook his head, no. "But thanks."

"Well," Rabbi said, "your Nalani and your couple, the married ones with the four-door Jaguar who preach and have visions on the college campus, Doctor Rosko, the translator, and Dolly, that's his wife, right, and is he the one who's always fainting, or is it her?"

"Her." Naum smiled and said, "Slain in the spirit."

Rabbi said, "Okay, then. And *gut mazi* to them. There they were in one of the brownstones on Rittenhouse Square, five-and-a-quarter million that building. Saw it in the Sunday real estate section coincidentally, right off the Square on Delancey Place.

"Turns out it was where Nalani's mother used to live. The three of them described their spiritual pilgrimage. Malka got it all on video. Said your Orthodox faith and church had served them well but was now a skin they must shed on their journey. Time to leave that particular body, to discard that shell, is how they put it, in order to progress toward uniting Shekhinah and Tiferet to restore God to a state of wholeness."

Rabbi saw Naum's bewilderment and said, "Which, as you know, Naum, is the ultimate good and goal of Kabbalah. No easy feat, of course, *restoring God* . . . good Father."

———

NAUM WAS EARLY when the Teuta Ladies Baking Society met in the church hall for their weekly meshe baking and Bible Study session.

The smell of the meshes rising, the sound of the ladies laughing and telling stories in the church hall . . .

They were gathered around Ramona's iPad, watching a video history of the parish.

"Oh, and look, look at the ladies bringing the platters of *lakror*." (Albanian spinach pie.)

"*Burek*, we called it." (Another regional name for the same dish the Greeks call *spanakopita*.)

"Oh, there's Thomaidha."

"Ooo . . . Thomaidha, smiling, always smiling."

"There, there, look. There's her Christie she lost in the war."

"Ah . . . look. He's putting his arm around her and kissing her. Ah . . . He loved his mother."

"She never got over that. Always crying out his name. Christie, my Christie. Lighting candles."

"And she was a widow even then. Can you imagine?"

"And the way that woman took care of her mother-in-law."

"Eugenia."

"And even with all that, neither one of them ever missed church. Her or her mother-in-law. Walked. No matter. Weather. No car. Sick. Nothing."

"And Saturday when the sun went down . . . Nothing. No washing your hair. No sewing. The meshe was already at the church so the priest could have the bread for early Sunday morning."

"Thomaidha and Eugenia."

"And they were always at the church, cleaning, polishing, decorating, saying the prayers, doing something."

"You kidding? Their generation? Practically lived at the church. Kept it cleaner than their own house."

"How long did she nurse that old woman?"

"Eugenia? Her mother-in-law? Had to be thirty years."

"Oh my. Can you imagine?"

"That's love. Thomaidha used to quote Shen Timotheu, 'Anyone doesn't provide for his relatives, and especially for members of his household, has denied the faith and is worse than an unbeliever.'"

"You know the both of them could read."

"And that was not the norm. The Turks wouldn't let the women learn."

"You remember the two of them teaching Sunday school?"

"Who do you think taught our Nina, who taught all of us?"

"That was faith."

"Yeah. Crazy faith."

Naum was watching with the ladies at the flour-dusted counter. Happy Naum.

At home he told Priftereshe Greta, "Big difference, our ladies, they just believe."

"Well," Priftereshe said, "maybe you'll finally learn. The fancy God talk? Suckers you every time, the Byzantine froufrou. Just got a knack for attracting those kinda birds, don'tcha?"

Naum opened a napkin full of kurabia, Bernice's specialty, butter cookies covered in powdered sugar. Greta loved the way they melted in her mouth.

She noticed he wasn't eating and said, "You already ate yours, didn't you?"

He nodded.

She said, "Go ahead, you can have one of mine, Mister Mocha Goat, only forty-eight dollars, tip included."

Sign

—⇒◆⇐—

THEIR TELEPHONE BLINKED RED when it rang. The doorbell too. Neither mother nor father could speak to or ever hear their only child. But their son, Bobby, he could speak and hear.

And he signed too. That's how they talked, him and Mom and Pop.

He was a tough guy, Bobby. Came to work at the putty factory in our neighborhood right out of the Marines. The man could fix anything.

Rode an old-school chopper with chrome Z-bar handlebars that curved out and back.

Wore little khaki short-shorts, even in the winter, and red ankle socks with cut-off T-shirts. Biceps like boulders. Jump-boots and a Marine Corps cap.

"Why?" I asked him.

"Just to piss people off."

We'd get in conversations at lunch on the loading dock, and dude never failed to bring up something about religion or the church.

I told my wife, Judy, "This guy's driving everybody nuts. All he wants to do is argue."

Judy's no dummy. She said, "Tell him to talk to Naum."

Yeah. Why talk to me? I'm just a civilian working at a putty factory. But religion? That's Naum's neighborhood.

Here were two custom-made pains in everybody else's rear when it came to ruining a conversation by always bringing up what Naum called "the one thing needful." Not a clue where he gets lines like that?

Judy, my wife, kissed me on the head and said she loved me.

Seemed like every day, good old Naum clenched his jaw, climbed in the ring, and kept stepping into the punch till it made his ears ring.

I told Judy, "I think Naum likes it."

It confused me when Judy told me I was less than an idiot. She said it was a kind of endearment.

I said, "Oh, okay." I was afraid to ask her what *endearment* meant.

Naum told Judy he welcomed any chance to offer a different way of looking at our relationship with a Being who was too simple for complicated concepts and too complex for easy clichés.

He said it was the only way he knew to fight the good fight and experience the reality of life not defined by separation and death.

Naum and Bobby got to be buddies.

Bobby told Naum, "I betcha we were shipmates in a previous life."

When Naum seemed doubtful, Bobby grabbed Naum hard by his wrist and said, "In fact, I have a strong sense we served together in the American Asiatic Squadron under Commodore

Dewey at the Battle of Manila Bay in the Philippines back in 1898, fighting the Spanish–American War."

Naum suggested they go over to the corner store across from Palmer Burial Ground and get a coupla radio balls—that's layers of water ice and ice cream we eat in the summertime with soft pretzels and mustard.

Bobby said, "I got a better idea. Wait here. I'm gonna spin around and get my bike."

People in the neighborhood saw the two of them eating water ice and pretzels down at Penn's Landing where Dewey's flagship, the *Olympia*, is docked.

Judy said, "That can't be right, Naum on a motorcycle, in his cassock?"

But it was.

If Naum needed to go somewhere no one else would go, in one of the neighborhoods with more questionable alleys than ours, he'd go find Bobby in the place you could always find Bobby, surrounded by every kind of tool you could imagine, squinting over his bifocals, sitting in the putty factory cellar where he ran the maintenance department.

Out in the yard by the railroad tracks he'd tell Naum, "The adventure begins, Padre. Get on the bike."

Naum'd straddle on back.

"And don't lean," Bobby'd tell him. "I'll do the leaning."

Naum only asked about a helmet the first time out. Bobby made it clear what kind of riders wore helmets.

They'd have theological shouting matches over the engine noise about the one thing Bobby didn't believe in.

Space aliens? Nope. Extraterrestrials were no problem for Bobby.

People turning into piles of smoking ash in their pajamas because of spontaneous human combustion? Bobby said, "People on the internet say it's true."

Ghosts. Mediums. Evolution. Who built the pyramids?

But when it came to God?

Bobby said he really wanted to believe, but no matter how hard he looked, he just couldn't find a sign.

But at the same time, God was all Bobby ever wanted to talk about. Any time he'd ride Naum somewhere—his every other word blowing back over the Z-bar involved some question about God.

Ballistic theology

Rotational force

Twisted cosmology

The interpenetration of science and mysticism displacing space, matter, and mile markers like quantum sparks as Bobby and Naum blew down I-95, eradicating time like string theory gone wild in Einstein's mind.

———

AFTER A YEAR, Bobby's father died. Mom a week later. The Catholic family hadn't been to church in years.

"Naum," Bobby said, "they believed. But the parish they'd been going to for years, the guy there hurt a lot of people. Did some weird shit. It got to be too much for them, for two old people, how they were raised, Baltimore *Catechism*, what they believed.

"And they didn't come by their faith watching TV or anything.

They may not have been able to hear or talk, but they damn well said their rosary together every day, the five mysteries, read Catholic stuff . . . read their Bible every night."

Bobby said, "I know you can't do your Orthodox prayers for Mom and Dad. Truth is, they never heard of you Orthodox. Probably never had a chance to . . ." He looked Naum in the eye and said, "Think God thinks that's their fault?"

Naum told Bobby he knew some pretty good Catholic priests. Monsignor Maurice Truen from Saint Veronica's in particular.

Father Naum loved Monsignor Maurice Truen. Monsignor, who never missed Great Vespers on Saturday evening. Monsignor, who carried the aroma of his ubiquitous cigar even when he wasn't smoking one. Naum knew he was there in the back at Vespers, even without turning to see him.

Monsignor, who said, "You still baptize by immersion, right? We used to do that, used the leavened bread too . . . I'd love ta come to the next one, just to observe."

Lately Naum had seen the white-haired priest slowly making his visitation rounds through the neighborhood or pulling his wire shopping basket store to store on the Avenue under the Tunnel, walking now with a cane. Had a dog he called Strawman, walked the same way, man and dog, both carefully considering each step, like a kid just learning to walk who couldn't stop looking at the bells in his shoelaces.

Gray-haired, jolly-faced Monsignor, one of the few who read the Fathers and knew the Pastoral Rule of Saint Gregory the Pope of Rome.

"Been a priest sixty years," Naum told Bobby, "fifteen hundred families—not people, families—he takes care of over there, with only one priest assigned to help him. Guy's a straight arrow, Bobby."

"Him," Bobby said, "I don't know from Adam. You, I do."

Naum talked to the bishop.

The bishop mentioned that in the old country there had been a section in the Orthodox cemetery set aside for non-Orthodox and a special prayer. He told Naum to find it.

At Donahue Funeral Home, Naum prayed the Trisagion Prayers. The people said the Lord's Prayer, and Naum ended saying what the bishop had advised: "Thy holy will be done in them, O Lord!"

———

ONE MORNING BOBBY didn't want to eat breakfast alone. He took a chance and went by the church while it was still dark. Naum was outside scraping ice in the frozen drizzle.

Bobby revved the bike up on the pavement. "You hungry?"

Naum said, "Betty's pancakes? Any time."

Bobby said, "I gotta go and clock out first."

Naum said, "Okay."

Bobby told Naum, "Did the overnight scheduled maintenance on the silicone sealant mixers, discharge extruders and shit . . . Forgot to punch out. Graveyard's not my usual . . . 'Sides, I left my leather bomber in the locker room."

Naum looked at Bobby, sitting there on his chopper in the rain, short-shorts, jump boots, the red ankle socks, the cut-off T-shirt, biceps like boulders, and the Marine Corps cap. He said, "You? You're gonna wear a jacket?"

Bobby smiled. "Just to piss people off." He looked to the back of the bike. "C'mon, Naum, adventure time."

Naum put the scraper against the wall and got on. He said, "Yeah, I know, Bobby. You'll do the leaning."

It was still dark when Bobby came off the putty factory loading dock pulling on the old leather flight jacket.

They blew across the Aramingo Avenue Bridge over Frankford Creek, past Bobby's parents' house off the park near Belgrade and Allegheny. The house with the beat-up pickup truck, and the boat, and the old motorcycle parts moldering in the front yard.

The blinking house with the year-round Christmas lights, the blinking telephone and doorbell, and every other blinking thing Bobby now owned.

"I hate getting out of bed in the dark," Naum told Bobby. "But I had to get the church cleanup done early. I could use some breakfast, warm me up."

It was Lenten March, rainy and raw. Naum ducked into the alcove at Betty's while Bobby parked the bike.

Overhead, red neon glowed from the Art Deco cup-and-saucer sign above the entrance. Naum looked at the weather and thought, "Not even an Orthodox pigeon would be out this early in this weather."

The 1940s-era coffee shop was crowded. Every booth was full. The buzz of conversation above the smell of scrapple, coffee, eggs, and toast made Betty's a cozy place to meet.

The waitress put a cup on the table and asked Naum, "Just you this morning, Padre?"

Naum held up two fingers. "Bobby'll be here, Carla." Naum

took off his coat and nestled against the wall in the well-worn booth. "Where's Lisette?"

"Day off." Tall, pretty Carla made a face when she heard Bobby was coming.

Carla was used to guys asking her if she was on the menu.

But Bobby? To Carla, Bobby was in a category all by himself.

Bobby came in, shook off, and stomped his boots on the mat. The rain down his neck made him shiver. He said to Naum, "Had to park a block away to get it out of the rain."

They ordered the usual.

Carla knew they'd be occupying the back booth for quite a while. With regulars in the neighborhood, it was expected.

Bobby said to Naum, "You think she's pretty?"

"Carla?" Naum said. "Yep."

"Go tell her I love her."

Naum said, "You go tell her."

Bobby said, "Her name's Carla."

Naum said, "I know, and I ain't going."

When Naum went over, Carla looked at him and said, "Yeah, I know . . . Bobby loves me."

It was funny at first.

Then they started going once a week. At first Naum thought it was just a cute joke. But as time went by, the "Tell her I love her" turned into "Ask her to marry me."

Naum told Bobby, "Nope. That's serious. If you're serious, you go ask her."

She already knew when Naum got up to the counter. "Yeah. I know. Bobby wants to marry me."

It was funny. A sort of weekly running gag.

Then one morning it got serious.

Too serious.

Like a bad translation of some macabre motorcycle joke.

Bobby looked at Naum and said, "I ain't gonna be here in six months. You gotta ask Carla serious this time."

Over the coffee and the hotcakes and the ketchup on the scrapple, torque gone wrong was displacing time and the arrangement of the checkerboard squares on the blue-and-white tablecloth.

Naum had a bad feeling. He said, "You leaving?"

Bobby didn't flinch. He took off his cap and set it on his knee, but he kept his eyes even with Naum's. "I'm dying, Padre. I got cancer."

It wasn't funny anymore. The joke was over.

Bobby said, "And don't you tell her I'm dying. I gotta do that."

Not long after, they married.

BOBBY TOLD NAUM, "I'd never keep her in the dark like that. She said she didn't care. She told me, open your eyes. Love is love. Marriage is marriage. A one-of-a-kind thing, both from God."

Bobby wanted her to have everything. The house off the park near Belgrade and Allegheny, with the beat-up pickup truck, and the boat, and the old motorcycle parts moldering in the front yard. The blinking house with the year-round Christmas lights, the blinking telephone and doorbell, and every other blinking thing Bobby owned.

Turned out the tough guy really did love her.

Turned out she loved the tough guy too.

That morning in the room

There was Sister Grace.

Monsignor Maurice Truen, who'd married them.

Turns out Carla went to Mass every week at Monsignor's.

There was Inez from the hospice, five-foot dark-skinned no-nonsense Latina nurse practitioner wearing happy nurse scrubs and a stethoscope around her neck.

A deathbed a day. Inez had seen it all.

Bobby's nephew Mel was there, home on leave from the Marines.

Carla was there.

And Naum.

Outside, springtime was making its neighborhood noise in the park down the street near the old stone church, and kids were taking off their coats and playing halfies and showing off T-shirts that made them feel like school was already out for the summer.

Naum was sitting on the edge of the bed, holding his friend's hand, when Bobby closed his eyes.

Inez the nurse took Bobby's pulse, did what she did, and pronounced him.

Over on Tilton Alley, the old red garage that housed Czerw's Kielbasa had no doubt Lent was coming to an end because the lines for Paschal sausage were out the door and around the corner.

The day was brisk, but it was sunny.

The good-looking Polish girl behind the counter at Syrenka's Restaurant Bobby used to tease when he went to buy takeout pierogis, potato pancakes, stuffed cabbage, and beets on the corner of Richmond and Allegheny—she heard about it from a customer later that day and sort of remembered the big flirty guy in the short pants with the little red ankle socks.

Little puddles of sadness bubbled up in her out of nowhere all that week. Somehow she never put it together and couldn't figure out why.

Carla had to go down the hallway, remembering the time Bobby embarrassed her at Betty's, serenading her with his Polish American String Band banjo.

Toward New Year's later that year, rehearsal at the Polish American String Band didn't sound the same. "Ya wouldn't think one banjo down would make all that much a difference." Joey Nowak and Bobby bought twin banjos back then, right after they were discharged. Twenty-two–fret plectrum open-back Gibsons.

Enlisted and did the buddy thing at Parris Island Boot Camp. Ate two plates apiece, shrimp and grits at Plum's South Carolina Café in Beaufort. Did the same two tours in Vietnam, Joey and Bobby.

Life rolled by outside Bobby's windows, ringing its bell rowdier than the #60 trolley riding the tracks out of Port Richmond, rattling under the El at K & A, heading out to East Falls and all points west.

Little boys were putting pennies on the tracks and selling the trolley-flattened souvenirs all around the neighborhood for a nickel, same way boys had always done. Same as Bobby did when he was a kid.

Probably not even the pigeons or the sparrows in the park, probably not even a squirrel, had any sense of the translation going on inside the room inside the house off the park near Belgrade and Allegheny.

Turned out he really did love her.

Turned out she loved him too.

And Carla didn't have problem one with the accounts later that month over at Polonia Bank.

Bobby'd taken care of everything.

Down the hall Naum could hear the comforting and the crying and the phone calls being made.

He sat in the room with his friend. He held Bobby's hand and prayed.

Bobby'd had the Catholic last rites. Monsignor saw to that.

Naum said to Bobby, and himself, I guess I'm praying for me.

Translate me, O Sovereign Lady, to the hallowed and precious arms of the Holy Angels, so that covered by their wings, I see not the impious, putrid and dark forms of the demons.

Probably twenty minutes went by

Probably more

He opened his eyes

Bobby

Bright blue and iridescent

Loud eyes

Loud enough to fill Naum's wordless prayer with silence

Shouting out as much as is possible for eyes so long closed

Jesus Son of David have mercy on me

Despite whatever it was all these years trying to rebuke him

Bartimaeus the blind man shouted out all the more

And that evil be not eternal—this indestructible bond should be cut away and dissolved, and that this body be dissolved from that of which it was fashioned, and that the soul should be translated thence where it will remain until the General Resurrection . . .

Naum couldn't leave Bobby.

He couldn't even call quietly for the others.

Sitting there alone, was it on the bike, with Bobby, or on the bed?

But Naum tried. He had tried.

"Carla. Carla."

Whispering over whatever was happening.

"Sister Grace."

"Monsignor."

"Somebody, please."

"Mel."

"Miss Inez."

"Please, somebody, come and see."

And as they came, what Naum saw, they saw.

Blue eyes wide open and staring away over the head of Naum.

As if there were no earthly person with him.

Bobby, on his back, signing.

Signing to someone up beyond Naum and the room. Somewhere above where the others stood.

No one spoke.

Finally, Naum said, "Bobby. What do you see?"

His sudden grip on Naum's wrist was so quick and unexpected. Bobby turned his head away from what he was seeing to look at his friend.

Bobby felt sorry for Naum.

He said, "I know you want to know, but I can't tell you right now."

When he closed his eyes, things were different.

Naum didn't know what particular argument remained untranslated on that particular day in that particular room.

Life rolled by outside Bobby's windows, ringing its bell rowdier than the #60 trolley riding the tracks out of Port Richmond, rattling under the El at K & A, heading out to East Falls and all points west.

Little boys were putting pennies on the tracks and selling the trolley-flattened souvenirs all around the neighborhood for a nickel, same way boys had always done. Same as Bobby did.

Probably not a pigeon in the park, black, mottled, or white, nor a single brown sparrow, nor a fat gray squirrel had any sense of the lyrical translation that had taken place inside the room inside the house off the park near Belgrade and Allegheny.

The house with the beat-up pickup truck, and the boat, and the old motorcycle parts moldering in the front yard.

The blinking house with the year-round Christmas lights, the blinking telephone and doorbell, or any other blinking sign Bobby could never hear calling his name.

Little puddles of sadness bubbled up out of nowhere all that week in every person who'd been in that room.

The room where only Carla remained, talking with her Bobby, kissing him.

Nobody actually suggested the others go out in the hall and talk in whispers, they just did.

Mel brought Sister a chair.

White-haired Sister Grace, eighty-three, one of Bobby's grade school teachers, sat like a Lladro figurine in her blue-and-gray habit, wiping her eyes, telling everyone, "To me, that was a puzzle I'm never gonna be able to put together."

Mel said, "I don't know, Sister. Could be. But to me, it's just another one more of Uncle Bobby's adventures."

"Who knows?" Monsignor said. "And maybe it doesn't really matter if we do or we don't. Maybe *better* if we don't."

"The thing that bothers me?" Mel said. "I just hate to think of Uncle Bobby out there on his own."

"That'd be a hell of a thing," Monsignor Truen, who lived alone in the rectory, said. "I could be wrong. But I don't think so, Mel. Not our Bobby. I don't think he ever really bought the existential lie that we're born alone and die alone, least not from what we just saw, not from what he told me. It was like that whole thing was him summing up his last confession. Hard to picture Bobby, or any of us, for that matter, ending up alone."

"We're not alone," Inez the hospice nurse said, "not from what I've seen."

A deathbed a day. Inez had seen it all.

The house was empty when Carla walked Naum to the corner.

Waiting for the trolley, she told Naum, "I just wanna be with Bobby by myself a little . . . before they come."

Naum said, "Understood. I guess Bobby got his sign, Car, signing with himself, or whoever he was signing with."

Carla said, "You know, Padre, I used to tell him, Bobby, Bobby, open your eyes. Look around. Look at us. We love each other. How'd that happen, Bobby? You think we did it? If that don't tell you nothing . . . then maybe there is no God for us. And if that's the way it's gonna be, then that's the way it's gonna be.

"But at the same time, Bobby, I gotta look at your mom and pop, the way they were. Maybe they were better off than us, sitting there all those years holding hands, saying their rosary, not saying nothing, not hearing nothing. They didn't have to. They knew there was a God. All they had to do was look at each other, look at their son, 'cause they weren't blind to what was right in front of them."

Naum couldn't say anymore.
On the trolley somebody was praying.
Naum could hear the prayer.

O Zoti Krisht
Open the eyes of our heart
That our understanding may be enlightened
That we may know the sign of Your calling

But with all the trolley noise,
He just couldn't hear who said it.

Others to See

He who has lost sensibility is a brainless philosopher, a self-condemned commentator, a self-contradictory windbag, a blind man who teaches others to see.

—SAINT JOHN OF THE LADDER

DEACON BOUTROS, when he was a teenager on his way home from school, saw the open front door of the Orthodox church. He passed it every day. Most weekdays it was closed and locked. He often wondered what was inside.

But one day the church was open.

On the sidewalk it was warm and bright. Spring was well underway. And although Pascha had come and gone, the cool fragrance from inside the church was familiar in a way he could not explain. Candles were burning. Someone had placed a row of them in a sandbox on stilts in front of an icon of two men holding a church. They were looking at the young boy, Boutros.

His friends said no. They were not going in.

He told them, "I'll see you at home."

Some people can't resist removing the thread of lint from the back of a stranger's jacket. Thirteen-year-old Boutros was like that. And by venturing inside and touching the icon of a woman called Matrona the Blind, he was touched by whatever mystical filament was woven into the fabric of the temple. It made him squeeze his eyes shut. Mysteries are seen with the eyes closed.

It recalled the day's biology lesson from Leonardo da Vinci. *Who would believe that so small a space as the eye could contain all the images of the universe?*

In a backlit shadow mitosis, the interior ecclesial silhouette reproduced itself on the inside of the boy's eyelids. The contour of the iconostasis, the cross atop, and the curtain across the Royal Doors, the asymmetrical distances, a vertical sliver of light down one deacon's door, surreal elongated proportions flattened in large-eyed, full-faced iconographic saints, analogion, candle stands, prayer rising on incense from where the psalti stood singing.

A dimensional entity. A living, life-giving liturgical portal, hidden openly in substantial symbols, abundant and elusive as black matter, dovetailing into an algorithmic Oranta Panagia, the outspread arms of the Virgin bearing Christ within—calling Boutros like a mother with open arms embracing him from the curvilinear apse rounding high above the altar.

The priest was in the forefront, vested on the ambon. When he turned to face the people, he was talking. He was looking directly at the boy as he spoke.

Boutros had seen this man before. Even when Boutros closed his eyes, the photochemical afterimage of each word, like the row of candles in the narthex, illumined the occipital lobe in the cerebral cortex of his brain.

WHEN BOUTROS WENT HOME and told his mother, Miriam, she was watching her shows. Her big galoot of a son turned off the TV and plopped in her lap. Whenever he was getting ready to take a big step forward, to grow, she noticed, he took two steps back.

He wanted to be held, like when he was a little boy. She embraced her son. She rocked him, put her face close to his, and reminded him, when he told her about the church, "You know, I'm Orthodox."

She'd always been so quiet when it came to her faith. A wife with a vow, living hope in love, sealed in a silence that spoke.

Circumstances had shaped her life and her marriage. It was a different world and time. She said, "Your father wanted you to be with him."

Malik, her husband, had pressure from Babba, his father, and from his family. They were not active in their Muslim faith, but the baby, Boutros, would follow his father.

Miriam remained Orthodox as best she could. Her inner life was her private life. She watched her son grow. She saw in him a longing for something more. She prayed.

"Be a wordless icon," her confessor had suggested. "Silently be Christ in your household. Weave a basket of faith by your prayer, like the sister of Moses."

Miriam's husband Malik never went to worship. Not even on holy days. His religion was his business; his business, his religion.

His faith was in his own strength and wit. "Trust God," he would say, "but tether the camels." Malik was a good man in every way, but in faith, he had set his son adrift. If his boy, Boutros, were to find a way to believe, he would have to find it in his mother.

More and more, Boutros was attracted to the Orthodox. He bought a Bible and hid it in his room. When he listened to the priest speak, he thought of Saint Peter, one of the men who looked at him from the icon of the two men holding the church.

Simon Peter answered him, Lord, to whom shall we go? You have the words of eternal life.

He knew his own name, Boutros, was an Arabic word for *rock*, like Petros, Peter, in Greek.

He had seen this man before, this priest.

To Boutros, it didn't matter what the priest did, it was what he said. He had the words of life given by Christ.

Boutros told his mother, "The priest said I should watch a movie called *The Island*. It's in Russian but has English subtitles."

Miriam said, "I have it."

"And a book, Mother, *The Way of the Pilgrim*. It has a foreword by a priest called Hopko."

She said, "I have that too." Miriam gave her son her own prayer rope.

"Shall I tell Father?" Boutros said.

Miriam said, "You can. You're sixteen now. He knows you've been going to the church on and off for the past three years. As long as you keep your grades up and don't bring the law to our door. You know your father. He loves you. But religion is not his thing."

Boutros said, "As long as Babba doesn't find out."

"We would never hurt your father's father," Miriam said. "Babba has our love, our prayers, and our respect. Always."

"Always," said Boutros.

The boy remembered that his babba had been to Saint Catherine's Monastery on Mount Sinai when he was a boy.

Babba told Boutros, "I touched the burning bush. They gave me a green egg for Pascha and a leaf from the bush. Prophet Muhammad, peace be upon him, wrote a letter and sealed it with his own handprint, that the Christians and their church there are to be protected.

"The monks have covered a certain step in a wire cage. One of our women from the *xhami*, the mosque, there inside the walls of the monastery, Boutros, this woman was going to light a candle at the church to ask the Virgin to help her daughter. She dropped her jar of oil, and it broke on the stone step. An icon of the Virgin appeared on that step, so they covered it with a protective wire cage, and that mother's prayers were answered."

By the time he was twenty, Boutros had asked his father's blessing to be baptized. Babba was dead. There was no one left on his father's side with interest enough to object.

Malik told his son, "I've always known your mother's secret, Boutros. She kept a journal. Now that she's gone, I am an empty man. She wrote in it every day. Every day, she prayed for me, and for you. She told God I was busy taking care of you and her, and that I really did love Him, but I showed it through my love for the two of you. She wrote that she never did anything to try to convert me, or you, to her way.

"But she wrote that she did pray that someday, you and I would come to see that being is life, and life is communion with those you love, and that true communion can only be achieved in God, not in politics, or nations—or in business. It must grow in and from something greater than we are. So, boy, go, follow your mother's heart."

When Boutros finished undergraduate school, he said to the priest, "Father, I have learned so much from you. It was hard at first, being obedient. Examples are hard to find. It's confusing, conforming to a new way. But in another way, it's like you gave me a key. Putting aside my individual way of living, finding the common life of the liturgy.

"You showed me the ancient writings, the prayers of all the generations before us. Taught me the tones, the chants, how to keep the fasts and the feasts. Gave me a seal and taught me how to make the meshe and prepare for Holy Communion.

"All the time you spent answering my silly questions . . . I don't know how you put up with me. Even if I myself wasn't always good, being obedient to good things somehow opened the door to something deep inside."

Boutros said, "Because of your diligence and patience, Father, I am here. I ask your blessing to petition the bishop to go to seminary."

The priest said yes.

The priest wondered, all these years, had Boutros seen? Had he put two and two together? If he hadn't put it together by this time, then probably not.

But Boutros *had* put two and two together.

When he thought of the trust and regard Boutros had shown, the priest promised himself, "I have to change. I have to start now. I can't stay this way."

But being so often alone and idle, something more than boredom would overtake the priest. Wavering back and forth, speculating on endless intellectual, moral, and ethical possibilities plagued the priest till his resolve to change dissolved in a self-absorbed existential hopelessness, and there he was, right back at the very thing he did not want to do.

Then the priest would accuse himself in the mirror: "You are a bad boy." Staring for a long time at his reflection, amused with his own unique cleverness, reveling in his poetic eloquence, smiling his standard-issue handsome-boy smile and scolding himself with a laugh, "My friend, you are a believing atheist."

———✦———

WHEN BOUTROS WAS THIRTEEN, his father said, "I have tickets to the ballgame. We'll take the train. Have a boys' night out. After, we'll go downtown to eat, wherever you like, and celebrate your birthday. Mother promised her special *tri leche* cake when we get home."

On the way home, Malik spotted the priest with a group of men and realized it was too late to divert his son. The boy had seen what he had seen.

There he was, looking directly at Boutros, laughing and coming out of the Merry-Go-Round, shirtless in a leather vest, backless chaps, cowboy boots with spurs, a leather Stetson Roxbury with rivets on the cowboy hatband.

Some people can't resist removing the thread of lint from the back of a stranger's jacket. Thirteen-year-old Boutros was like that. It made him squeeze his eyes shut.

Who would believe that so small a space as the eye could contain all the images of the universe?

Even when Boutros closed his eyes, the photochemical after-image remained.

Malik put his arm around his son as they walked to the train. "Your mother always tells me, from the Bible, 'What if some did not have faith? Will their lack of faith nullify God's faithfulness? Absolutely not! Let God be true and every man a liar.'"

They went home. Nothing more was ever said.

Not long after the time Boutros married his sweetheart, Lucille, and left for seminary, the priest became ill and died.

At the funeral, the priest's wife took the young deacon aside. "He wanted you to have these," she said to Deacon Boutros.

He left Boutros his vestments and all his books. Including the *Ladder of Divine Ascent*, a book by Saint John of Saint Catherine's Monastery at the base of Mount Sinai, a book the priest knew very well.

Along with Saint Peter, Saint Paul was the other man in the icon of the two men holding the church, the saints who had called to young Boutros all those years before.

Saint Paul wrote to the church he had established in the city of Corinth:

Every man's work shall be made manifest: for the day shall declare it, because it shall be revealed by fire; and the fire shall try every man's work of what sort it is.

Deacon Boutros knew he was, at least in part, the result of the work of the priest he had seen that night coming from the ball-game with his father.

Boutros had always been obedient to the priest in all good

things. The priest had never suggested anything immoral or illegal.

Boutros chose to remember the good. A monk at the monastery told him, "Everyone we meet is either an icon or a warning."

Boutros knew, as time went on, he and any good work accomplished by God in his service as a deacon to God's people, he knew he and that work would be tested too.

After he was ordained a priest, Father Boutros, it was noticed, never walked directly or quickly into the church but stopped here and there, praying along the way, and then kissed the doors, and once inside, stopped again before entering the temple.

When asked, he told people he paused to recall the time long ago when as a boy he would pass the closed locked doors on weekdays and wonder what was inside.

And that was partly true.

After many years, he confessed, when asked about this practice by Father Naum, the new priest at the parish.

Father Boutros answered, "I ask God to show me my coffin in its place before the Royal Doors of the iconostasis. And me in it. And I am afraid to enter not discerning the Presence there. And I am afraid to enter with any judgment in my heart regarding those faithful who struggled to live the life in Christ before me, and have now gone before us to their rest, or even those who will come after. And I beg God not to leave me alone to rely upon my own devices to serve His people, to help others to see."

God Is Good

I

THE YOUNG BOYS WITH THE PIT BULL didn't question when the tall lady with the gray braids told them, "See that white man with the beard over there? Go and take him around the corner to that deserted yellow-brick church."

Slick drizzle was icing off the end of the day and turning the late-afternoon pavement to glass. When his pit-bull escort left him in front of Holy Savior Orthodox Church, the front doors were gaping open on their hinges and banging in the wind.

The three-bar cross on the roof tilted to one side, and there was a blackened gash in the rounded right rib of the copper-green cupola.

Naum made the cross and went in.

Gray daylight slanted through the broken ceiling in slow swirling columns mixed with drizzle and mist. The icon of the Pantocrator, suspended by a single canvas thread, swayed from its place in the overhead dome and stretched toward the floor.

The entire temple wept at the storm of destruction visited by the sons of disobedience.

Every icon on the iconostasis was black-eyed, pierced through and spray-painted.

The angels on the deacon's doors were defaced.

The Royal Doors sagged on their hinges, and the throne, what others call the altar table, stood centered in its place like an oceanside rock ravaged by a storm.

Peacock mosaics embedded in its cold stone face were visible through jagged slashes torn in the gold brocade of its cover.

The altar top was molded over with pigeon droppings and chaff from the blistered ceiling, and like those of the table of oblation that stood nearby, its braided-fringed skirts were thick and twisted with the silted debris left when the tide receded from the grimy tiled floor.

Naum took the epitrahilion from his bag and made the vesting prayer.

He would not enter through the Royal Doors.

He venerated each icon on the iconostasis.

The south deacon's door hung open. He kissed the angel and went in, praying not to find the tabernacle violated with its contents strewn . . .

"Thank God," he said. There was no tabernacle. But where were the chalice, the diskos, the spear, and the spoon?

Noticing the purple silk and brushing aside the soggy mess on the altar top—Naum couldn't believe it had been left there—the antimension. The square icon cloth signed by the bishop, giving his blessing for the community to gather in Holy Savior.

Naum cleared a space. Where was the seven-branched candle stand? He took off his gloves. He removed his scarf and spread it as a tablecloth on the empty altar top.

The eileton, the purple outer silk cover, was slightly damp. Naum went slowly, opening the purple cover that had been folded in thirds. There inside, the antimension was intact and dry. He made the cross and unfolded the wheat-colored linen antimension.

The icon of our Master Christ's entombment, the Evangelists, and even the flattened sponge, they were all perfectly dry and undisturbed. He wondered, *How did the vandals miss this? Why did the priest and the congregation not . . .*

Naum stopped his wondering, and though he couldn't see well enough to read the inscription, he venerated the relic in the center. He noted the name of the bishop who had signed the antimension, refolded it in the eileton, put it in his bag, and went to check the rest of the church.

All the way around, from the steps leading down to the church hall in the basement to the steps in the back winding up to the choir loft . . .

Classrooms and cloakrooms
The kitchen and the pantries
Utility rooms and restrooms
The floors all covered
With shredded cover-torn church books
And accordion-paged Bibles
Vestments
Every festal color
Altar coverings
Broken glass
Incense and charcoal ground underfoot to pebbly grime
Where was the censer

Each step along the way would have taken Naum days to clear
and clean, to salvage and retrieve.

The aftermath was too much for one man . . .

One old man alone and cold and not believing what he was
hearing and seeing . . .

Crunching snapped beeswax candles
Shards of votive glass
Paschal red, Virgin blue, Pentecost green
Every step echoing sadness
As he felt his way
Through the dimness, the dankness, the blight

Naum climbed over the splintered bishop's throne, wedged on
its side where it had been jettisoned to the floor at the partially
flooded bottom of the dank, narrow stairway. An empty episcopal miter box, satin-lined, lay open in the damp.

He straddled analogion and icon stands
Large free-standing brass candelabrum
They broke the legs
Music stands
Memorial tables
Marriage tables
Crowns in a tangle of smeared silk ribbon
All wedded in a heap
He saw the kouvouklion
The bier from Holy Friday
Upside down
And when he exhumed the Shroud
From the remains
Naum carried it on his shoulders

A sacred offering that had come to an end in a winding sheet

Heartbroken Naum righted the baptismal font, tried pushing out the dents, but couldn't.

The tables in the church hall

The ones that were not spilled on their sides

Were set in an almost formal fashion

Silver settings

Soup bowls and tureens

Coffee cups on saucers

Glasses for water, glasses for wine,

Children's settings in front of high chairs

Cloth napkins, serving dishes, and plates

A long table on a dais seemed set for the clergy. The vases lay on their sides. There were stains on the embroidered cover where water had spilled and flowers lay wilted in front of headstone-like placards naming the ghosts of those meant to occupy each esteemed padded chair.

The ornate chair in the middle had the emblem of the bishop. It made Naum think of the empty miter box. Where was the crown?

It looked as if the hurricane had blown in out of nowhere at the end of a peaceful Sunday liturgy as folks were gathering in the church hall and sitting down to eat.

Naum could picture them fleeing. How could this happen, here, in a modern American city? What kind of culture could reduce a human being to this kind of violence?

Too much for one old man to understand.

II

OUTSIDE, AFTER SECURING the building as best he could, stupefied Naum lowered himself into the sheltered doorway at the top of the wide front steps and wondered if there were any of the parish faithful who still lived within a mile of the church. Naum could not imagine how long the church had been abandoned—it must have been months, a full festal cycle. He wondered if there was anyone who remembered or cared.

A tall woman using a collapsible wire shopping basket for balance took her time carefully crossing the sidewalk as day faded and a crackled skin of ice formed over the pavement down in front of Naum.

When she saw Naum she stopped.

Just her face.

The eyes.

Her demeanor.

The length of her oversized coat. The braided graying dreads coming from under her embroidered woolen cap. The way they framed her face when she tilted her head, her knit gloves and boots . . .

Naum wanted to cry when the lady with the complexion of a kalamata olive pulled her scarf from her nose and said, "You okay, mister?"

She took off her glasses, breathed on them, polished them with her scarf, and put them on again to get a better look at the man with the beard huddled in the corner at the top of the steps.

He told her, "Yes. I'm okay. Thank you for asking."

"God is good," she said.

He knew the traditional response. Naum said, "All the time, sister. All the time."

When he stood he said, "Those were just the words I needed to hear. Be okay if I come down and thank you, Miss . . . ?"

She said, "Uriel. And yes, you may."

When he took her hand and bowed, she said, "You a preacher, aren't you?"

He said, "Yes, ma'am."

Uriel said, "Ma'am is for my mother," and she smiled.

"How shall I address you?"

"Just put a handle on it."

He said, "Okay . . . Miss Uriel."

She looked up at the doors and said to him, "You been there, on the other side, haven't you?"

Naum nodded.

She could tell he was at the edge of his strength. The man was shivering, and his eyes were looking beyond her and beyond the street to somewhere she didn't want to know about, not yet.

Miss Uriel said, "Twenty years, more, I been going by here. You name the day. Mostly on Wednesdays, but 'specially Sundays. Them people, mostly white, no offense, pretty much all white, never said so much as good morning to me.

"I did try to peek in. Once. One time I even got up to the top step on a Wednesday when it was all shuttered up, and the window on the door had some brand new glass. I got up on my tippy toes. It was like I had wings. Place was *pretty* . . . *so* pretty inside I could hardly believe it. I never saw anything like it down here on earth. I just stood there like my toes was almost levitating trying to figure it all out.

"I swear it looked like a portal could take you straight back to heaven if you could just get yourself in there and get lost in its . . . its shapes. Its spaces. The colors and the light. You could smell the holy through the door. The way the whole thing was laid out was like some kind of language other than talking. Some language the angels on them doors must 'a' spoke when they listened to God like Moses did and built the tent the way they built that place, causa that's the way He told us to do."

"Sounds like you did more than just peek through that portal, Miss Uriel."

She laughed.

The woman had that handsome kind of face that was made even more appealing by the gap in the middle of her upper teeth. Naum could tell, back in the day, Uriel probably had the boys lined up in front of her mother's garden gate.

She said to him, "So, Pastor, *do* you know what they do in there?"

He said, "I thought I did."

She put her hand on his shoulder.

She looked around.

The sounds in the street were changing. Working people were in a hurry to get in out of the weather. Streetlights were coming on. A different population was emerging. One with no cause or purpose. A people more accustomed to neon lights and the meaningless action that ended life in death after dark.

Miss Uriel said, "You be feelin' better, honey, but right now, me and you, be better for people of our persuasion to be home and indoors."

Naum didn't want to admit there was something in her

gray-blue eyes that knew more about this whole thing than he could understand. Seemed to him she was speaking in lost words he once knew. She had him trying hard to remember things he didn't know he'd forgotten.

She said, "I know what you're thinking, but now not your time. And you be wasting your time thinking what you're thinking. You *do not* want to know how that place got tore up—you feel me?"

He said, "Will I see you again?"

It was that same sadness within a smile when she said, "With you, Father Naum, ya never know, but prob'ly not, not this side a the iconostasis, but I know that ain't gonna stop you from trying, now is it?"

She knew he'd be looking out the window of that amber-light trolley interior, trying to see out into the darkness, wondering how she knew his name.

She turned her face toward the #47 trolley.

She let him see.

In the dark, toward morning, the icon of the archangel, the one he saw or thought he saw when he sat up in bed, was Coptic or Ethiopian . . . ? Or maybe he was half awake or not awake at all . . . toward morning, sitting up in bed, making the cross.

III

ON THE AVENUE under the Tunnel in the back room of King Baby Pawn, a man who didn't like the questions they were asking said to Naum and Pastor Stephen Jerome, "Can you prove it?"

The seven-branched candle stand

Hand-painted festal icons
Two enameled chalices
Two diskos stars
One enameled diskos
A jeweled pectoral cross
Two cherubic processional fans
Two processional banners
A bishop's miter—no box
Communion spoons
Five liturgical spears
Three censers, chains tangled together
Strung between two censer stands
The tabernacle, intact

They called the man King Baby because he'd fathered twenty-nine kids, only two with the same woman, and every "mother's day," the day of the month when the checks came, he drove his Benz around the neighborhood collecting his cut—"Break me off my piece"—from each baby's mother.

People said the man looked like an oversized baby.

Just not to his face.

"You claiming they're yours," King Baby said. "Can you prove it?"

"No," was all Naum could manage.

"Then you can visit," King Baby said, "but that's all."

Pastor Stephen said, "How much, K-B?"

"All?" King Baby was doubtful.

"Yes." Pastor Stephen was known in the neighborhood, even to King Baby.

"Okay," K-B said. "You da skin-diving pastor and this old

Albanian over here, say he's my cousin, right? He brought you, right?" King Baby showed his gold teeth and put two fingers on Naum's shoulder. "So, you gonna *show* me, or just . . . what?"

Naum looked at Pastor and said, "You don't have to do this."

Pastor said, "No, we do."

IV

FOR SOME REASON, Pastor Stephen understood early on, "I just lucked out when it came to having a good mother and father."

His father was Pastor Emeritus CJ Jerome at Saint Yared's, the congregation that met in an old factory over on Frankford Avenue.

Pastor CJ was an old-time Bible college working pastor who spent his pastoral life as a full-time second-shift custodian in the Philly schools.

No young person aspiring to serve God's people could have had better icons of sacrifice and service than old Pastor CJ Willard Jerome and his wife, Matilda, whom everybody in the neighborhood called Miss Tilly.

The old couple lived in the senior housing complex built by Saint Yared's next to the parish school and the playground across from the big lot where the church parked their buses.

White-haired, bearded Pastor CJ knew there was a time when there were two chalices offered at some Orthodox churches in some countries, one for the colored . . .

"We Orthodox not there yet," he used to say, "but we always on the way."

"Right here in America," CJ said, "when that archbishop on the cover of *Life* Magazine walked in his robes and hat with Reverend King, people in his own parishes down South sent death-threat letters, on church stationery, signed them too, and told him he better not come . . . En route, but still a ways ta go. That's us."

Pastor CJ used to tell his son Stephen, "Sometimes the distance between persons and God is only thin as skin."

"A navy diver," CJ used to brag about his son. "Going down on wrecks, aviation, military, big boats, civilian pleasure craft, retrieving bodies."

That was Stephen Jerome prior to discharge. Prior to finishing his undergrad studies and working nights cleaning with his father to finish law school.

"Boy passed the bar first time," Pastor CJ said.

Tall young man. Good-looking kid too. Smile that would've made you think he'd never seen what he'd seen doing what he did, diving for the navy.

Kind of smile that fooled other people.

Kind of smile made other people glad thinking Stephen wasn't sad. But he was sad. That deep existential kind of *never be satisfied as long as others got the pain* kind of sad.

Perfect pastor material. The man knew a little something about how to offer ordinary people a chance at being salvaged.

But that little girl who saw him around campus and fell in love with him? She knew the other side too. She knew the boy had hope beyond the facts.

"Malvena," Stephen asked her. "You picture yourself a pastor's wife?"

"Never," she said.

"My mother'll tell you it ain't always an easy life," Stephen said. "I guess I can't blame you."

"Never mind what your mother told you," Malvena said. "Maybe she and I talked about something you didn't even know you don't know."

Nowadays, Malvena and their kids were in it up to their ears helping around Saint Yared's. Yeah, she had the educational certification, was a curriculum advisor at Penn Treaty Junior High, but how she let her Stephen talk her into starting a K–8 grade school at the church . . . ?

The light-skinned girl wasn't always happy with his religious theorizing. "You overthink things," she would tell him. "Just get to work, boy."

Old Pastor CJ, his father, told him, "She right, son. You gotta put work boots on your faith and get ta steppin'. After all, son, we did accept the gospel when Saint Mark came to Africa, and you know Jesus Himself lived in Egypt. We freely heard it. Freely loved it. Freely lived it. Then the other two came at the point of a sword. Islam and the slave religion our young folks rightly rejecting.

"And nobody telling them about their roots? I gotta carry that and try and do something to get us back to the original love. I been steppin' and praying God keep me in that love."

Love is love.

And when they walked through our neighborhood holding hands—Pastor Stephen, their daughter, Cordella, their son, Karl, in the middle between Pastor Stephen and Malvena—well, wasn't nobody around our way had any doubt they were in love.

V

PASTOR STEPHEN did a deal with King Baby.

Naum knew Pastor wasn't gonna tell what he said to King Baby. But he also knew Pastor was an attorney. He knew Pastor no longer worked nights with his father cleaning schools.

Everybody in Fishtown knew Pastor had a badge, an office staff, a city vehicle—the whole thing. Everybody who ever had a visitor's pass or some shady reason to be up at CFC Prison knew Stephen Jerome was deputy director of the city prison system.

It was too bad it didn't work out.

Too bad the people who could've made it work wouldn't give a blessing to work.

The bishop wanted Pastor Stephen to move his family full-time up to the seminary for at least a year, preferably two.

Hard to give up a six-figure city salary, pull the kids out of school, lose the health benefits, have Malvena quit her job.

What were they gonna do with the house, and who'd be there to bring the faithful of Saint Yared's along on the road to being received into the canonical Orthodox Church?

Who'd maintain the Rehab Building Renovation Program? What would happen to the men and women released from the prison Pastor hired and trained: plumbers, electricians, laborers, roofers, every kind of woodworker, tile specialists, painters, carpet installers, hardwood floor people, painters, metal-workers, bricklayers and masons, who'd keep that going? After all, these were the people who volunteered to rehab Holy Savior.

Hurt a lot of people if Pastor were gone.

They were walking through the renovated Holy Savior church building with the bishop.

Naum was begging.

The bishop said, "How can a parish depend on one man? Not healthy."

Naum said, "Master, you're our bishop. We all depend on you. He's catechized his people. They're used to the sound of his voice. What will they do for a year? With online schooling now, and our two communities so close, there's got to be a way to vet and prepare him in our midst . . . Maybe a few days a month at seminary. He gets thirty days' vacation every year . . . Or he could spend two weeks with you in—"

The bishop cut him off. "There's an agreement among us, no one bishop may ordain unless all are in agreement. And a year minimum at seminary is part of that agreement."

Naum said, "So?"

Peshkopi said, "We're not."

Naum knew most times it was better not to try and out-guess the bishop. They knew things they couldn't say. Confession was confession. Besides, Naum didn't have the nerve to say what he wanted to say:

And not only what will happen to his flock, but then what? When he finishes two years, him and his family living like paupers at the seminary. How many of our seminarians are told to go on welfare? And after seminary, what viable parish do we have in the diocese that could come close to supporting him and his family to the degree that they now provide for themselves?

Naum felt the note in his pocket.

Many potential vocations overlooked by clergy who don't consider encouragement of vocations to be part of their calling.

Christ-loving men left on the vine for lack of any provision to prepare them other than an academic model adopted from a scholastic culture foreign to our ecclesial ethos.

It wasn't the first time the bishop had encountered a self-righteous priest who thought his ideas were unique. He was kind when he told Naum, "We'd be out of line bringing up the sins of others. We have none of our own?"

Then he said, "Father, we'd be out of line pushing this any further. So let's not embarrass ourselves. How long have you and I been ordained, forty years, more? We know better."

The bishop was right.

Still, something a lot like spite was itching Naum like a mosquito bite in the middle of his back, wanting to say that the Sunday collection at Saint Yared's was over twenty thousand dollars each week, in cash, because their people tithed, and they had armed men in the counting room, but what did it really have anything to do with . . . ?

Naum handed the bishop the key to Holy Savior.

The bishop said, "The crew of craftsmen they sent over from Saint Yared's training school. I gotta say, they did do a nice job restoring this old place."

Naum asked the bishop's blessing.

"The problem now," the bishop said, "is what are *we* going to do with this building, in this neighborhood? Very few of the faithful are left, and none of them live within ten miles of the place."

The bishop gave his blessing.

When old Pastor CJ heard what had happened, he said to his wife, "Don't make no sense."

Miss Tilly told him, "Not seemly for us to judge. You're the one always telling me, CJ, don't let your good be spoken of as evil."

VI

BRIGHT WEEK, NOT YET light. April cold. Rainy and raw. Naum ducked into the alcove at Betty's and closed his umbrella. Overhead, red neon glowed from the Art Deco cup-and-saucer sign above the entrance. Naum looked at the weather and thought, "Not even a pigeon would be out this early in this weather."

The 1940s-era coffee shop was crowded for a Monday. Every booth was full. The buzz of conversation above the smell of scrapple, coffee, eggs, and toast made Betty's a cozy place to meet.

The waitress put a cup on the table and asked Naum, "Just you this morning, Padre?"

Naum held up two fingers. "Pastor Stephen's coming." He took off his coat and nestled into his regular spot up against the wall in the well-worn booth.

Pastor came in, took off his hat and his long black raincoat. It wasn't a long walk from Saint Yared's, just long enough to give Pastor a good soaking.

Naum's neighborhood wasn't all that big that a thorn from a bishop born far away and over the water could stop two neighborhood boys from having a cup of Betty's coffee.

Looking at Pastor, thinking how he would explain about the bishop's decision, about any promises he may have held out to Pastor, Naum had to reproach himself for usurping the bishop's pastoral prerogative and for his unkind thoughts about the bishop.

What if I were sent to serve in a far country, born far away and over the water? What if I were a stranger in a strange land?

What arrogance makes me think I would be able to understand the dynamic that separates Ishmael and Isaac?

That I, someone who might not even have command of the local language, would know what brings the diverse peoples of that land together?

To be a bishop, you gotta know that much. You gotta believe our faith reaches across languages, cultures, and borders.

Takes a lot of faith to be a bishop. You got that kinda faith, Naum?

Pastor slid into the booth and said to Naum, "We love this place, don't we? Malvena picking me up later."

Breakfast at Betty's. The African Orthodox pastor and the Orthodox priest met there early mornings once a month and talked patristics, liturgy, family, and food.

It was the same rendezvous spot where Naum met with Pastor Cal from Holy Communion Protestant Church, with Rabbi from the temple across the street, with Monsignor Truen from Saint Veronica's, with parish people who needed to talk, and with lots of folks from the neighborhood.

The waitress, Betty's daughter, Lisette, took Pastor's cup from the shelf behind the counter. On the side of the red cup it said, *Believe Anyway.*

She poured his coffee and gave Naum a refill.

Naum's cup said *Urata*, "he who blesses me."

Both took it black. Lisette knew their orders. Regulars were a mainstay at Betty's.

On the wall over the booth was a round vintage mirror advertising Old Reliable Coffee. An outdoorsman in a beaver brown cap and a red woolen double-breasted work coat stared at Naum over a logo that said *Always Good.*

You got the antimension in your pocket, the one you found in the mess, don't ya? Forgot to give it to the bishop, didn't you? Sure . . . you forgot, that's all.

If ya ain't got the nerve to give it to Pastor Stephen, then go over yourself on Saturdays and celebrate the liturgy for the people of Saint Yared's. And after a while chrismation will come.

Pastor saw him gazing off into the mirror. "You okay?" He knew what was bothering his friend.

"I can't figure it out," Naum said. "The mirror . . ."

Pastor Stephen looked at the mirror. "God is good," he said. "Always good."

And there *she* was, in Betty's alcove, a Samaritan good enough to stop and ask, "You okay, mister?" The woman with skin the color of a kalamata olive.

"Will I see you again?" he'd asked her.

"With you, Father Naum, ya never know, but prob'ly not, not this side a the iconostasis, but I know that ain't gonna stop you from trying, now is it?"

In the dark, toward morning, the icon of the archangel, the one he saw, or thought he saw, when he sat up in bed and made the cross, was it Coptic or Ethiopian? Or maybe he was half awake or not awake at all . . .

And here, toward daybreak, in the alcove, under Betty's neon cup and saucer, on a raw and rainy Bright Week morning . . .

She let him see.

Pastor Stephen looking at him kinda funny now.

Naum lifting his cup toward the door, saying, "Yes He is, Miss Uriel. All the time."

Miss Ruthie

—◆—

M ISS RUTHIE PROBABLY cleaned bathrooms belonging to other folks as many times or more than she cleaned her own bathroom.

Seventy-two years old. Still cleaning bathrooms.

Miss Ruthie was tired.

The woman had thirteen grown children. She lived in the projects people called Six Bedrooms.

Housing the city called the Columbia Avenue Courts.

What neighborhood people called CAC.

What people living there called the Courts.

Six of her kids had done good. Gone to college. Out on their own. Families of their own. Professional people.

Mostly the older ones and the younger ones.

Why that was? The woman could never figure.

Miss Ruthie used to tell people, "I raised them all in the same house. The same way."

She would shake her head and say, "Don't ask me to explain why some turned out one way and some the other."

Seven of her grown children lived with her.

Miss Ruthie's unit in Six Bedrooms had four bedrooms.

"Don't ask me 'bout that either—I had six? Heaven knows I don't have nobody to help me with the four I have."

And some of her seven grown kids had kids of their own living there too. Grandbabies crawling underfoot. There was no end to caring when you loved people.

Miss Ruthie got one day a week to herself.

Sunday.

Up early. Out the door showered and smelling new.

The only lady at the stop wearing a Sunday dress and gloves. Sometimes the only passenger sitting up front behind the driver on that first trolley out of Brewerytown heading over the tracks to Fishtown.

The only lady at our little Saint Alexander the Whirling Dervish Orthodox Church wearing a Sunday hat.

What Miss Ruthie called her crown. Wore a different one every week. And a fine outfit to match. Handbag. Shoes, gloves too.

Saved the black one for Holy Week. First time we saw her was Holy Friday at the Tomb.

Saved the white one for Pascha and Bright Week.

Sometimes our Miss Ruthie was all in red.

Still and all. Most times the woman sat alone.

Was lonely too. And it felt that way. Except for the presence of the priest and the deacon behind the iconostasis.

Miss Ruthie could tell by the way they looked in her direction whenever they did a peek or processed out from behind that curtain.

They must at least 'a' wondered. Back there thinking. *Why that woman in the hat left to sit alone?*

How could they not wonder, right? I mean, once a year they

read Him talking about welcoming strangers, visiting the sick, and all that sort of thing.

Had to come to some conclusion hearing that year after year with a person sitting out there on their own all alone week after week.

Miss Ruthie didn't know a whole lot about priests, but she thought he had to be asking himself, *Is there something I'm doing wrong, or something I'm neglecting to do?*

Or maybe washing his hands . . . *Got nothing to do with me. People just are what they are.*

Be a damn shame, Miss Ruthie thought, *if they're not back there coming to some kinda conclusion.*

Then again, she reasoned, *Some neighborhood dogs do make a lot of stops and take a lotta detours and give a person time and excuses putting off getting to a place they didn't necessarily want to go in the first place. And coming to conclusions can be like that too. Allow people to stay awhile in their denial.*

She just wasn't sure *she* had the kind of soul could get used to walking a lie on a leash.

She figured eventually the priest, at least, had to part the curtain and address, with *somebody*, why it is one of God's children was left to sit alone in Christ's church.

'Cause that situation ain't church.

Wandered her own damn self over to coffee hour.

Nobody *seemed* to mind. A lotta folks even said "Hi."

One time a rascal of a woman called Raskova made Ruthie sit with her. They did a lot of laughing. Next few times, though, Ruthie didn't see Raskova's big blue eyes.

And most times, since Miss Ruthie was used to years of

coaxing herself with little white lies so she could get through what she had to get through . . .

She'd tell herself that was all okay. Sitting alone on Sunday was just the way it ought to be. For now, anyway.

Just what she needed after all week of endless people pestering and pleading and pulling at her shirttails.

Coaxing herself.

Smiling inside.

Some inner voice whispering.

Peaceful time.

Rare time.

My own damn time.

Time nobody gonna give me.

Time I never get unless I take it.

Savored.

Me time.

Staring at Him up there on the iconostasis.

Him staring back.

It was all right.

Sitting there seeing eye to eye with the One who knew the truth about the coaxing lies she had to tell herself, and why she had to do it.

And how she'd employed that self-tricking strategy all these years just to fool herself into getting up weekdays in the dark.

Put on her clothes with her eyes half closed. Go sleepwalking out of that apartment with everybody else and all her grown children tucked in warm and sleeping.

Bend her neck against that wind that always seemed against her. One cold foot in front of another.

Counting all her bones.

Show up smiling at whatever house she was cleaning and do it all again.

He knew.

The Man up there in purple and indigo.

Walked that walk Himself, carrying his own Cross and all of ours too.

She knew that.

The Man who said He was the truth.

Staring right back at her.

He knew the truth.

All she wanted to do was walk up there and touch His robe.

———

THE MAYOR WANTED TO KNOW, "How in the hell did you end up at that church?"

That's what Mister Williams, the man they called the Mayor in the Courts—that's what the Mayor wanted to know.

Walking around CAC patrolling and pontificating.

Everybody right down to the toddlers knew to call him *sir*. All up in everybody's business. Bullhorn Mister Williams.

Had the straw hat thing going on with the Bermuda shorts halfway touching his bony knees. Basketweave no-socks buff-colored summer slip-ons. The short-sleeved crisp white shirt open at the neck.

Called it his summer sling.

Winter you could hardly see Mister Williams's face, wrapped up like he was. Top to toe in so many layers you woulda thought he was a second-grader snowsuited by his momma with his name sewed in the cuffs of his clipped-on mittens. Was only the straw hat tied over his ears with a tartan scarf that gave the Mayor away.

"How I ended up at that church is how the Lord ended me up there," Miss Ruthie told Mister Williams. "You know I was cleaning for that couple for years."

"The ones with the big house downtown on Rittenhouse Square?" Mister W said. "They go over to that church?"

"Yep," was all Miss Ruthie was willing to say on the matter.

Why the Mayor needed to know about her asking that lady about that icon out in the hallway, the long sheet with Jesus being buried and all the people a complexion she'd never seen before in a picture like that, why tell the Mayor? The man had no interest in church. Hadn't been in years. You think people can't see what you're aiming at under that hat?

"Well, if you ain't gonna talk to me . . ."

Mister Williams had an idea about his stature in the neighborhood that allowed him the pleasure of feeling insulted whenever he damn well pleased.

"Then you and your summer sling can just go about your business, Fred. And ain't you got a wife at home wondering where in the hell you are all day, 'stead a be going around bothering all the widows in the Court?"

And with that she dismissed the man in the straw hat and settled down to sitting on her front steps sewing.

Thinking about how her and the Orthodox came to meet through her scrubbing and scouring and singing church songs while she worked at that rich lady's house, songs she'd learned as a child.

She spent her money here and there
Until she had no, had no more to spare
The doctors, they'd done all they could
But their medicine would do no good
When she touched Him the Savior didn't see
But still He turned around and cried
"Somebody touched Me"
She said, "It was I who just wanna touch the hem of Your garment
"I know I'll be made whole right now."

———◦———

IT WAS BACK A WAYS . . . back when she was young. Before doctors were a part of her life.

Back before she had to come down from her second-floor CAC apartment scooching her butt down a step at a time. In those days she could've skipped down those steps if she wanted to. And sometimes she did.

Now to tell the truth, back then, young Ruth Blossom Craig didn't like James Major Blue when she first saw him.

The man was too stiff.

And serious? Too serious for a young man. And way too serious for a man who couldn't read or write. But damn if he couldn't fix a truck or car. Any truck. Any car. Anything with a motor or an engine for that matter.

"Boy got a good job," is what Ruthie's mother said the neighbors all said. "Work for the city. Like your daddy did before he died."

Ruthie remembered her father talking about the man who worked where he worked. Man called James Blue.

"That young man they hired gonna be something someday," her father said. "Boss told 'im, 'I tell you what, son, you take that engine there, the one all in pieces on the ground? You put that heap a shit together and it run . . . I hire you.'"

Ruthie's father, Gaylord Craig, and the other men in the city auto pool yard couldn't believe it when the boss said, "One more thing, kid," and that old white man tied a red handkerchief around James Blue's eyes. "You got to do it blindfolded."

"And damn if he didn't," Gaylord Craig told Ruthie and the family when they were eating supper that night around the kitchen table.

James Blue told everybody it was love at first sight. "When I saw Ruthie . . . boy, I was like, there is no other girl."

Ruthie told everybody, "I hated him. Trying to follow me to the bus stop talking nonsense. I told him, I don't talk to strangers."

Two months later, maybe three, they couldn't wait no longer, is what Ruthie said. "So we just did it and got married."

First couple in the community to own their own house, James and Ruthie Blue. First ones to have a new car. First ones to have more than a dozen children.

People said, "No wonder James died young."

Ruth Blue had no choice.

Working as a housemaid downtown at that big hotel on Broad Street after getting the kids off to school, that's where she met the woman who got her into doing private-duty cleaning.

The priest, Naum, was introduced to Miss Ruthie by Pastor Stephen Jerome and his wife, Malvena. They co-pastored the

Saint Yared African Orthodox Church that met in an old factory on Frankford Avenue.

Malvena told Naum, "If you're looking for someone to make that old cassock of yours look new . . . Miss Ruthie," Malvena introduced them. "Padre here needs a little mending."

Miss Ruthie looked up from her scissors and sewing and said, "He does look like he's coming apart in some critical places."

Pastor Stephen's father was pastor emeritus at Saint Yared's. It was the old pastor who first read about the ancient Church and traced the apostolic roots to the Orthodox. "But as far as getting in the door?"

Naum once heard the old pastor say, "Sometimes the distance between persons and God is only thin as skin."

Miss Ruthie knew it to be true.

Especially on Sunday mornings.

Naum came out of the altar. The prayers of Proskomedia were completed. The preparation of the bread and wine for Holy Communion was something he liked to do slowly and in a quiet way. Naming each person. Placing a particle of bread for each soul. Building on the little golden dish, around the cube of bread in the center that represented Lord Jesus, building an icon of the life of the local church, one particle, one person at a time.

It did bother him, seeing Miss Ruthie, a person in the pew but no particle on the paten. God knows the fullness of His Church. It bothered Naum a little less now that they'd come to know each other.

Miss Ruthie looked up from her sewing as he came out the deacon's door. "Morning, Father," she said. "Putting the finishing threads to your cassock. Every stitch a prayer."

"Miss Ruthie." Naum was happy to see her. "I don't want to disturb your prayer," he said.

She said, "Don't worry about that. You can't. Not all by yourself. Takes all the people I got pulling at me all week to unravel that thread."

Naum thought about that for a minute, all the people dependent on her, all the things she'd been through. Then he said, "I often wonder why we end up where we do in life."

"I don't know," Miss Ruthie said. "But I did notice when I was down the Shore, they did tend to put the strongest, thickest pilings where the water was the deepest and the waves was the roughest, holding up that pier we was all standing on."

Naum said, "You wanna do me a favor, Miss Ruthie?"

She said, "What's that?"

He said, "Stay today. Be a good sermon if you give it. Tell the people about the pilings and the rough water and the pier."

The way she said no made them both smile.

"Well, if I can't get you to do the sermon," Naum said, "then can I ask you a question, while it's just me and you?"

She said, "Sure."

He said, "We both know of a certain couple, living in a certain brownstone on a certain gentrified old Philadelphia square. Got more gold than the whole neighborhood put together."

"Maybe we don't," Miss Ruthie said. "Maybe we might."

Naum said, "Well, this is the problem."

Asking Miss Ruthie's hypothetical *what-if* guidance on couples having problems.

The woman in the front pew in the pretty Sunday dress with the crown hat and pristine gloves on her lap, sitting there looking at Naum over her glasses like a boy trying to hide a hole in the knee of his new dungarees from his mother . . .

Him going on and on about the lady with all her houses and cars and money and closets full of clothes, saying so and so, and such and such . . . No right to be unhappy but doing nothing but murmuring and complaining . . .

And him, the husband, richer than King Solomon. The man oblivious as one of those stone frogs sitting in the fancy fountain in the square that's supposed to be spouting water but hasn't for years.

Miss Ruthie was packing up her sewing kit.

Sad, Naum, every time she got ready to leave.

She held up her scissors. Solid and shiny. Looked to Naum like eight-inch knife-edged dressmaker shears. Had the kind of heft that could've cut the moon in half.

Force and the blades of a simple machine. A pair of wedges in the shape of a cross. Miss Ruthie in her energy made them pivot around the fulcrum and alternate positions in space, severing the liturgy from the morning in wide sacramental swaths of time that cut across eternity.

She started to open and close the blades. Slowly at first.

She looked at the moving scissors and said to Naum, "This one thing, or two?"

The essence of the woman saw him without apology.

She said, "Moving in different directions, or the same?"

He may have blinked.

Ruth Blossom Blue didn't blink.

There *was* no blink in the woman.

She said, "You wanna put your finger in between?"

Naum knew that was the only comment she was gonna give on getting between that rich couple or any couple, and he said, "No, thank you, Miss Ruthie."

When she looked at him, Naum the priest could see the eyes she'd been staring at, the eyes of the One on the iconostasis.

Naum once heard old Pastor CJ say, "Sometimes the distance between persons and God is only thin as skin."

Miss Ruthie knew it to be true.

Especially on Sunday mornings.

She finished her packing up, pulled on her gloves, and said, "Take more than scissors and sewing, Father, to get us all together."

Sad, Naum, every time she got ready to leave.

Miss Ruthie told him, "I'll have those other vestments ready next Sunday, if that's okay? But I got to be up at Saint Yared's today. You know I'd like to stay . . . But your Little Harry's waiting."

Naum said, "I really appreciate this, Miss Ruth."

She put her glasses in, snapped her purse, and said, "God is good."

Naum said, "All the time, Mother, all the time."

Outside, Little Harry was waiting at the curb in his '71 Stepside C10 Chevy pickup, the light blue junkyard jalopy with the dapple-rust patina.

He got Miss Ruthie seated and closed the door.

She said, "I appreciate this, Harry. Save me taking the trolley and two buses and being late getting all the way up to Saint Yared's. You know Pastor Stephen says the choir sounds better with two sopranos."

Harry said, "I don't know how you do it, Miss Ruth."

She said, "Seventy-two now, Harry. Still cleaning other people's toilets. Still scrubbing and scouring. Still singing church songs, and boy, I'm still tired."

The woman had a way of knowing what a boy was thinking by the way the boy went to start, and then stopped—knowing Harry wanted to ask her something, probably the same thing the Mayor wanted to know, what first made her come to Saint Alexander's.

And she let Harry know—the boy could tell by the way she looked out the windshield—it'd be better if he didn't.

Was that Friday last Lent Doctor Baks told her.

That evening. Wearing her black hat.

Resolved right there at His Tomb, looking at Him and His Mother and all the people with a complexion she'd never seen before in a picture like that—on that long winding sheet with Jesus being buried—resolved right there at His Tomb just to sing the Lamentations and not tell a soul.

Looking at Him and His . . . and all that wailing going on around Him. Miss Ruthie knew it wouldn't do anything but get 'em all, church and home, just hanging on her even more.

Too tired.

Kinda be nice, just to stop.

Put the scrubbing and the scouring and the scissors aside.

Spend at least part of her last year singing church songs.

She could tell by the quiet sitting there in the truck with them that Harry didn't want to disturb her.

So she said, "Little Harry?"

He said, "Yes, Miss Ruthie?"

And Miss Ruthie said, "I'm ready."

Matty Nat

———⋙⋅◆⋅⋘———

S HE SAID, "NAUM, the next thing I knew, it just happened."
Naum was backing out of the narrow church drive, twisted
in his seat, navigating between the thick wrought-iron gateposts
and the palm trees on either side, when the priest's wife decided
to tell him.

Her telling Naum that, then and there?

That's how he got the dent in his new used car and smashed
out the taillight.

After liturgy, her husband, Father Andon Flynn, the priest
of the parish, had told them, "You two go ahead. I'll meet you
there."

He often stayed behind to talk with parishioners who were
having problems. He was a good priest that way, Father Andon.
Today he was meeting with a young woman taking religious history classes he was offering at a nearby college.

Everybody loved the priest Andon.

He'd been ordained a long time and was one of the first priests
to offer to go south and start a community in the American Bible
Belt.

Andon's grandfather—the old priest Father Andon Terrova,

Andon the First, born and ordained in the old country, who had his name changed to Andon Flynn at Ellis Island—had died years before Andon's birth.

Father Andon the First had appeared to baby Andon's mother in a doorway of her home, warning her that his namesake and grandson—her baby, Andon—was smothering.

The tall man with the priestly beard stood like a silhouette in a doorway of light and drew her to the room at the end of the hall where her baby napped.

"Nusa," Bride, he called her, and the man in the incorporeal cassock turned into her baby's room.

Fearless when she looked up and saw the stranger, Florence, the young mother, advanced with only her broom for a weapon and only her love for courage.

But when she entered the room, the bearded man in the cassock was gone, and she couldn't see her child.

In the crib, Sultan, the family cat, was sitting on her baby's face. Her little Andoni was blue. She shooed the cat away and breathed into her child, again and again, and slowly, the color of life returned. The first and most intimate community, mother and child, cried together.

———

IT WAS LATE WINTER when the bishop sent the newly ordained Naum south to cover for a number of retiring priests. Father Andon allowed Naum to serve with him on Sundays when the young priest wasn't needed elsewhere.

Andon was approaching retirement, living in a fifty-five–plus deed-restricted community with all the amenities—clubhouse, pool, walking trails lined with palm trees, and bougainvillea.

Naum was invited to stay in the extra bedroom, sit on the sofa with Father and Matushka Natalie in the evening, and watch Hercule Poirot and Miss Marple. The couple loved British mysteries and tea in the evening, decaf for Andon.

But the local Holiday Inn Express had a free buffet breakfast, and at the end of the day, Naum knew they preferred relaxing with their socks off.

Him too.

That morning after liturgy, Andon told Naum, "Go ahead, Naum. Take Matty Nat. I'll be along presently."

Natalie was fifteen years Andon's junior and a beauty to boot.

"Go to the café and I'll meet you there." Andon pulled at his long graying beard, looked at her, smiled at Naum, and said, "I should never have married a younger woman."

Most of the people at the parish were retired from up north, and most were of Slavic background. So Andon, the people called Batyushka, little father. And Natalie, the mother of the parish, they called Matushka, little mother.

Some of the younger men had a hard time concentrating on the prayers when Matty Nat came in to light her candles.

Women too.

One woman in particular, an MSW/clinical psychologist, told Naum, "A skirt that short? An hour in my office, at least, for every inch above the knee."

Long-legged Natalie, the Iowa-born, blonde-haired, corn-fed quintessential American girl and former fashion model, at liturgy in heels. "Nobody cared when I was a lipstick Evangelical," she said. "And if my husband doesn't say anything . . ."

Natalie, *la zeste de la vie*—the very lifeblood of being. The primal heat the old women denied they'd once known and now chose not to recall.

Natalie, the *dynami zois*—that dynamic female force of life that once boiled in their being, the very force of life the nunnas now buried in the laundry basket where the old men hid the dancing shoes their Natalies used to wear.

Natalie and Naum sat across from each other at the café.

The waitress with the tattoos said, "Two, Nat?"

Natalie said, "Three. He's coming."

Sarah the waitress said, "Father Andon be getting his regular?"

"You can count on him being regular." Natalie and Sarah sharing a laugh, a standing joke.

Naum sat there like a cartoon ghost.

Outside, the sky had that Sunday-after-liturgy brightness. Every variant of green in the palm-tree palette, from light to dark, olive to avocado, jungle to pine, pistachio to lime, took a turn showing its face as the breeze fanned the fronds across a too-blue sky.

But Naum couldn't shake the coldness of her matter-of-fact statement, "It just happened."

It had his mind escaping up north where the branches were still spindly-grim and winter-barren. He couldn't help seeing them twisted across the rust-belt sky like the scratches she described down her boss's shirtless back.

Sarah the waitress left, and Natalie thought she had to go over it all again, in detail.

"Why're you telling me this?" Naum asked.

It was like vinegar in his coffee.

Natalie didn't answer right away. She had some coffee and said, "Confession."

That made about as much sense as her leaving the spoon in the mug as she drank. All Naum could think about was her poking herself in the eye.

"Confession? Here?" he said. "To what end?"

He knew she could tell he was looking out at his taillight in the parking lot. Naum couldn't believe she was smiling.

But she was so pretty, so . . . women that age . . . men didn't know what to call it. Naum didn't, and Natalie knew it.

She said, "I know you haven't been ordained that long, Naum, but you are a priest, and I guess what I really want to know is, should I be receiving Holy Communion or not?"

Sarah the waitress came back with two globular pots, one with a brown top, the other orange. "Decaf or regular?" she said.

"Regular," Natalie said. She looked at Naum and said, "For both of us."

He sat there looking into the steam. Maybe he was thinking there'd be some kind of a simple solution to this bad dream swirling up like a genie from his cup.

There wasn't.

Bewildered Naum said, "Look, Matushka, you know I love you. You two are like family. Mentors. Role models to me and to my wife, and we love you. And Greta and I respect you and your husband. We look at you two and hope someday we'll have what you have, but then with what you've told me . . ."

All that got him was her smile, again. But this time, a smile a half a shadow sadder. What seemed to Naum a smile that was a little more *little-girl* subdued.

He told her, "The bishop has me down here doing supply for the next month or two, filling in, covering different parishes where the priest is retiring or on vacation. I'm scheduled back at your parish in two weeks. That'll give you, and me, time to think this thing through. Time to change your mind. You're an educated woman. Theologically astute. You and Father have been ordained way longer than I, and you, as a woman, have more insight into this than probably I *ever* will. But at the same time, you know this just doesn't fit with our life in Christ. Hurts your boss too. He married?"

"Yes," she said.

"Kids?" he asked.

"Yes, Naum." Natalie wasn't smiling.

"What? Did he tell you he was going to leave his wife?"

"We're making plans," she said.

"How old is this guy?"

"Does it matter?"

Naum waited.

She said, "Little younger than me."

Naum said, "Oh boy."

There was no way she could hide what she was thinking.

Naum wanted to ask her if she could still get pregnant.

So he did.

She said, "Why do you think I'm asking you?"

"No?" he said.

And when she saw she'd fooled him, she felt sorry for him and laughed. She said, "I can, but I'm not. Not as far as I know."

"How long's this been going on?" Naum asked.

"Almost a year," she said. "And you know, I have my suspicions about him."

"Your boss?" Naum said.

"No, Naum, not my boss. Your precious Father Andon. With a girl from the college. The one he's probably with right now. Spending too much time, inappropriate amounts of time in my opinion. I've tracked him. I've compiled a dossier, receipts, cell phone bills, evidence, printouts from social-media sites, hard evidence. Almost two years' worth."

Matty said, "Men have their midlife crises too, ya know. So what? What was I supposed to do? Take a betrayed spouse overdose like that other matushka when she found out about her husband? It's not that easy down here to find Darvocet or Oxy anymore since they shut down the pill mills. Try getting painkillers, you know, unless you go downtown, on the street."

It took his breath away. Naum tried not to show it. He'd heard what that poor matushka had done years after she'd found her husband had been unfaithful.

Years after the guilty priest confessed and thought he'd been reconciled with his wife . . .

Years after he was sure they'd found a way to go on with the work of the gospel . . .

Natalie said, "It's a particularly toxic hypocrisy, Naum. Hits different people different ways. Maybe they're not even to blame, somebody gives up on the light and gets lost in the dark. Never know what a person might be driven to when the priest wears one face at church and another when he thinks nobody's looking."

Maybe the young matushka couldn't figure out why she was

doing what she was doing or what exactly it had to do with the priesthood and her husband, but at least she didn't lie to herself, or to Naum.

She said to him, "Don't look so hurt."

Natalie was nobody's fool, except maybe her own.

Naum said, "One thing you're not, Nat, is naïve. You're a pretty sophisticated person."

"So perhaps there's more to married life and to my particular situation than you might first have imagined?" she said.

"Nonetheless," Naum said, "don't tell me you believe your boss hasn't run that same game on someone else. And if that's the regard he has for his wife, not to mention his kids, how is he different from that priest whose wife committed suicide? And what's gonna happen when some new girl in the office catches his eye, maybe somebody his own age, maybe somebody younger, and he stops seeing you?"

Natalie had turned to stone.

If Father Andon hadn't suddenly appeared, Naum had no doubt she would have come across the cold Formica booth top, poured his coffee in his lap, and put her spoon in his ear.

"Hey, you two." The man was always smiling. "I gotta go wash my hands. Be right back. Nat, you order for me, my usual?"

Up until now, they'd been very private people.

Naum couldn't tell one way or the other if she'd confronted Andon with her secret dossier. Naum had no clue if Andon knew or was aware of her adulterous actions or her accusations against him.

And Father Andon?

If he knew, he couldn't have acted more in-the-dark

unperturbed or done a better job concealing his reaction if he'd hidden her and her unfaithful boss and her entire catalog of contemptible charges in his bushy gray beard.

Naum watched his friend and confessor walk toward the back. His cassocks had to be special made. He was broad and muscular, with a thick neck and chest. If he'd been an athlete, classic Greco-Roman wrestling would've been his forte, every match, no doubt, shoulder to the mat.

The stout powerful build he had inherited from his father, Two-Beer Eddie Flynn, was typical of many of the men of our background. But unlike most, Andon was more than six feet tall—like Florence, his American mother.

Andon had worked construction in the beginning. The men on the job site knew Andon the laborer had a religious side, and that might've opened anyone else to torment and teasing. But no one on the work site wanted to mess with Eddie Flynn's son, Tony the Pit Bull, who could carry four five-gallon buckets of stone in each hand, no sweat.

Naum said to Natalie, "Will you tell him?"

She said, "Will you?"

She knew he couldn't. But was this a confession?

She looked over her shoulder at Andon as he walked to the restroom. Turned to leer at Naum and said, "I'm not stopping."

Some people can cry on cue. Some people can hold the tears back at will. Naum was sitting there right in the middle. In the middle of two friends. In the middle between someone facing a choice that could affect a lot of people's eternity.

He said, "Then can I ask one thing, Matty? Just one."

"Sure," she said.

"Hold off on receiving till we can talk again in a . . . a better setting," Naum said. "And then, if you want, we can talk it out some more. Not so much for me, Nat, but for you, for your husband, give your marriage a chance, for the other guy and his family too. Please. From what I hear, these things never turn out well. You might have a change of heart. Pray. Maybe talk to a more experienced priest or matushka. And promise me you won't do it again with this guy. Look for another job. Please. This is serious."

"Wherefore whosoever shall eat this bread, and drink this cup of the Lord, unworthily, shall be guilty of the body and blood of the Lord. For this cause many are weak and sickly among you, and many have died."

Natalie knew.

She helped the women of the parish prepare for Communion. She instructed them in the way we'd been taught from the beginning. It's not water, our mothers taught us. So why would she continue in this soul-destroying activity?

Naum didn't think even Natalie herself had a clue as to why she was doing what she was doing, just some kind of pheromone jones reaction to whatever clergy wives had to deal with on their own.

She said, "Okay, Father, I won't receive."

He sat next to her, Andon, and brushed back his full head of hair, still thick and black.

Naum had never seen Andon happier. They were holding hands in the booth, laughing and being silly, like only loving couples are silly.

He didn't look at Naum, not once, but once in a while during their silliness, she'd stare at Naum till he looked away.

But when Naum did look at them, Batyushka Andon and Matushka Natalie, he couldn't help it. He loved them, and dumb as it was, he said, "I love you, Batty Tony. I love you, Matty Nat."

Three women in the next booth overheard their silliness and started mocking Andon and Natalie. Naum knew the cafe served alcohol. Most twenty-four–hour operations did.

The language on the other side of the booth-back got racier and racier. Naum's booth rocked right along with the raucous party next door.

When matushka stood up to complain, they cursed her back down.

Andon stood, straightening his cassock and stroking his beard. "I'll have you know you're cursing the wife of a priest."

The way he smiled at them, the way he said it, Naum couldn't tell if he was being serious or still being silly.

"Oh! Apologies, handsome!" The three women stood in a chorus and saluted him with their drinks. "To the handsome priest!"

"Accepted." Andon turned to sit down.

For some reason that struck the ladies as over-the-top comical and started them laughing and mocking. They goaded each other in a crescendo of curses, one trying to outswear the other, purposely rocking the booth with ribald charges of nothing under that cassock, child molestation, dicey bishops, and collection-plate pilfering. Macbeth's three witches couldn't have concocted a more malignant malediction.

That was Naum's cue.

Day was fading, and the thick subtropical landscaping made

the café parking lot look pastel pretty in orange-sunset azure hues.

Andon stood with his arm around her waist and nodded toward the broken taillight and the dent in Naum's car.

Naum looked at Natalie.

"I was backing out, not paying attention at the church," Naum explained.

She looked up at her husband, then looked back in Naum's direction, shrugged, and said, "The next thing I knew, it just happened."

Married People

—◆—

AFTER FIFTY YEARS TOGETHER, old Samuel Elias told his wife, "Magdalena, we'll give it another fifty, and then we'll make a final decision."

She gave him the look.

Magdalena knew he was an idiot. She knew it when she married him. That's why she loved him. She loved him even during the years she couldn't stand him.

She would walk around the house singing, ignoring him, maybe on purpose, doing whatever she was doing, and hear the old fool talking to her mother. "Is the girlie singing, Muttie?" old Samuel would say to her mother's black-and-white picture hanging in the hall.

When they left her mother's house all those years ago, the day of their wedding, Muttie said, "Take care of her, Samuel, and God will save your soul in her."

He said, "Muttie, I promise."

Samuel knew men and women were not equal in the modern sense. Men had bigger lungs. Bigger muscles. Bigger brains, so they could serve the woman.

The day of his wedding, his father told him, "She's the gate to heaven, son. You were in a woman nine months. If there's only one seat, she gets it. If there's only enough to spare, her and the kids get the new shoes. You make do. Open the door for her. Never let the hands that cradle your babies clean the bathrooms. That's your job. You are not her equal. What the soul is in the body, the woman is in the world.

"What? Do you think the snake in the Garden couldn't have gone after Adam if he wanted? No. He knew which soul to wound, the one more spiritually sensitive, and the man and all the rest? A piece of cake."

Samuel knew what his father meant. There were times early in their marriage when he could stand on a nickel and tell if it was heads or tails, when he could caress the buffalo with his big toe. Magdalena would look at his boots and give him that look when he came home from the loading dock.

"How many times can you take the same pair of boots to Jacob the shoemaker? Those old boots know their way home by themselves."

"I don't need new boots, girl, I hate new shoes." He'd put the unopened pay envelope on the kitchen table. "They give me shoe-bites, new shoes."

But she knew the finances. She had a natural talent for doing the bills. So when she said, "It's time, Samuel."

Then he'd relent.

"New steel-toed boots for the putty factory." He looked down proudly.

When he looked up and saw her over there where she was making the holy bread, the way she looked at him and dusted the flour from her hands, he didn't know which way to jump.

So he said, "What a waste of money, new boots three months before retiring," and knew right away he'd jumped in the wrong direction.

But his Magdalena didn't say a thing. She just sent him on his way with a kiss and the lunch she packed.

Every day Magdalena was looking more beautiful to him, and lately more like her mother too, her mother who'd been gone for many years.

"I think you're pretty," he said, backing down their porch steps on his last day at the factory, stuffing the lunch she'd made into the oversized pockets of his hooded denim work coat, the one she'd patched so many times.

Behind the door she made the cross and closed her eyes.

"Fifty years." Magdalena said when she thought back, "It took that long, Samuel, for your eyes to soften and my heart to unharden."

———◦———

HE MADE HIS USUAL before-bed around-the-house routine. Windows. Doors. Outside lights. Is the gas off? And lately, before bed, it seemed like he spent more time in the bathroom than she did.

It was okay.

She liked to read propped up on her pillows by the bedside lamp with the faded shade. She didn't seem to mind waiting for her Samuel to finally come and snuggle in close to her.

Samuel was an action junkie. He had to *do*. He couldn't *not* be doing.

Magdalena, on the other hand, didn't always have to do. She merely had to be. Her being was her doing.

Samuel Elias had always had a sense that he felt his way through the world, his life, and even his house by means of measurements and tools, like a blind man feeling his way around a blueprint with a cane.

But his Magdalena?

She walked in light by her gift of just being Magdalena.

He lucked out and found a girl who danced to the rhythm of God's creation. A girl who never had any use for so-called instructions or prefab one-size-fits-all measurements or the schematic blueprints used by those who fancied themselves general manager of the universe and needed to oversee and orchestrate every little detail.

She looked up from her book. "Yes," Magdalena told him, standing there with his flashlight. "Like you, Herr Meister des Universums."

Her eyes would read a sentence, then take a rest. And on the inside of her eyelids she saw the two of them together when they were young, in front of their icon corner, lighting the oil lamp and saying the prayers before bed.

Now the lamp was a flickering lithium-battery LED tealight, and as he made his rounds in the dark, he could hear her in the bedroom, whisper-singing the hymns of the Church.

Samuel looked in the corner and could've sworn it was the genuine article. He wouldn't have lied to himself and denied he smelled incense and the warm oil of a real flame.

When the kids were little the family prayed together—before meals, before bed, in times of trouble, on name days and feast days, around the birthday cake, or when someone was anxious or worried, when someone died, or when a baby was born . . . lit the lamps and prayed the prayers.

They showed their boys how to make the cross without moving their arm each time they heard someone taking the Lord's Name in vain.

Magdalena told them, "Not take—bear. Bear the Lord's Name in vain. Don't call yourself a Christian and not struggle every day to grow in being a bearer of His likeness in your heart and in your actions toward others, bearers of His holiness. Just like the oil carries the flame, so we bear His Name."

Magdalena made sure the twin threads of faith and thanksgiving were woven into the fabric of their daily life. Especially gathering her boys in front of the icon corner after Saturday Vespers, lighting incense and candles, and asking one another's forgiveness, saying together the prayers of preparation before Sunday Holy Communion.

But now the boys were raised and had lives of their own. Sure, they called here and again, maybe even a visit now and then . . .

Ah, why lie? Not even for Pascha.

Not even a telephone call on their fiftieth anniversary.

Lonely, bittersweet birthdays. The bright sadness of lighting candles every week at church alone. They never called or came around unless their parents called them first. Who wants to be a nag?

But Magdalena and her Samuel knew, even though the icons were still there in their icon corner, old and cherished ones, along with the ancient holy bread seal from Albania and all the holy things from their parents . . . and their parents' parents . . .

Even though at morning prayers, they shared a nibble of the nafora, the holy bread from Sunday that others called antidoron, and sipped the holy water—still they knew that there were bound to be shadows, even in a sunlit life.

Every year the list of the living for whom they prayed became shorter. And the list of those gone to be with Lord Jesus . . .

And lately, most vividly, when either was alone in the house, it was as if they could hear all the wise things their mother or father used to say.

Magdalena, walking through the stillness of a silent house, and Samuel, by himself with a push broom, sweeping out the cavernous unheated putty factory warehouse, talking with those gone before, communing with "the great cloud of witnesses," with the saints and angels who had walked with them since childhood.

Now that they were old and it was just the two of them, every time they took their meds—"Thank God for . . ." and they'd name each doctor by name. And the pharmacist too.

Have mercy on those who have no doctor or medication or access to hospitals or health care . . .

Every time the old car started, or they did their wash—*God has blessed us . . .*

When they unloaded the groceries—*God have mercy on us for having so much and on those who don't have enough . . .*

Thanks be to God, for health, beauty, goodness, intelligence, yes . . .

And yes, Lord, for our Love of Thee . . .

For keeping us safe and free from all serious injury, illness, incident, and harm, and out of the hands of those who hate You, O God . . .

For refrigeration, indoor cooking and plumbing and running water . . .

Every sunrise, every snowfall, each new blossom in the spring, rain running in the gutters, new shoots on the trees . . .

Each time they saw the ocean, it was new—*Yonder is the sea great and wide . . .*

The sunset, the moon and the stars—*How wondrous are Thy works, O Lord . . .*

A beggar or a man walking with crutches—*Have mercy on my brother . . .*

Loud happy children on their way home from school, raucous boys shooting hoops at the playground, cars in a procession around Palmer Burial Ground—*In wisdom hast Thou made them all . . .*

The wordless icon of thanksgiving just came out of them, neither looking at the other, both together, making the sign of the cross.

Nowadays, seeing each other first thing in the morning or napping at midday, or eating in front of the TV at sundown, or sitting on the porch in the evening, most days . . .

The man and the woman were the only icons either knew

One to the other

Icons of reciprocal love-bound existence

Married people

Icons, one to the other, the other to one

The Holy Spirit, sent by the Son, proceeding from the Father, enlivening the space between

One in the way they touched

One in the way they felt when she moved close on a dark restless morning

A closeness that gave such comfort that before Magdalena

knew it, Samuel was back to snoring as they sank again together deep into that otherworldly sleep.

A closeness of being

A oneness in breathing

An unshakable solace during lightning in the middle of the night, when thunder elicited psalms from their dreaming souls and drew them forward together like moths, toward the dawn of the day without evening.

———

WHEN THE PAIN CAME, Samuel's pain, and she touched him, joy resounded in the heaven of his heart. He looked at her and said, "Don't leave me, Magdalena."

Magdalena took him in her gaze and said, "I never will."

How could she let go his hand?

He, who sat on her bed all those nights when she wasn't feeling herself. When the young doctor needlessly changed her meds. Meds that had worked perfectly well all those years. And after three days of worsening misery, he took her to the ER. They kept her three nights, while he went home alone to an empty house and neither slept, nor ate, nor did his nightly routine.

And when he brought her home, every time she looked up, she didn't even have to ring the bell he placed on the bedside table. There he was, staring, holding her hand while she slept, trying to be nonchalant, like she hadn't caught him praying over her and making the sign of the cross.

How could he not hold her hand?

Wasn't it Magdalena who had kept her head and called the

EMTs the time he collapsed, when they shook their heads like there was no hope for the man motionless on the pavement?

"Silly," she'd say, every time she caught him staring. "After all these years, still looking at me. I don't know what you're seeing."

"Never enough," Samuel would say.

"Silly."

Her voice?

That's all he needed.

As long as he could hear the sound of her, what matter were the words?

What matter if it was two beds now, close together, now that she was always too hot and his feet were always too cold? They could hold hands at night across the space, couldn't they, and who would need to know?

"And a restaurant, why?" Samuel told Naum. "When her cooking is love made edible."

The ritual of morning coffee together. Taking turns doing dishes, singing songs from the sixties . . .

Eating cream cheese on rye toast, feeding crumbs to the blue-jays jumping down from trees in the yard . . .

While he scrubbed the bathrooms and said the prayer, Magdalena did the bills at her table and said the prayer too.

Sometimes he would come home and find her sleeping in his bed. "For the smell of you." She would smile up at him, hugging his pillow.

Something in Samuel, each time he saw his Magdalena, called prayer out of his heart, if she was rolling up the vacuum cleaner cord or doing the dishes, every motion a petition.

Three times.

Three little kisses.

She knew Samuel was thanking the Father, and the Son, and the Holy Spirit for his girl with each kiss.

"What? You think I don't notice?" she'd say.

"Notice what? What do you know?" He'd get shy like a kid caught peeking at a girl he thought was pretty.

Magdalena wouldn't answer.

But they both knew.

She did the same.

When she watched him pushing the mower, each pass over the grass, each heart saying the Jesus Prayer without words, each heart beating.

Her behind the curtain.

Him out in the yard in his ancient bib overalls and battered straw hat. Out there where it was too hot for a man his age to be traipsing around in the sun.

Maybe their hearts did sync like he always said, the old fool. Maybe it was her heart that kept his beating, maybe the other way too.

Still, Magdalena wouldn't rest easy till she brought him his lemonade. He loved her homemade lemonade, and he was out there in his lawn chair admiring his yardwork, sitting under his tree, eating Cheez-Its, wearing his battered straw hat and reading his Bible till his beard rested on his chest and he admired his yardwork to sleep.

Slowly through the darkened house, jiggling locks, double-checking, triple-checking, now did I do that lock already?

Ah, habits, automatic habits.

Probably did. But better check again, won't hurt.

Samuel, making his rounds, thinking of how things went at home and how different they went at church.

Samuel Elias and Magdalena were among the few left of our founders. They worried like a father and mother about how God's people treated each other at our little Saint Alexander the Whirling Dervish Orthodox Church, how easily offended they were, how stubborn, how slow to forgive or repent.

"My goodness," Samuel Elias said to the priest, Naum. "I think of all the Orthodox, we Albanians have the thickest heads and the thinnest skin."

"And we also have the best annual shish kabob picnic at least once a week," Naum told Samuel. "We grill each other every Sunday over the glowing charcoal of the smallest offense, intended or imagined. Doesn't matter to us, we'll work with whatever the devil can give us."

At coffee hour, both parties insisting on their version of what the Church holds while completely missing the Cross and our Master, who to Samuel seemed to watch from the estavromenos in front of the iconostasis while armor-plated egos hammered more nails.

"Ah, who knows? I suppose I do it myself," Samuel said to the dark, and waved his hand at a mosquito who'd somehow slipped in past his best effort to secure the screen door without letting in those things that fly in the dark.

At home, when he and Magdalena had a disagreement, "And thank God," he said to the mosquito, "our arguments are like your bites, my friend, itchy and annoying, but less and less substantial and usually gone by morning."

Samuel knew emotions ran high in families. Blood was thicker than water, no doubt. People took things seriously, maybe too seriously.

He and Magdalena did it too.

But unlike some at the church, neither Magdalena nor Samuel ever listed their contributions to the household as a defense for bad behavior, or turned the hot handle of the samovar toward the other by pointing out their shortcomings.

Besides, what good would it do?

When it came to shortcomings, Samuel admitted to the mosquito, "I, no doubt, got her beat by less effort than it takes to stay awake during one of Naum's sermons, which Naum himself admits could anesthetize an elephant."

Blood *is* thicker than water, but chrism is thicker than blood—at least that's what Father Naum said.

And though Magdalena and Samuel did not share blood, they were one in the chrism of the chalice, and one in the blood of their sons, as all their forebearers were present in them, one in the Blood of Christ Jesus.

Yet at Saint Alexander's lately, they were rolling up their baptismal certificates and beating each other over the head with long-festering charges prepared against their brothers and sisters in the chalice. Charges that usually had very little to do with the life in the New Covenant of Christ.

And that bothered Samuel and Magdalena the same as when their children used to fight.

Their marriage, their household, and the household of God's communion in the Church? Hadn't they finally, after fifty years, become one and the same?

Or had they always been so, and now, finally, after years of struggle together to lead the life in Christ, the truth of shared being could be seen with the softening of the eyes of the heart and the unhardening of the heart of the soul.

The natural bonds, the covenants—God and His people, husband and wife, mother and daughter, brother and sister, father and son—were still there, but now, in Christ, in the Church, those covenant bonds stood for more, didn't they?

Naum told the people, "In the Eucharist of Christ, the biological blood relationships are no longer confined to individual households. They become symbols of a greater existential truth, of an eternal covenant. There is truly only one Bridegroom and one Bride, one household not built on sand, and it is His, and it is Him, and we are in Him."

"So how are we treating Him," Samuel wondered, "when we treat each other so carelessly?"

Magdalena made the cross and said she knew of "three Persons united by love of the other . . . and a myriad of individuals divided by love of self."

Naum wanted time to think that over.

For Samuel and Magdalena, how could they be cruel to one another, or to anyone? After all they'd been through, the tragedy with their sons, what they called their greatest sadness—one forever lost, the other walking wounded.

And even after that, by the grace of God, they still never gave up on Christ and His Church. Something deep down made them know He would never give up on them.

Some deeper truth, they understood, came home only in suffering. Each one loved, loved even the stumbling and missteps of the other.

WAITING FOR HER SAMUEL to come to bed, knowing he was double- and triple-checking? Made her smile, really.

Foibles and failure? Even for those, they thanked God.

The children of Samuel and Magdalena, having witnessed in their parents, in all their growing up, the day-to-day struggle of ordinary people to live the prayer before Communion—to work out the salvation of their family with the help of the Holy Spirit in a hymn of life offered to the Father in thanksgiving for His Son—a husband and a wife, married people, openly confessing and asking forgiveness for failures and foibles . . . "Boys, we're not perfect, we make mistakes. We're sorry. We're a family. Let's try again."

A mother and a father repenting, the heartbreaking regrets of parents trying to learn parenting as they go, anguishing in their beds over wounds uncovered at the end of the day that can't be kissed better, having no way of knowing that at night in the midst of the garden, one son would wound the other, put him in a pit, and sell him down to Egypt for twenty shekels as a slave . . . Parents in Christ, who "tear their clothes and put on sackcloth, who go down to Sheol mourning . . ."

Can they be blamed?

Can they be embittered?

Can the plague on their house be any less poisonous than the second angel pouring out his bowl and turning the sea to blood?

Long ago, when they told the priest the older boy had abused his brother, Naum told them about the priority of covenants.

"You and God, then you and your husband or wife, *then* the

children, then your parents, then the parish, your work, you know which to situate where. Keep the covenants in order. The order changes as life goes on, but always with you and Magdalena first with Christ Jesus at the center, and He will sustain you to persevere together in faith—if you keep Him as your center and the covenants in the right order."

"Lord have mercy . . ." Samuel prayed. "Please, Lord, let our center hold us." Samuel kissed her hand and said, "Let us cleave to one another . . ."

———◆———

THE DAY HE FINALLY STOPPED being by doing and sat down in his lawn chair, she looked out the window and knew.

She could tell, when he said he couldn't get warm and asked for that damned threadbare crook-eyed four-button blue cardigan sweater, with the one button always dangling by a thread and one button missing, two buttons always in the wrong hole, making the whole thing hang funny . . .

She could tell by the way the lemonade glass tilted in his lap.

By the way his beard rested on his chest.

By the way the sunlight filtered through the leaves under the tree and sprinkled shadows on his dented straw hat.

By the way he sat there admiring his yardwork. Bible open on his lap.

Her Samuel, no longer hearing the cooing turtledoves.

First Samuel—the open page animated by an unseen breath.

Hand spread over the page like a blind man seeing proto-images of the garden through the tips of his fingers.

His final words, "At least they're not Phinehas and Hophni . . ." spoken like a memory of heaven ascending just above the leaves.

Brokenhearted Samuel Elias, who had fought the good fight, finally surrendered to his pain, to the double-barreled brutality of sons who "having accepted the image, preserved it not."

Samuel's finger on the verse, his own Joel and Abiah . . .

When the pain came, his pain, he did not fall over backward in his chair.

She touched him, walked slowly to his chair and touched him, and joy resounded in the heaven of his heart.

"Don't leave me, Magdalena."

She heard his voice clearly, though his lips never moved.

She took him in her gaze and said, "I will never."

A week later, maybe less . . .

Magdalena curled around his pillow and joined her Samuel.

How could she let go his hand?

Inside Out and Backwards

—◆—

An angry person is like a willful epileptic who, through an involuntary tendency, breaks out in convulsions and falls down.
—SAINT JOHN CLIMACUS

"CAN YOU IMAGINE," Naum said to the priest who had come to confess, "what would have happened if the person in that car hadn't pulled away?"

On the outside, Father Zaza said "Yes."

Inside he was seething. Still boiling. Petting his anger on the head and nursing his grievance on a bottle of formula overfilled with ego, entitlement, and what Father Alexander Schmemann used to call "a morbid desire for supernatural respect" . . .

Imagining ways he could harm the moron who had provoked him and embarrassed him in front of his son.

Naum said, "Your son was there?"

"Yes." Zaza seemed regretful. "I've prayed and prayed about this temper of mine."

Naum himself had prayed against anger, and become angry with himself for not being able to control his anger.

He asked the priest in the dark blue cassock with the long black beard, "What would you say is the first step in dealing with this?"

Zaza looked down at his bare feet and sandals, kicked some invisible dust in the air, and said, "To kick myself in the rear."

Naum said, "I have to go over to the Garden to see Emma and Izzy. Will you walk with me? Emma's in an isolation room and suffering with toxic reactions to almost everything. Izzy is a hero. He loves her so much."

When Zaza hesitated, Naum said, "Only if you have time, Father."

Father Zaza didn't really want to go with the old windbag. He was only there because the bishop had sent him. He just wanted to confess, get absolution, and go home. He'd come a long way from his suburban parish, and the later it got, the more of a traffic nightmare he was going to have to endure on the Schuylkill Expressway.

Irritate Zaza?

It did. But how repentant would he look if he showed it?

"Sure," he said. "Why not." He fiddled with his prayer rope and said to himself, *I suppose this boring torture is Naum's idea of teaching me patience.*

As they locked the door of our little Saint Alexander the Whirling Dervish Orthodox Church, Naum asked, "Father Zaza, have you thought about the first step?"

Of course Zaza knew the answer. He had an MDiv—from the *smart* seminary. "Being aware of my anger."

Naum said, "I like that better than my own first step."

Zaza felt good. Of course he knew that much.

"How does one become aware?" Naum said.

And as they started off down the street, Zaza noticed that the old priest, Naum, had his cassock on inside out and backwards, and across the street waving was another unzipped old idiot, Rabbi Aaron, outside his synagogue, sweeping the pavement. "Naum, come see me!" Rabbi was shouting like a neighborhood huckster.

Ever since young Vlad, a giant from the parish, had brutally beaten Rabbi's ninety-year-old wife, Maureen, Naum felt guilty every time he saw the kind old teacher.

When they reached the other side, Rabbi said to Zaza, "What a beard! I love your beard." And he touched the young priest's long black beard. "I remember," he said, squeezing his own long white beard to a point, "one time when I was . . ." And then he smiled. Rabbi put a finger to the tip of his nose and said, "Naum, I'm so tired of being talked at by old men . . . Come, sit."

Naum asked Zaza, "Do we have time?"

Rabbi said, "You're Orthodox. You'll make time."

Great, Zaza thought. *More wisdom from the ages.*

When they were having tea in the temple library, Naum said to Rabbi, "Father came to visit and made my day."

Father Zaza said, "Father, please."

"I wish somebody'd visit me," Rabbi said.

Naum knew his neighbor the Rabbi had more visits a day than the Liberty Bell.

Zaza said, "I had an incident I wanted to discuss with Father Naum."

Both older men waited.

Zaza said, "My temper got the best of me and I almost lost

it." He waited . . . and then told on himself. He said, "But you two probably have things other than me getting in a fight to talk about."

"No," Rabbi said, "I need some material for my Saturday sermon. And who ever heard of a bearded Orthodox putting on the boxing gloves?"

Zaza acted like he was giving in. He said, "I was with my son . . ."

"Dressed like that?" Rabbi said.

"No. Thank goodness. I was in civilian clothing."

"Incognito is best if you're bent on belligerence," Rabbi said. "It's unseemly for a clergyman . . . I mean, Moses, for goodness' sake, when he threw down the Commandment stones, no worries that time. God knew that particular anger was against idolatry. But the rock? Striking the rock with his staff? No. No. Won't do. The people were only crying because they were thirsty. Is it a sin to be thirsty, after all? And look, it cost poor Moses the torture of seeing the land of promise . . . His anger became an idol. But I guess even an incognito disguise wouldn't have fooled God." Rabbi caught himself and said, "Sorry. No more interrupting, Aaron." Admonishing himself. "Please, go on."

Zaza said to himself, *Why not? I guess this is Naum's plan to lead me in the paths of righteousness to the valley of humility by letting me* further *embarrass myself . . . As if living the humiliation of my parking lot fit and scalding and cutting myself wasn't enough, now I gotta tell on myself.*

"There were two of us backing up at the same time. I could swear I was first out, then this idiot in the big SUV starts on the horn. I jam on my brakes. Our back bumpers kiss. I slam it in park, jump out, and next thing I know I'm at the driver's window and every foul thing you can imagine is coming out of my mouth . . . My son gets out and is standing there watching me. I'm daring this imbecile to step out and . . . I broke the side-view mirror. I was swinging my arms, and the next thing I knew . . . I grabbed my kid and got in the car and drove off."

Father Zaza was reliving it right there in Rabbi's library.

"I see it every day. Anger demolishes rear-views and relationships," Rabbi said. "People smashing property and other people, and in the end, it all leads to self-destruction."

Zaza said, "It was like I blacked out and woke up in a sweat, balled fists, grinding my teeth, clenching the SUV's broken side mirror in my bloody hand, and my son yelling, 'Dad. Dad.' Standin' there feeling like my pants were on fire."

"You know the Talmud, Naum," Rabbi said. "You *borrowed* my set, three years you kept it. I hope you at least read some of it."

Naum said, "Twenty volumes, beautifully bound. One page English, one Hebrew. It made a great wall display in the parish library. People actually suspected I might be smart."

Rabbi quoted the Talmud. "'The life of those who can't control their anger is not a life.' Also, it is written that breaking things when angry is as sinful as idol worship. One who becomes angry, even if he is wise, his wisdom leaves him."

Zaza said, "I was furious with that . . . idiot."

Naum said, "If I were twice as smart I'd still be an idiot."

Rabbi said, "I wonder, how does someone in that kind of a rage look to you? Wise? So, how do you think we appear to others? And your poor son, watching his father act out of anger? Perhaps you were the idiot?"

Naum said, "Inside, when I'm boiling, hoping I'm hiding my frustration, sometimes it makes me wonder, what is God seeing?"

Rabbi shrugged, looked at Naum, and said, "If God lived on earth, people would break His windows."

Zaza said, "I guess against my stupidity, even God is helpless."

Rabbi said, "As a young man I realized I lived much of the time as an angry horse's behind. And when I got a look at myself, thanks to a woman who loved me—God bless Maureen, my wife—I began to practice, to model my behavior on what I knew, what little I knew at the time, of God's ways. God is slow to respond angrily to provocation. As the prophet says, 'At a time of anger God reminds Himself of God's own mercy.'"

Zaza said, "I found out today I know little about myself and less about God, and less about love. And even with that, I'm still afraid of my own anger."

Rabbi said, "Get some holy water from Naum."

Zaza said, "What?"

Rabbi said, "A Hassidic rabbi I knew in West Philadelphia would dispense holy water to his people and tell them he guaranteed it would eliminate all domestic quarrels. Whenever a husband or wife had an urge to argue or fight, he or she was instructed by Rabbi to hold some of the water in his or her mouth without swallowing for as long as possible."

Rabbi took a sip of tea and held it for sixty seconds.

"And as it turned out, this water proved to be so effective in stopping arguments and diffusing anger, the congregation began bottling it, and now today, you would recognize the brand in your supermarket as a best seller. We built a new temple out there on the proceeds." Rabbi winked at Naum and said, "Can you believe it?"

Father Zaza looked at Rabbi and Naum smiling at each other like two mindless inmates in some senile religious ashram somewhere in hippie heaven. He didn't know whether to laugh or invite them to the Honey Sit N Eat Diner for the Early Bird Senior Special—then deny he knew 'em and leave 'em there.

"Now me," Rabbi said, "I never allow myself to get angry unless I first go to my vestment closet in the temple and put on a special set of garments I call my *angry apparel*. Father Zaza, I had them specially sewn by Manny Laden's wife, Renée. And the buttons, zippers, ties, and loops for belts, not to mention the shoes and hat, the Velcro, and the snaps, are so complex, Gordian's knot puzzle and the Rubik cube? Nothing. By the time I get out of my regular clothes and into my outrage outfit . . ."

Zaza couldn't help smiling when he pictured the process.

"And," Rabbi said, "I keep a set in my trunk for road rage or incidents like yours. Good thing I wear boxers."

Rabbi looked down and realized he was unzipped.

"Again?" he said.

Even Naum had to laugh.

"You know, Rabbi Yisrael tells a story about something in the Talmud . . . A man who was insulted by his wife goes and that night he sleeps in the cemetery. He explained that the man did so with the hope of breaking the pride that was urging him to respond in anger."

Naum said, "Being angry like that is as if you've killed yourself."

Rabbi said, "Another good reason I try to be slow to anger is that I may not have my facts right. I was once waiting at the airport car rental and started yelling at the clerk, thinking she was giving away my rental. I snatched the paper on the counter from this kind young lady, and pointed. She looked at me, took the paperwork, turned it right side round, pushed it front of me, and said, 'Is your name Janis Anne Zercowski, sir?' Boy, was I embarrassed. The woman there, whose rental it was, said to me, 'Maybe time to get some glasses, eh, sir?'"

At the temple entrance, Rabbi kissed Naum and whispered something to Zaza.

Outside, Naum said to Zaza, "Rabbi noticed my cassock, inside out and backwards."

As the two priests walked toward Girard Avenue, Zaza said, "He whispered I should tell you."

Instead of asking why Zaza had let him go out like that, Naum thought it better to ask how long the weather permitted the wearing of sandals.

<hr />

OUTSIDE BONITA WONG's martial arts dojo, loaf-round, five-foot, shiny-headed Eddie Gjarper was holding a handkerchief to his bloody nose.

Naum said, "Eddie?"

He said, "I deserved it, Father. I shouldn't have squeezed her . . ."

Naum said, "I get it, Eddie."

Inside, people were stretching and sparring. The yellow walls of the training studio were covered in posture posters, diagrams of striking patterns, and placards announcing upcoming tournaments and events.

FIGHT LIKE YOU TRAIN, DON'T TRAIN LIKE YOU FIGHT

PRACTICAL APPLICATIONS OF ANGER

ALTERNATIVES TO ANGER

PAIN IS A GIFT; ACCEPT IT GRACEFULLY

UNKNOWNS BECOME KNOWNS AS YOU CONQUER YOUR ANGER AND ALLOW YOU TO GAIN CONTROL OVER THE OUTCOME OF CONFLICT

Black belt Bonita Wong, all four-foot-ten of her in her white *karategi*, was telling the advanced class, "I believe that if you practice martial arts to grow in harmony with God, your fellow human beings, and the universe, rushing to rage is a counterproductive strategy.

"And truthfully, being angry has never been all that useful for prevailing over an opponent, either."

She looked out the plate glass window where Eddie was tilting his head back. When he looked in, Bonita smiled and bowed to him.

Eddie waved and mouthed, "My bad."

Bonita said, "Anger will prevent you from effectively employing your hard-earned skills. Timing, precision, coordination, and sensitivity to the moves of your opponent decrease during emotional peaks and valleys. Try to stay with a mind like the moon—placid, focused, and reflecting their aggression back to them. Capture their energy and turn it."

Bonita noticed the two priests from the corner of her eye. She had not missed a Sunday liturgy in more than ten years.

She said, "Anger, fear, and anxiety are natural human

responses to stress. Better to run away, better to not get into a fight in the first place. That is the best way to win, because the risks are significant and the outcome is unknown."

Naum saw her look over at Zaza and say, "You may be facing an opponent you've underestimated, and your anger will be used against you. You may hurt someone you love or the loved one of another. You will go that night to the morgue or the police jail, but you will not go home to your own bed."

When she saw Naum, Bonita instructed the class to lie prone on the floor, eyes closed, doing the lower Dantian breathing exercise, employing what many believe to be a major energy center found slightly under and behind the navel.

"Father," she said. "May I have your blessing?"

And then, to Zaza, "Father, please." And she received his blessing too.

Bonita gave Father Zaza a yellow belt for his son, and after a small tour, the men left.

The overcast morning had bowed like Bonita and given way to the afternoon sun. Now afternoon was preparing the way and sweeping the leftover clouds from the sky for the early arrival of evening.

As they walked, Naum said, "So, awareness . . . Someone who loves you and lets you know your cassock is on inside out and backwards . . . Then what?"

"Repentance?" Zaza said.

"How about reflection?" Naum answered. "Reflecting on who you are, honestly. Saint John of the Ladder says we angry people are willful epileptics."

Zaza sighed.

Naum said, "I know now who I am. I am a willful epileptic. I think, Father, you know how and who you'd rather be."

And then Naum quoted Saint Paul writing to the church at Rome. "The trouble with me, I am all too human, a slave to sin. I don't really understand myself, I wanna do what's right, but I don't do it. Instead, I do what I hate."

Zaza said, "I get it. I get it all too well."

Naum said, "Look, man, once you get it and you're aware of it, and you reflect on what triggers it—pride, self-will, ego, all that—then ya got a start. You practice. You go over it in your mind. Debrief the unpleasant incident. Analyze. You lie awake at night and say, 'Okay, here's what would've been better . . .'"

"Then repent," Zaza said.

Naum said, "Yep. Then that long hard process of change begins. It's not like the guys over at the putty factory sitting at lunch break on the loading dock who remove a wart with a razor blade. It's more like Compound W—dissolve that thing a little at a time. Sure, you're gonna fail. Ya get up. Ya do it again. Same as Great Lent. Takes time to reorient hotheads like us, get us back to His way."

Father Zaza said, "Any suggestions?"

Naum said, "What's the opposing virtue to selfishness?"

"Selflessness? Sharing. Generosity?"

"How about anger? What's the opposing virtue?"

Zaza said, "Peace?"

"I like that better than my answer," Naum said. "Keep applying that Compound Peace . . . Once in a while you'll forget and go back to being a maniac, but that's our main sin, forgetting. Forgetting who we really are, where we're really from, and where we're called to go. But keep at it and it'll come back to you, your true identity in Christ. You'll remember the future, given to us in the past, constitutes our present. That's from Schmemann."

"Thank you, Father," Zaza said.

"One beggar telling another beggar where to find bread," Naum told him. "Keep pulling up the old weed of anger and replacing it each time with the good seed of peace. Or else the weeds'll grow back."

"Yes, Father." Even now Zaza was becoming impatient.

Naum said, "Humility, self-reproach, patience, obedience, and discipline . . . They lead to freedom. Keep planting those seeds. You remember what our Master said: *that* one—" Naum, not wanting to say it, pointed down, and Zaza understood. "When he came back from the dry places and found the house empty, clean and swept, what did he do?"

It hit Zaza.

He bit his lip and said, "Went out and got seven worse than himself. And came back to occupy that house."

Naum said, "We can't stand still in the spiritual struggle, Father. Me and you, all of us, we're in a procession, an ascetic struggle, from the garments of skin back toward the first coat we wore in the Garden, the one we prodigally tear up with anger. And any pause, any letting up in our shared pilgrimage is a regression. Don't let it get worse, Father. Fight it, please."

Zaza said, "We going back to the church soon, Father, for absolution?"

Naum looked out at traffic and said, "I think absolution's coming to us."

ZAZA STOPPED WHEN THE WINDOW went down as the big silver SUV rumbled in fast over the trolley tracks to the curb and pulled to a halt where he and Naum were walking along busy Girard Avenue.

Some believe in coincidence.

"Hey, Padre." Pastor Stephen Jerome and his wife Malvena copastored the Saint Yared African Orthodox Church that met in an old factory on Frankford Avenue.

Naum turned to Zaza and said, "I love this man."

Naum said to Pastor, "Where ya headin'?"

"Over Getzy and Little Harry's Salvage Yard."

Naum noticed.

Zaza didn't need to.

When Naum introduced Father Zaza, Pastor Stephen said, "Always good to meet a brother."

Malvena waved from the passenger seat.

Naum looked at the SUV and said, "Shame."

Pastor said, "Yeah. Some out the neighborhood fool, yelling at my Malvena, jumped outta his car . . . Man was in a fury. Had his kid there too. Little boy out on the pavement pleading and screaming at his pop to stop . . . Man knocked my side view right off . . . *and* cut his hand." Pastor lifted the bloodied mirror from the seat and showed Naum. "Malvena saw him in the rear camera, man was yelling at his kid, not paying attention. She tooted, trying to get his attention, but he was so hopping around in there and intent on something happening in his car . . ."

"Malvena?" Naum said. "You okay?"

She said, "Yep. Now I am."

"Shaky. But you know her. Locked the doors, got ready to call nine-one-one."

Malvena said, "You boys don't have to worry about me."

Naum said to Pastor Stephen, "You? You okay?"

Pastor said, "Good thing I wasn't there. I woulda had ta do some serious preaching ta that boy. Lotta lost souls out here, Naum."

Zaza wanted to . . .

But before he could, Pastor said, "Man wearing cargo shorts all wet down the front, and sandals, and a raggedy old T-shirt. Had a Z-Z-Top beard." Pastor gave Zaza a slow peruse and said, "But he couldn't 'a' been no priest, not the way he was acting."

Zaza was steeling himself, not really wanting to, out of shame, but knowing he needed to look Pastor in the eye, admitting inwardly he needed it to heal, almost wanting it: *The righteous chastisement that was impending against him.*

Pastor said, "Man needs to let go of his narcissistic anger. Let go of his need to control. Resign as General Manager of the Universe. Brother'd find he was happier. Everybody around him too."

Pastor Stephen said to Zaza, "And like Naum here always says, 'How else can a relationship blossom and begin if we let opportunities that could go either way get by us?' Man coulda made a friend today, a good friend in Malvena and her talks-too-much husband."

Naum said, "We'll pray, the four of us, God forgives this man."

When Pastor looked around to Malvena, she put both her hands on his shoulders. The pastor leaned out the window, reached his hand to Zaza, touched hands with Naum, bowed his head for a second, looked up, scoped the oncoming traffic, and said, "Already done."

Malvena said, "We been praying for him and his son, lit candles back at the church."

Pastor gave a few quick taps on the horn and flowed out over the trolley tracks, waving back over the roof.

Zaza said, "I spilled my coffee in my lap."

Naum told him, "Time, Father. We're done enough walking. Go back to your car. Rush hour's gonna be heating up. Can you find your way in the neighborhood?"

Zaza said, "I think you showed me a good way."

Naum said, "You'll be okay." He kissed Zaza's hand and said, "My good Father, I have to get to the Garden."

Naum, meandering through the neighborhood in his backwards-inside-out cassock on the way to see Emma and Izzy, who lived on Beach Street in the Garden by the river.

Already There

LATE MAY, AND DESIRAE SHTËPI could still not blink the January sprinkling from her eyes.

The seven Epiphany priests of the Philadelphia Brotherhood still floated in the happy sky of her memory like stringless balloons in the blustery wind of the blessed New Year.

Seven reckless crazy cassocks. All beards and brocade. All sailing too close and bumping one another out over the precipice of the very slick, very shiny, very slippery edge of the river jetty at Penn Treaty Park.

Vestment-colored celebrants of every stripe and size. All tangled chains and pectoral crosses, silver, gold, and wood. All service books and basil bouquets bunched for blessing.

Inflated shapes Desirae had never seen, swinging incense from silver chains laced with ringing bells and fingers chilly stiff from tugging bright skufia caps tight to heads bowed in deference to the water and the wind.

Each priest unnested in his turn and tongue, each successive red-cheeked matryoshka priest praying waves of words above the waters, supplicating God in His mercy to reveal the Delaware as primordial and blessed at His creative Word.

It was five months ago when the sweet green basil bound in the hand of the priest called Zaza came up out of the golden font in a single liquid arc. Something more than swirls of flying water found something more than the head and eyes of Desirae Shtëpi.

Linear calendrical January had no hold on the water.

Once inaugurated, the Epiphany within Desirae Shtëpi came unbound. The Paschal icon already present in the woman was called forth like Lazarus from the grave.

But it was not so long ago, Desirae remembered, that she had hesitated alone on the precipice, looking out over the bleak Delaware with no reason to believe that the heaviness she carried left her any option other than to sink.

Now she stood with no hesitation on the precipice of an unimaginably green Penn Treaty river promenade in an unimaginably bright yellow Paschal dress, in an unimaginably bright yellow post-Paschal May.

Probably it was Naum who first spotted her that January day.

"You okay?"

She said, "The tea bag."

Naum repeated, sensing it was the beginning of a list, "The tea bag."

"His pants in the escalator." She waited for Naum.

"His pants in the escalator." Said by Naum in a way to let her know it was her turn to go on, if she wanted.

"Their baby was born Downs," she said. "And he said he wanted to put it in a burlap bag and drown it in the river."

Naum was afraid.

"And when I asked the homeless man who sleeps behind the Hashemite limestone column toppled at the edge of the quad to marry me," she said. "I mean, I gave him money every day, he looked at me, and said, 'That's all?' And laughed and turned me down and crawled back in his box."

Naum said, "I am sorry."

And immediately, she didn't like Naum.

He could tell "sorry" had been the wrong thing to say.

It had been wrong to speak at all.

And so when Naum went to Father Zaza and looked back at the woman in the thin green dress shivering in the icy January breeze coming in off the Delaware, before Naum could speak, Zaza was already standing next to Desirae, bent so he could hear her whispers.

And offering his arm, he led her in a gentle procession to the front of the assembly, where they bowed together before the icon of Christ's Baptism on the blessing font table.

Desirae was not herself.

It wasn't hard to see.

She held the basil Zaza placed in her hands, held it like a bridal bouquet. Raised it close and inhaled the fragrance.

Was it the water or the basil that was so sweet?

Desirae wanted to open her mouth, wide. . . . It was all she could do to resist spinning around and backing off the crowd, wielding the basil with a threat. Then encircle the whole soaking bunch with her lips. Leaves, branches, stems, and all, and suck the whole bunch dry like a who-cares crazy lady. Seize the golden font from the table and drain it in a swallow. In a gulp.

Turning to stare at the crowd, Desirae was thinking, *Really, how could any of you object if poor dehydrated Professor Shtëpi,*

shriveling in front of you like dried fruit, moved this bouquet of
life-restoring liquid close to let it brush her lips?

Would it really matter?

Would it be seriously sacrilegious if she took just a little of the moisture with the tip her tongue?'

She closed her eyes when Zaza removed his riassa and placed it around her shoulders, saying, "Is it okay? I myself am too hot and think maybe you're a little chilly?"

⊷•⊶

THE TEA BAG INCIDENT.
Maybe that was it, in the professor's lounge at the university where she had tenure . . . That could be where it started.

"Yes, in fact," she told herself. "That's what did it. That tripped the trigger."

"Poo Poo Pu-Erh Tea." She was pacing the chrome-and-white-leather staff lounge repeating, "Who in the *hell* drank my Poo Poo Pu-Erh?"

Her Monkey Picked Loose-Leaf Oolong had been the previous victim of this insane tea-leaf thievery. And now her Poo Poo?

Her tisane glass infuser just sat abandoned there on the window ledge in the sun. Leaf residue coagulated at the bottom, sadder than an orphan staring out the window of an uncoupled train car sidetracked and left to corrode.

Desirae Shtëpi, PhD, Professor of Phenomenology and Existential Philosophy, coming that morning from teaching her landmark course, "On Being Bored in Bala Cynwyd."

A course that examined books, articles, and movies supporting the notion of not being productive and validating the value and contribution to society of not wanting to do anything.

"Boredom," she said, "is an exaggerated state of excitement in which the aim is repressed." An idea she borrowed from a man named Otto Fenichel, and to which she added, "And so, in the end, if nothing means nothing, why not admit it's all just a boring, pointless sham and . . ."

She never *could* think of a way to end that particular thought except to unfurl the 8 x 10 Jolly Roger she kept in her purse as a wrapper for her Sig Sauer P239 pistol and say, "Next time, class, maybe we'll just get it over with and consider a life of piracy as a means of collective slow-suicide."

It might have been Otto Fenichel's exaggerated state of excitement, or something like it, that set her off that morning.

It sure as hell wasn't boring, and there was no Jolly Roger way she could say her aim had been repressed, not that morning. Not the morning her tea was shanghaied.

At the high crime of hijacking her Poo Poo, when her anger at everything and everyone who didn't see the truth "that there is no truth" finally reached the boiling point, Professor Desirae erupted like Vesuvius spewing over Pompeii. "If there's nothing that's true, then even saying there's nothing true is false. It's all a lie. I'm a lie, a living, breathing lie!"

She blocked the door, waving the Sig Sauer, and menaced every tea-thieving collegiate colleague cowering in the lounge.

The morning her rage wreaked havoc in the lounge.

The morning—thank goodness—she forgot to put an ammo clip in her pistol.

The morning that screaming Professor Shtëpi received a

mandatory, involuntary, "I don't want it, I don't need it, and I won't take it" mental health leave of absence.

The morning Campus Security—a serious-looking woman on each of her elbows and another carting the unwieldy box—escorted seething Professor Shtëpi, tisane glass infuser, monkey-picked-tea-stained custom-bound Boredom course syllabi, Serenity Zone CD Yoga collection, aloe plant, and all, out through reserved faculty parking and down to her dark blue Honda Civic.

Mornings after that, she had time to hang around downtown at the Chock-Full-A-Nuts Coffee Shop on Chestnut Street two steps from her subway stop.

She liked to sit in the window and watch the ties and skirts do the morning run. Seeing their reflection in the mirror behind the counter and then out the window. Running to punch the clock. While she spun back and forth at the counter on her high-backed spinning stool.

Mirror. Window. Mirror. Window.

She pftted at the futility of the morning rush. *These elevator jockeys . . . Cubicle gorillas . . .*

Saw the same white-haired baggy-pants banker every morning, umbrella in hand. Carrying his *Wall Street Journal*, heading down the subway escalator in his brown tweed suit. Tie over his shoulder. Old-school horn-rims and oxblood wingtips. Ew! Oxblood.

She sipped her coffee and said to her window reflection, "Wouldn't I like to bash him in the head with a copy of Ayn Rand?"

Then came the morning she was late exiting the subway and there he was, Mister Oxblood, on his back. Snagged in his baggies and screaming near the top of the escalator, holding on to the railing for dear life and pleading for help.

The cuff on his baggy pants had caught in the teeth of the moving escalator steps, and the old man was going inexorably down.

The professor in her had some theories about what needed to be done, but not until much later, when it was all over.

Thank goodness Nicky Zeo came along, a quick-thinking electrician heading to a job down at the Navy Yard. He dropped his tool kit, quick unbelted the old geezer and while a crowd gathered and Desirae watched, the old man's pants ground into the gears as he slithered out and Nicky pulled him to his feet.

The man stood red-faced, umbrella in hand, panic-spotted pinstriped boxer shorts, black ankle socks, and oxblood wingtips, cursing Nicky Zeo.

Nicky said to the cop who came running, "Good thing he was wearing baggies or we'd 'a' never got his pants off over his shoes."

———

FATHER ZAZA LISTENED. He waited to make sure it was all out.

Then Desirae said, "Don't I know you?"

After the Epiphany blessing they sat together having coffee in the church hall at our little Saint Alexander the Whirling Dervish Orthodox Church.

"Didn't you teach at the university?"

Zaza didn't want to get into it.

Material Religion, Religion, Affect, & Emotion, Science & Secularisms, had been his chair.

"Yep," he said, "that was me."

Zaza, with the long hair and dark black beard wearing the

year-round sandals. Walking the campus in Che Guevara camouflage sweats before he was ordained. Tall and broad like a Greco-Roman wrestler. The man was hard to miss.

"And you left?" she said.

When she saw him hesitate, Desirae had it figured.

She was just about there herself.

"No complicated reason, eh? Just not doing it for you anymore."

"That's all," he said. "What about you?"

"Me?" She told Zaza, "I expelled God so I could take control of my life and of my world, and the opposite happened. I sneezed and creation cracked. Existential anarchy. I mixed a cocktail with water pilfered from Epiphany and imagined myself a creator, can you believe it? Even the glass I mixed it in was borrowed. I'm my life's only inhabitant. My only enemy. My only friend. Some lonely shit, Z . . ."

Desirae Shtëpi had wrestled with *why* all her life.

Her insides were worn down, beat up, and bored raw from the contest, from the endless variations on a strategy for trying to pin this bastard down.

The fact that she hardly had a match, intuitively or intellectually, made her tolerant and suspicious at the same time of anyone glib enough to offer an easy answer, or any kind of answer for that matter.

When it came to the tea-bag incident, or the man with his pants in the escalator, or her associate who wanted to drown his Downs baby, or the homeless man turning down her proposal of marriage, Zaza listened.

And she could tell he cared. But she also understood the response of his silence.

Desirae Shtëpi recognized the truth that any response worth anything probably lay beyond words.

She smiled and nodded.

She was happy someone finally got it. "Yeah," she said. "Why ruin it?" Then she told him, "I'm gonna go get more coffee."

When she returned, she saw Zaza holding his empty cup to his mouth, making an echo tunnel, saying, "Injustice. Absurdity. Senselessness. The obscene lies that there's life without the primeval instinct to communion. God, please help our Desirae." She took his cup and said, "Let me getcha a refill, dummy."

When Zaza mentioned the women's monastery, Desirae said she was willing to visit Mother Stephania.

Maybe they had too many cups of coffee after the Epiphany blessing on the river.

"She's the one to talk to," Zaza said. "Like a big ear."

Professor Desirae Shtëpi, still on leave of absence, for some reason waited till Holy Week, attending all the services of Great Lent, didn't miss one, and then on Holy Thursday, she went to see Mother Stephania.

At the women's monastery, the room where they met had a fireplace going full blast. Mother and Desirae had tea and Lenten cookies.

Desirae Shtëpi was thinking she had known Mother, and that Mother had known her, for a long time, though she knew, chronologically, it wasn't possible.

And then Mother said, "Time is a chalice."

Desirae filled the chalice that day.

She told Mother of memories that time had forgotten. She

told Mother her memories of the future the past was having a hard time trying to forget.

It was as if Desirae Shtëpi *had* swallowed the blessing font that day on the river, and now the waters of time had her swirling in a Coriolis force of remembrance, close and bumping out over the precipice of a very slick, very shiny, very slippery waterfall Epiphany.

Novices and nuns were busy with every phase of vestment making

From buttons to thread

Young women spinning spools of galloon

Taking orders off the internet

Listing prayer requests

Tying prayer ropes out of black woolen strands

And boxing beeswax candles dipped in the dark that very morning just before light came in the window behind the altar.

Ever-present incense from the open chapel door and the meal being prepared in the large commercial kitchen were giving the brick inner-city mansion that served as Holy Nativity Monastery a fragrance of home that blended together longing and contentment like precious ointment in a vessel of prayer.

Mother Stephania listened while she crocheted.

Desirae confessed all that God gave her to confess that day. *Including*: the tea bags, and the escalator, the Downs baby, and her marriage proposal to a homeless man.

Desirae told Mother, "Mother, I was not myself. I was standing at that blessing table clutching the basil like a bridal bouquet. I remember raising it close and inhaling the fragrance. Was it the water or the basil, or the blessing that was so sweet?"

"Mother," Desirae said, "I wanted to open my mouth, wide . . . It was all I could do to resist spinning around and backing off the crowd, wielding the basil with a threat. Then encircle the whole soaking bunch with my lips. Leaves, branches, stems, and all, suck the whole bunch dry like a who-cares crazy lady, and seize the golden font from the table and drain it in a swallow."

"That's all?" Mother had a way of making you feel bad about brandishing a pistol while making you feel better by reminding you that you were probably not cut out in the first place for hoisting the Jolly Roger.

Mother said, "Please, when you see Father Zaza, tell him to pray the prayer of absolution, for you, and for me."

Five months ago, when the sweet green basil bound in the hand of the priest called Zaza came up out of the golden font in a single liquid arc, something more than swirls of flying water found something more than the head and eyes of Desirae Shtëpi.

Linear calendrical January had no hold.

Once inaugurated, the Epiphany within came unbound. The Paschal icon already there in the woman Desirae Shtëpi was called forth like Lazarus from the grave.

Now a woman stood with no hesitation on the precipice of an unimaginably green river promenade in an unimaginably bright yellow Paschal dress, in an unimaginably yellow post-Paschal May.

Desirae Shtëpi, who not so long ago hesitated alone on the precipice, had considered the bleak Delaware with no reason to believe that she would have any reason to do anything but sink.

Desirae said, "Something in the blessing."

Mother said, "Yes, the blessing. But it didn't add anything to our dear Desirae. It simply married the symbol of His love for creation to what was drying up. It refreshed you and opened the eyes of your soul, like the man at the pool of Siloam. It allowed the good truth that was already there inside you to be revealed. It healed the lungs of your soul so that you could again inhale the Breath of our Garden home."

Full of Soup

———≈◦≈———

THERE WAS ACTUALLY A GUY with a pole in each hand, wrapped like a Yukon mummy, skiing without a sound down the middle of Sepviva Street, along the park past our little Saint Alexander the Whirling Dervish Orthodox Church, right before first light the morning after it snowed all night and buried Fishtown under five feet of snow.

Would've been a beautiful thing too, for old Naum, standing up, stretching out his back, leaning on his shovel to catch a breath and take a break.

Seeing the park and the trees and the skier and the snow blown like new stripes of fresh-painted pointing between the bricks on the old two- and three-story row homes.

Tarpaper rooftops, new-day bright and pretty.

Our little fieldstone Orthodox temple, standing like a catechumen about to be baptized. Radiant and pure in a brilliant white vestment.

And the vapor from his breath steamed out without so much as a sigh and added to the quiet of the after-storm stillness that descended over it all like a prayer without words.

Yep.

Would've been a beautiful thing if he wasn't digging out his old beater, that '66 two-door lemon-cream Impala. Good thing Little Harry came from the junkyard early the day before and helped him roll the snow chains on that big rusted junker.

What Naum knew, but what people forgot year to year, was probably, when he was just about dug out, the city trucks were gonna come plowing down the street and bury him back in.

But for now, that was something he was too busy digging out to think about. Probably better anyway, 'cause there was nothing to be done about it except try to beat the snowplows and hope that maybe it'd be like the years when they just cleared the main drags and left half-ball side streets in neighborhoods like Fishtown unplowed till spring.

Probably some old person who got up daily at dawn out of habit, looking out their dark window wondering, "So where is that priest going now? Somebody musta died, or be dying."

Took Naum forty-five minutes that morning to get into his snow gear in the dark and another fifteen to pull on his boots.

Not wanting to wake Priftereshe Greta was how he explained to himself why he was moving so slow. Had nothing to do with these old bones creaking in the cold.

He couldn't sleep anyway after her telephone call.

"It's me, Robin. Sorry to call so late. You weren't sleeping, were you?"

"Nope." Midnight and he'd been deep in dreamland.

Naum said, "How ya been, Robin? How's Vito and the kids?"

"We're doing okay."

"Thank God," Naum said.

"Reason I'm calling, Father, Mom's in the hospital."

"Jenny?"

Naum hadn't see Jenny in church in thirty years.

"Yeah, Father." Robin's voice had that *resigned to it, trying to be brave, but knowing it was probably time* kinda tone most grown daughters have when they find themselves telling relatives, "Don't look good. Doctor said it don't look good. Could be days. Could be hours."

———

ONCE A YEAR Naum would go to visit Jenny at her house, and once a year she'd tell Naum, "God might be good for other folks . . . But if I haven't learned by this point in my life what I shoulda learnt in kindergarten, how to be a moral person, then hanging out with you Sundays for an hour or two ain't gonna do a damn thing for me, Padre. Pardon my French."

Car-shaped piles of snow were lined up nose to tail in the early morning shadows. In a few hours people would shovel them out, one after another, along both curbs.

Shoveling reminded Naum of the time he was skating his wire-wheel cart over unshoveled pavements to go shopping on the Avenue and saw Jenny shoveling her pavement.

Jenny stood up, took the cigarette from between her lips and said, "Ya wanna yak?" She pointed to Naum with the first two fingers of her right hand, always did it on purpose, the ones with the tips missing, same as her cousin Mira, Pandi's wife.

Jenny made sure the priest noticed. She said, "Doc had to amputate 'cause a the goddamn smoking . . ." Naum knew that couldn't be quite right, but he knew Jenny too. Now was not the time. "Pick up that shovel over there and ya can do some good while you're pontificating."

Jenny had a way about her.

She handed Naum a flat-end double-wide coal shovel and pointed to the wide section of the pavement closest to the corner.

Probably thought to herself, "Might as well put the pain in the ass to work where the ice's the hardest."

Naum spent an hour that day breaking ice and shoveling, and another hour thawing at the kitchen table having soup and crusty bread from Schmidt's, listening to Jenny tell about her grandfather's father fishing the Delaware for shad.

"That's how we knew it was spring, hucksters yelling shad was back. Peddling oysters and shad in their carts and wagons. Going down to the docks. Meeting the shad boats. Place down there, this was way back, ya understand, place they called Fancy Hill, lotta men worked down there. Big-ass nets. Filled sixty, seventy wagons a day during the spring runs. Why ya think they call it Fishtown?"

Naum liked to listen. Jenny's practical-mindedness had its appeal.

When he said, "More to the gospel than morality, Jenny. Someday maybe you're gonna tell me your thoughts about family. Other people. God. Being together. Eating together . . . Things that make life life . . . What happened that you don't come to communion? What happens after we die?"

She told him he was full of soup.

"Good soup," Naum said.

"'Course. When you make it yourself, ya know what's in it."

Jenny gave him a stub of an old yellow pencil, flattened a

brown paper bag on the table, and made him write her grand-father's Fishtown recipe.

"Your wife Greta likes soup, right? Bony as hell, shad, and oily too, but *you* like it, she's gonna like it.

"Okay, Naum, so what you're gonna need is, first, you're gonna need some soup makings from a five-pound roe shad . . ."*

She told him the whole recipe, and he wrote down every word.

Finally she said, "Ya got all that?"

Naum said, "Yep."

Jenny looked at the bag and said, "Well, look at that."

———◆———

NAUM FOUND JENNY'S RECIPE in his pocket that morning, the morning after her daughter called.

A year later. It made him sad.

He smoothed it on the kitchen counter before he left.

Dressing in the dark

Digging out

No food or drink

We don't

Before Communion

Prayers

Packing the Communion kit

Driving all the way over there in silence

Finding parking—paying for parking

Hospital security going through his bag

Getting the look with the cassock and the beard

---

* The full recipe may be found at the end of this book.

Every time

Smiling—explaining

Naum drove east on Girard, straddling the trolley tracks all the way till he got to Broad Street. Cars were sliding out of control sideways into each other when he made the slow wide turn south toward center city.

Off in the snowy distance he could see William Penn high atop City Hall looking out over the grid of his snow-covered green country town.

Windshield wipers scraping ice, all vents blowing, and the heater keeping his feet warm, the old priest somehow managed not to slide sideways on the ice as he navigated the City Hall circle and headed west on Market Street, thinking, *I got this, no problem.*

Once across the Schuylkill River, Naum thought of stopping to see Father Agron, dean of our cathedral, but the thought of getting stuck on the unplowed side streets made him think better of it.

It was only forty-five minutes, in good weather and normal traffic, to do the ten miles to Delaware County Memorial Hospital out on Lansdowne Avenue in Drexel Hill. And now, by some miracle, he was almost halfway there.

Naum made the cross.

Police were up ahead, out there in their cold-weather gear and watershed storm boots, waving flashlights, detouring traffic south down a little side street near Sixtieth called Redfield, just past the Church of the Apostles and Prophets . . .

. . . And it was on the corner of Redfield and Chestnut, in front of the sweet home of Emmanuel AME Church where a space had been plowed for a funeral that had been postponed due to weather, that dumb-luck Naum came gliding to a stop, like it was part of the divine plan, just as his old lemon-cream '66 Impala shivered its exhaust and gave up the ghost.

The dude down the block shoveling the pavement pointed inside when Naum reached the Swank, the bar on the corner.

Inside, the bartender said, "Use this phone, Padre," and motioned Naum to come back behind the bar.

When there was no answer from Father Agron, the dean at our University City Cathedral, Naum called Father Boris, head of the Philadelphia Brotherhood.

"Father Boris, please." Naum explained the situation.

Father Boris lived on Argyle Street, less than a block from the hospital. He said, "I'm not driving, let alone walking out in this mess for less than a hundred dollars."

Naum was using his scarf to wipe the frost dripping from his beard. "You're funny, Father."

"No. I am not. I'm serious."

Naum was quiet. He wished he had a hundred dollars, but he didn't, so he said, "I understand, Father."

"I should hope you do," Father Boris said. "I pray you do. Person hasn't been in church thirty years, what does that tell you? I mean, what does that come to, three dollars, thirty-three cents a year?"

The calculation was too subtle for Naum.

Millard, the bartender/owner of the Swank, said to the man who'd come in from shoveling, "Booker, hold the fort, man."

Mister Millard took his coat off the tree behind the bar, put on his hat and an oversized pair of army-issue mittens.

"I'ma run this here preacher out dat' Drexel Hill hospital, hear? I be back shortly, Book, and I don't wanna hear no shit 'bout you-know-what when I get back. No matter what she say, you tell her I'm on a mercy mission, and I be back when I get back. Hear?"

Booker said, "Understood."

Beyond that, Mister Millard didn't have to say anything.

Naum followed 'round back of the Swank, and when Millard revved it up, Naum satcheled his bag crosswise over his shoulder, got behind Millard on the snowmobile, and damn if he didn't arrive alive, ten minutes to two at the hospital's main entrance.

Millard waving bye without a word, disappearing in the winter wonderland, leaving tracks in the snow on his way back to the Swank.

Heading up the hospital walk, Naum heard Millard's motor coming around again.

Millard spinning the snowmobile back and catching Naum at the crosswalk. "Need a ride back when you're done, Pastor, you call me, hear?" He handed Naum a card, said, "I'll have lunch ready by the time you're done."

———◦—◦———

ROOM FIVE IN THE CICU was all blue beeps and digital blips. The gown on Jenny was blue and open in that peculiar way only hospital gowns come open.

It made Naum look around the room and notice things. The mounted TV he could tell hadn't been on. The dry-erase white patient board with the name of the Nurse on Duty / Today is:

Day—Month—Year / Your Room Number / Your Doctor / Your Pain Level—Zero to Ten.

And the tube down her throat. The tube taped to her mouth. Lines in both arms. Swollen and discolored. Her uncovered feet. Both hands, palms up at her side. A funny kind of breathing. Eyes tight.

An icon of Her holding Him taped to the monitor made Naum wonder who, and when, and where are they now?

The bag hanging across Naum's shoulder was beginning to weep as the snow turned to liquid in the heated room.

A nurse came in and made some adjustments. She looked at Naum and smiled but left without saying anything.

He wanted to thank her for taking care of Jenny, but he'd been lost in his thoughts and tangled in a prayer that *might* have made sense to another person, probably, probably not.

It didn't matter.

He was there with Jenny.

Same as he was Memorial Day in Palmer Burial Ground.

"WHY?" Jenny was clearing weeds from the grave. "You wanna know why, Naum? Ask that priest, the one before you."

Jenny made the cross the way we do, still had all her fingers back then. Kissed her fingers and her thumb held together, you know how we make the sign . . .

Then she touched her mother's headstone in a blessing and sprinkled the *grure*, the boiled wheat, around the gravesite, saying, "*Në qoftë se një kokërr gruri nuk bie në tokë dhe nuk vdes* . . . Unless a kernel of wheat falls to the earth and dies."

Eventually the other priest admitted he was wrong not to bury Jenny's mother.

He told Naum, "The woman had been involved early on, was one of the founders of the parish. Dedicated. Sacrificed, her and her husband. Half of the shad money they earned went directly to the parish.

"Even after he died, she was still out there pushing that damn cart and working for the church. Loved Krishti. Loved the Holy Mother.

"I was new. What did I know? I'd never seen her in church. I thought she was just another old person ended up in a nursing home . . .

"So I refused to bury her. Said she wasn't a paying member. Jenny tried to tell me . . . But I had an MDiv . . . Turned into a shouting match. Got ugly. Bad feelings.

"Even years later, when I got it and tried to make it right. Don't think I'm not ashamed. I pray for them every day, and for forgiveness."

———

SO, NAUM, HERE YOU ARE, looking down at Jenny in her hospital bed, squeegeeing tears from your beard. Answer yourself an honest question. Ya got the guts to do that, Naum?

If Jenny could open her eyes. If she could speak with you. If she could remove all those tubes and open her mouth to be received into the heaven of Holy Communion . . . ?

Old Father Cere's epitrahilion, the first priest to serve the parish, was the priestly stole Naum carried in his bag. He placed it around his neck and laid it over Jenny.

The prayers of the Church. That's what Naum prayed.

The nurse came in and stood with him. When he finished, the young woman with the Island accent kissed his hand and thanked him.

He kissed her hand and thanked her.

She said, "You be careful going home in the snow, now, Reverend. It's more than slippery out there."

Father Agron from the cathedral, bundled in snow gear, was in the lobby waiting for Deacon Boutros to bring his four-wheel SUV around. He said to Naum, "The daughter called you too."

Naum said, "I wondered who taped the icon."

"They just like to cover all the bases, don't they? Long as they get one of us to come. Prifti is prifti, I guess."

Naum wanted to say, "They have no idea what it takes . . ." But he didn't.

Father Agron and the deacon dropped Naum a short walk from his car. Agron told him, "Get home safe."

It was only after the taillights of their SUV turned the corner that Naum realized his car that was sitting there in front of Emmanuel AME was going nowhere. "Naum, you dummy."

His '66 two-door lemon-cream Impala, right in the space where it had conked out. Both doors wide open. The seats missing. The radio too. All five tires disappeared. Spare included. The steering column was sticking up like a dandelion without a flower. That was a classic, that steering wheel.

The hood and the trunk were popped open, and the only thing left in either was a snow-covered mess. Getting dark early, and dusk was getting ready to dump another round of snow.

Sixtieth Street El stop was about a block's worth of trudging over unshoveled pavements through knee-deep snow. Naum was happy he had two pairs of socks under his boots.

He got off the elevated train at Girard Avenue a little after five in the afternoon. It was already dark. The street was a storm-abandoned boulevard. A riderless trolley slid along the tracks without a sound. The sky had cleared.

He thought about funerals and memorials and discernment and listening and Jenny in that cardiac ICU and who buries us or remembers us when the priest won't. A starry winter night and nobody knew. But Jenny knew.

He got that crack-your-heart smile when he remembered her telling him, "When you make it yourself you know what's in it."

Him and his theology.

He *was* full of soup.

Head down. One foot in front of another.

Heading home.

Frozen tired old Naum
What a risk it is to be
A person called to being
The image of God
Wake up in an ICU realizing
Our so-called self-sufficiency
Is totally inadequate
To be what we're called to be
Like Him
Even in our fallen state
The separation of sin
From God and from others
Can be the starting point of participating

In the miracle of salvation
Life in Christ.
It made Naum shiver the whole walk home.

STANDING DOWNSTAIRS, the overhead streetlights glowing like a halo around her head, lawn chairs shoved in shoveled-out spaces to save parking places, there on the pavement in front of their home, Greta, in the oversize sweater she'd knit for him, gloves and boots, hat and hoodie, scarf around her neck.

Their flat-end double-wide coal shovel leaning against the door jamb. Priftereshe Greta, with a broom, sweeping up the last of the snow she shoveled at the far end of the walk.

Greta came to meet him, took the bag from his shoulder, and slid her arm around his waist. She kissed him on the cheek above his frosty beard and made him smile when she wiped the moisture off his mustache with the back of her glove. Naum closed his eyes and sighed.

Ten steps out in the clear cold air, Naum could smell crusty bread and Jenny's Sow Shad soup. They walked up to the kitchen holding hands. Things began to thaw.

TOWARD ELEVEN the phone rang.

"Father Naum?"

"Yep."

"You weren't sleeping, were you?"

Naum said, "No."

"Slight problem, Father. We're having trouble getting the money together to bury her."

"What about your mom's house, Rob—?"

Robin said, "Mortgaged to the hilt."

Truth was, aside from the house, Jenny never had much to begin with.

Naum said, "Tell ya what, Robin, tomorrow we'll go over together, see Donahue at the funeral home."

———

THAT EVENING LITTLE HARRY was heading out in the junkyard flatbed to grab what was left of Naum's Impala from in front of Emmanuel AME when he saw something you never see in our neighborhood.

Killed the engine
Cranked the window
Sat back
Inhaled
Let the cold roll in
Through the unfamiliar hush
And down windscreen
Comes a Yukon mummy
A pole in each hand
Skiing Sepviva Street
Past Saint Alexander
Along triangle park
Two nights
After snow
Buried Fishtown

Five feet deep
A beautiful thing
The park and the trees
The skier and the snow
New stripes of fresh pointing
Blown between
Pockmarked
Ben Franklin bricks
Tarpaper rooftop
Row homes
Two and three stories
Snow-light acolytes
In a circle around
Our thrice-illumined
Fieldstone catechumen
Radiant and pure
In her frozen white vestment
The vapor from Harry's breath steamed out the cranked-down window without so much as a sigh and added to the quiet of the after-storm stillness that descended over God's winter world like a prayer without words.

Woulda been a beautiful thing too . . .

Savvy

"WHEN I'M EIGHTEEN I'm becoming Orthodox."

She was seven when her father first brought her to liturgy.

She stood up front and didn't blink.

Her eyes were little girl garden eyes.

She could see every sound.

She could taste the liturgy like sweetness on her tongue.

Every color, she could hear.

Each iconographic shape made a tingling on her skin.

The choir of her five senses intoned a harmony so strangely familiar that her heart recalled a memory of the future in a language she knew but hoped never to learn.

Why father and daughter had come that morning?

Naum didn't know. He didn't think they were Orthodox.

Naum had consumed the Gifts and was unvesting.

Her father said he'd taken her everywhere to try to get an answer to her questions.

Naum listened.

To illustrate her questions, this child needed no crayons beyond the rudimentary colors contained in a beginner's box.

One hundred fifty-two colors in his grown-up Crayola case, and still the eloquent rainbow of primary simplicity that colored her questions persistently eluded Naum's attempt at retelling, and left him with nothing but broken crayons and byzantine scribble.

The priest Naum had to settle for, "She asked it better than me, but . . ."

"If I love God and I go to heaven, I'll be happy there with Him, right?"

Naum said, "Right."

They stood, the three of them, in front of the iconostasis.

"If my mother and father don't go to heaven too, will I be not as happy?" she asked while ignoring Naum and processing back and forth along the portal wall, running her hand along the iconostasis, visiting for a moment with each angel and saint.

Stretching on her tiptoes to kiss the feet of the Master with the open book, with what seemed to be the happy reciprocal recognition of family who had not seen each other for a long, long time.

She stood smiling at the icon of the Child in the embrace of His Mother.

What she said to Naum and to her father, the questions she asked, she expressed more eloquently.

There was no way either could do it justice.

Maybe they could only blame the Sandro Botticelli *Virgin and Child with Saint John and an Angel* expression the kid carried in her hazel icon eyes.

Maybe they could blame the hopeful sadness that called out from somewhere deep within the child, a hopeful sadness only she knew, but not in the fashion of this world.

Maybe it was her lisp or the way she said *Amen*.

Maybe it was her being halo blonde and so naturally at home, lost in a liturgical reunion her father and Naum could only hope to fathom, running her fluent fingers in Braille-like revelation over the familiar faces of the icons in her good shoes and Sunday dress, softly kissing each one and whispering, "It's me."

Both could see, but why only one father wondered about the light dancing from her fingertips . . . ?

When someone told Naum,

It's the mystery that clarifies the knowledge, not the other way around . . .

Naum said, "I understand."

But he didn't.

Then the Botticelli child asked another.

"God knows everything, right?"

"Right," Naum said.

"And God knows ahead of time, right?"

"Right."

"Then why does He make people He knows ahead of time won't love Him?"

The child was serious.

"And so they make themselves go to hell forever?"

No cookie-cutter answer, Naum. No pithy quote.

"Why doesn't He just make people He knows will love Him and go to heaven with Him, if He loves His creation?"

Naum said, "You want a doughnut, sweetie? C'mon, Dad, let's go to coffee hour."

Dad shook his head, took her by the hand and told Naum, "I still don't savvy."

Naum always said our Master told stories, parables.

He said, "Outside liturgy, all I have are stories, coffee, doughnuts, and more stories."

On the way to the church hall Naum said, "I met a guy once, food and beverage manager at a big downtown hotel, Peter was his name. He said as a kid he'd been an unruly altar boy. One Holy Thursday he was running around the front yard at home, raising dust devils, while his old nunna was dyeing red eggs.

"She came out wiping her stained hands on her apron and grabbed him by the ear and stopped him in his tracks. She'd had enough. She told him, 'Peter, look up.' He did.

"She said, 'Now spit as hard as you can.'

"When he looked down, rubbing the spit off his face, Nunna was back inside finishing the Paschal eggs.

"Peter told me that the meaning of what she taught him that day without explaining or saying a word has never been exhausted, but in remaining unexplained, it has taken on a significance apropos to the relentless changing conundrum we call life.

"Peter said, 'I've become my nunna. She dyed me in her love. I put all my red eggs and everything I don't even know I don't know in His basket, the basket she wove in me.'"

After hearing Peter's story, the girl's father said, "Sometimes I wonder, if God sat me on His lap like a little monkey and explained it to me in baby language—if even then I'd understand."

Naum smiled and quoted Mark Twain: "The only reason God created man was 'cause He was disappointed with the monkey."

That got a laugh. At least from Naum.

Naum said, "But I get what you're saying. Sometimes I feel

like a clever monkey. A monkey who learns to sign and recite riddles just to get ambrosia.

"I just like being inebriated by the cup without ever really knowing the truth of what ambrosia means, or the love required to make it be . . . Selfishly content in my oblivious monkey failure to relate to *the Offered and the Offerer* . . . to what Dylan Thomas calls 'the close and holy darkness' . . ."

———•—•———

RASKOVA, OUR "FOREIGNER," was wiping tables when she overheard.

She bowed her head, put her right hand on her heart, and whispered to herself:

In the close and holy darkness

The Unanswerable is a star for us to follow

A companion to hold hands with

To talk it over with

Again and again

Along the road to Emmaus

It might be that

A certain kind of answer

Would only hinder our growth in

The Blessed Unanswerable

Raskova put her finger to the right side of her forehead and slowly tapped three times.

Maybe the persistent beggar

Is an eternal beginning

A daily renewal of the blessing

A constant opportunity

Not meant to be dismissed with easy answers
Easy alms which cost me nothing
She extended her right arm, Raskova, and touched her first two fingers to her thumb.

His cross
She made
Over her
My mind—my heart—my strength.
Maybe better to accompany one another
We and the unanswered question
Until the ripening of the grain and the season of the harvest
And together make the bricks for our oven
Gather the wood and fire the hearth
Grasp the heavy stones
We cannot handle on our own
Erect our mill
Grind our grain
Ask God's blessing on the water
Infuse the Unanswerable like leaven
A little at a time
Slowly rising, knowing
And being slowly known
In His season
In the breaking of His bread
Our Raskova, who had survived Dachau, Siberia, and a forced immigration from the homeland of her youth, found her broom and started sweeping.

Prayer disguised in simple motion.

Raskova hid the gift in mundane movement.

A habit developed through suffering. A habit that saved her, soul and body, whenever she found herself in a place where prayer became imprisoned by her words.

Once, on a spring morning, Naum came unnoticed upon Raskova. She was holding out three fingers as a perch, talking with a kaleidoscope of butterflies in the back garden.

"A love that is trivialized," she was saying, "is made silly and diminished when we try to prove it. That is a love turned to dust, like when we try to grasp the wings of a butterfly. There is a love that makes no worldly sense, but that is nonetheless beautiful in flight."

———

AT THE TABLE, her little-girl feet didn't reach the floor.

She laughed at Naum and called him "the Church Keeper."

Naum liked that.

Raskova set aside her broom and came to the table. She asked the little girl, "What kind doughnut, please?"

And when she pointed to the chocolate cake doughnut without icing, Raskova gave her two. "For you, my dushenka," *dear little soul.*

Dushenka looked toward the temple and told Naum, "I saw Jesus in the incense."

She continued dunking the doughnut in the milky coffee Raskova set before her. "Mommy and Daddy were with Him."

She said thank you to Raskova, who gave her a napkin.

"But they weren't big people. They were little, like me."

Raskova sat next to her and leaned in to listen.

Behind Raskova was an icon of the Descent into Hell.

The little girl said to Raskova, "And He was holding their hands, like when we cross a big street." She pointed and said, "Like them."

Raskova looked over her shoulder at the icon, Adam and Eve and Him taking them by the hand, and said, "Ah." And nodded.

"They were all happy," the girl told Raskova.

She looked at Naum and twirled her napkin into a blessing wand. "Like all of us," she said, and waved her little-girl blessing over the coffee-hour hall.

Father Naum wanted to say, "And then what?" But he didn't.

Dushenka, the little soul, said, "Then they forgot."

Naum wanted to ask, "Why?" Instead he took some coffee.

She said, "Because they got big."

Naum looked at Raskova and then at the little girl.

He said to the little soul, "Well, that answers that."

She just smiled and told Naum, "You're silly."

The girl become Orthodox at eighteen, studied in England, and went on to graduate from Orthodox seminary. She married a young man who became Orthodox too. They have kids. They never miss liturgy.

She serves the poor in a neighborhood shelter.

Kid's probably got more unanswered questions than ever, and her little-girl garden eyes in which other worlds were revealed, they may have softened over time, a little.

Eyes often do.

But wonder can return.

Far as Naum knows, she still eats an occasional chocolate cake doughnut, no icing, at coffee hour after liturgy with her dad, who nine years after her embraced the Faith.

Dad likes to say, outside the liturgy, he still doesn't get it.

He says, "When my daughter was a child, she could see what I could only understand."

It reminded Naum of a quote from Saint Gregory of Nyssa, a quote Naum truly loved but kept forgetting to make room for in his box of broken crayons.

Concepts create idols; only wonder can understand.

No wonder Naum could only savvy coloring outside the lines.

Money–Sex–Power

⟫◈⟪

THERE IT WAS AGAIN, the big car, occupying the prime
space in the church parking lot. The space everybody knew
to leave open for 105-year-old Olga. Not that Nunna drove, but
her 65-year-old son, Teddy the Horse, who sold used cars at Auto
Heaven on the Avenue, he drove her every Sunday to church.

Not this guy. He parked that big champagne-colored Lincoln
Town Car wherever he wanted. How many liquor stores did he
own? Who knew?

His old man, Koli, and a couple of the old guys in the parish used to have a business cleaning out cellars back when they
first came to America. And not with trucks, mind ya, but with
pushcarts.

When they got a horse they named him Lucky, 'cause that's
how they felt to finally not have to push those carts full of junk
down to the scrapyard using what Chicky Cilligan called "Nor-
wegian steam, meaning we pushed them carts our damn selves."

Kosta Koli had parlayed his old man's pushcart junk-hauling
concern into a liquor emporium empire.

Inside St. Alexander the Whirling Dervish parish, they were
arguing back by the *pangar*, the candle stand.

"Six thousand dollars," Nicky Zeo was saying. "And that ain't half a what he gives every year."

Two-Beer Eddie Flynn's father, Andon, had been a priest, and Eddie had a son named Andon who was a priest too, but Two-Beer Eddie rarely came to church. "Today though? For this baptism?" He said, "Kosta Koli coming to church? To be godfather to this family he brought over? Not missing this."

Kosta Koli had the look. The Frank Sinatra *Pal Joey* look. With the fedora tilted just right. The skinny silk tie and the royal blue sharkskin vicuña suit. Very costly fiber. With the black patent leather lace-ups and the see-through black socks everybody in the neighborhood wanted but could no way afford. Even had a cigarette angled in the corner of his mouth, in the narthex of the church, and who was gonna say anything about it?

He was the king of the interstate cigarette thing. Better not ta mention that particular nighttime enterprise in the light of day. Not around Koli, anyway.

And if Kosta Koli didn't go to Lefty the barber three times a week, then explain the head a hair on a man that age. Straight-razor sharkskin sharp. If nothing else, ya had to give it to Kosta Koli, the man had style.

Slide into that big old cream-colored enamel chair with the black leather seat. Get the crisp striped barber cape snapped around his neck. Pumped up high, telling Lefty, "Not too short, Lef, I'm gonna make it grow."

And when Lefty finished him off with aftershave and a twirl of duster-brush talc, and popped that pinstripe cape and let that hydraulic chair go down slow. . . A smooth, cool Kosta Koli stood outta that throne newborn every time, smiling in the mirror through a Pinaud Clubman haze, and every shoe-shined step broadcast nothing less than barbershop fresh and razor-strap clean so the whole damn neighborhood could sit up and see.

"And ya couldn't smell the incense for Kosta when the man with the tan sauntered into church." What Sharky always said.

"How's the kid, Kost?" Lefty asked when Kosta came into the narthex.

"Ekaterina? Growing up, Lef. Nineteen now, off ta college with one a the cousins, Melia. Payin' for her freight too. We only had the one, but the kid's my heart, my Ekaterina. And better if ya call me Mister Koli in public. Appearance, Lef, know what I mean?"

Kosta never lost his composure. You could tell by his smile. You could tell by the shark-tooth smile he pasted on his face whenever he saw Father Naum, or any priest, for that matter. The smile that let you know what Kosta Koli was thinking: "Whadda schmuck."

When Naum came into the narthex, he gave Kosta the news quietly. "It would be better if we talked another time, privately, about the baptism today," Naum said. "After we first spoke at your office, I did try to meet with you again to explain, but your secretary told me you were unavailable. I can meet whenever you like. I know you're busy." Naum handed Kosta a folded paper.

Kosta faced Naum and put both hands on the priest's shoulders. He turned his face to the candle stand to smile at the boys from the Black Bridge Gang, named for the iron railroad trestle that spanned the tracks at American Street.

Then Kosta Koli turned to look Naum in the face. "Whatever you got to say, Father, you can say right here. Lefty. Two-Beer

Eddie. Teddy the Horse. Nicky Zeo. Sharky. Chicky and me, we grew up together. Had a real job. Not just talking theory. Pushed carts together. Hauled junk. Cleaned out cellars for my old man would've gagged a maggot. Slept many a summer night on the old Black Bridge. Went to war together. And we all came back. No, Naum." He fanned Naum's face with the folded paper. "You wanna talk, talk. That's what you do, right, words? That's all you're giving me here, right?" He fanned Naum again with the paper. "So give it to me, baby."

"Please excuse me, Mister Koli," Naum said. "I have to get things ready for the baptism."

Kosta watched Naum walk from the narthex into the church. He looked at his boys. "We shoulda had Lucky the horse haul his ass away a long time ago."

"C'mon, Kosta." They all knew Lefty never used profanity. "We're in church," Lefty said.

Telling Kosta Koli *no* was just one rung below asking him to curb his language. Most people didn't want to get on his list.

"I don't know, Lef," Kosta said. "I gotta a feeling that priest is gonna cost yas." Kosta Koli crumpled the folded paper Naum had given him. "What I'm offering and what he's offering?" He pushed the paper into Lefty's hand. "Where's he think his salary comes from? Prayers don't pay the light bill. Some people don't know which side their holy bread is buttered on, or where the communion wine comes from, and I ain't talking about grapes." He winked and said, "He like hittin' the juice a little, him, dat it?"

When the priest came back, Kosta could tell by his shoulders Naum had come to his senses. Kosta could smell submission in another man. Kosta Koli never lost his composure. You could tell by his smile.

He bent to hear Naum whisper, then turned to the men at the candle stand and said, "I gotta go."

Nicky Zeo and the boys could feel the money-off coupon scheme dripping like cherry water-ice melting out of the pointed bottom of a leaky paper-cone cup and evaporating all over a hot August pavement.

Upstairs in the church hall they had rows of shopping bags full of money-off beer and wine discount barcode certificates, and cigarette money-back coupons the people clipped. Kosta processed them through his outlets and gave the parish pennies on the dollar.

The same slate of candidates who sanctioned the coupon scheme were nominated and elected to the parish council year after year.

"Easier," is how Anthony Albert always put it every time he proposed casting a single ballot to re-elect the entire current board. "'Sides, they're doing good keepin' the place in the black and nobody else really's interested anyways."

"I thought it was a three-year term limit." Philoxenia raised the same objection every year.

The parish council president said, "Noted." And they moved on.

Teddy the Horse had a bookkeeping course in high school. He agreed to be treasurer, temporarily, he used to joke, "Eleven years ago. Temporary." Teddy would point to the rows of coupon shopping bags lined up in perfect rows like the headstones in the veterans' section over at Palmer Burial Ground and say, "Never had our operating account fat up so fast."

No one on the parish council ever told Naum the details about the arrangement with Kosta. Maybe they didn't know exactly what objections the priest would've had, but they knew he would've found something wrong with it, that's for sure.

They knew "You can't achieve good by evil means" was one of his favorite patristic quotes.

"Better ta stonewall a guy like that," was what Eddie Gjarper said.

And what Kosta did with the coupons once he gave Teddy the cash? Only Chicky and Two-Beer Eddie ever speculated how Kosta worked that angle. Both had made night runs up from Carolina.

Kosta told them, "You ain't payin' the freight. It ain't your truck. Don't worry about what's in the back. Take your goddamn money, go down ta Shooky's, have a beer on me and be happy."

Sharky, who ran his own truck hauling for the putty factory, would've refused outright if he didn't know Kosta Koli. He told Kosta he had too many outstanding tickets to take a chance going interstate, let alone on the overnight. That's how Sharky got out of telling Kosta *no*.

Chicky and Two-Beer Eddie did it the once. Both said they'd never do it a second time.

Told Kosta since coming home from the war, all that sitting in the truck going long distance was hell on their legs. "'Sides, Kos," Chicky said, "the old night vision ain't what it used ta be."

———✦———

NAUM RANG THE BELL at the Leka house, but no one answered. He could see movement behind the front-door window of the old brick row home.

It was the youngest daughter, Melia, who called him back as he turned to walk away. "Father, don't go. We want you to bless the house."

Melia and her older sister, Angeline, had a reputation at church.

"Skirts that short. Where's their mother?" Ramona, who always wore a different colored bandana, didn't care if anyone heard. Not even Pia, the girls' mother. Maybe she wanted Pia to hear.

Naum asked Ramona, "What's a higher quality, Ramona, honesty or mercy?"

"Honesty," Ramona said.

"So, if I am born not as fortunate as you in the looks department, Ramona," Naum said, "and I walk into the room, you're going to say, 'Wow, is that man ugly!' loud enough for me to hear it?"

Ramona wouldn't answer. She bit her tongue till Naum was out of earshot whenever Pia brought her girls to church.

Angeline, Pia's older daughter, was petite and full-figured like her mother. Pia saw herself in her older daughter.

Pia and Angeline did all they could to avoid a fight. They were good at not hearing what they didn't want to hear. People said Pia was too old-world passive, and Angeline was much the same.

The row of candles Angeline lit in church, she told her mother, "One for each of the ladies I hear whispering my name."

Now Melia, the younger daughter, stopped coming to church. She was her father's daughter. "I'm not a phony," she said. "If I were, I'd join the Teuta Ladies Baking Society and make cakes and smash them in their faces."

Melia believed in action. "Too much talk only leads to trouble," she would say.

Carol, who always wore a hat to cover her wig, to cover her early-onset androgenic alopecia, told Ramona, "You never know what goes on behind someone's front door, Mona." Carol, who had no children, made the cross and said, "Thank God, Ramona, you have children, beautiful children of your own."

Carol saw and heard more than her fair share of gossip at her Village Thrift and Consignment Shop. "I've seen their mom. Our Pia. Maybe the poor thing thinks the makeup covers it, but it doesn't."

Plain-Jane Bernice bit her tongue. She had daughters too. "I cross my fingers," she said. "It's not easy."

Madeline the nun or Madeline the theologian is how the other members of the Teuta Ladies Baking Society teased her because Madeline was *religious,* she said, "God cares what they wear? At least they come. At least Pia brings those girls to church. But I get it. It does distract, the way they . . . Well, enough."

Madeline knew every kind of icon had its impact. She wanted to say, "Each one is affected from without by what's within. And the reverse." But she didn't.

Pia Leka's house was so neat and sparse it made Naum nervous. Most homes didn't smell like disinfectant. Most working-class homes had comfortable furniture in the living room. A TV. A place to put your feet up and relax after a day out in the world.

Pia had arranged the dining room table with an icon. A shallow bowl of water. A bushy sprig of basil and a votive candle.

Naum kept himself from reacting to the bruises on Pia's face.

Gregory, her often sullen husband, the father of Angeline and

Melia, led the procession through the house, carrying the cross. Angeline and Melia held icons. Naum sprinkled the blessed water with the bushy sprig of *borzilok* and chanted the prayers, room to room. Pia followed with the small home censer, and they made a circuit, upstairs and down and back to the dining room table.

Each one kissed the cross and Naum's hand as he touched their heads with the basil after dipping it in the bowl of blessed water.

The girls set out bowls and spoons. Pia ladled soup. Gregory sliced bread. Demitasse cups of coffee were served. Together they said the Lord's Prayer, *Ati yne*, in Albanian. Naum made the blessing.

Tall, handsome, muscular, silent, sullen Gregory began to sob. Pia went to comfort him.

Angeline, the older girl, said, "Daddy, don't."

Melia looked at Naum. She said, "The priest knows."

"We wanted to come to America so bad." Gregory sobbed. "He's rich. He's sponsored so many of us, his relatives."

The distraught man could not continue. He pounded the table. Soup jumped out of the bowls.

Gregory cried so loudly a well-meaning row-house neighbor knocked.

Melia told the woman, "My father was hammering to hang a picture and hit his thumb."

"Both the girls, and me." Pia said.

Naum took both of Gregory's hands in his. He turned them over, back and forth, looking at the scrapes and bruising. "You hit her?" he said.

"Only when he drinks," Pia said. "He doesn't mean to."

"He drinks all the time now," Angeline, the older girl, said. "And punches the walls in the cellar."

Melia didn't know who she hated more, Kosta Koli or her father. The younger sister said, "Someday I'll kill them both."

When Pia finished night school, she left her husband Gregory. She was full-time at the hospital. Pia was respected on the oncology ward for her dedication and compassion. Her older daughter, Angeline, stayed with her.

Kosta Koli had paid for the younger girl, Melia, to go to an out-of-state college with his daughter, her cousin Ekaterina.

Melia rarely came home.

Now Uncle Kosta, the man who sponsored so many "relatives" to come to America, wanted to be godfather to another family of new immigrants, more young relatives he recently sponsored from the ancestral village at home.

"I gotta go," was all he said, there at the candle stand in the narthex, hat in hand, bent to hear the schmuck's whisper in his ear in front of the Black Bridge Gang.

None of them knew the truth.

Naum went in to wash Kosta's cologne off his nose.

"Maybe he really did get an emergency call," Sharky said when Kosta went out the door and got into his big Town Car.

"You think it was something Naum said?" Lefty couldn't figure it out. Kosta Koli wasn't staying? He was supposed to be godfather at this baptism.

"I betcha it was a family thing," Chicky said. "Or more likely business. Gotta come first. Ain't easy running an empire."

Teddy the Horse said, "Well, money or no money, Kosta was never here much anyway. And whenever he did come, all he'd do was sit in the back with his legs crossed checking his bank accounts on his smartphone."

"I think he was insulted the woman in the short skirt he was godfather to didn't kiss his hand," Nicky Zeo said. "You see the heels she was wearing? They think this is a nightclub or something, these new ones."

"Another buncha relatives he brought over," Teddy said. "Taking a free ride to America on rich Uncle Kosta, who wouldn't?"

"Good-looking kids, too, the new ones," Chicky said. "The whole family. Men and women."

The new immigrant family was gathered around the baptismal font in front of the iconostasis.

"Father Naum looked pissed though," Sharky said. "'Bout something."

"Naum? Pissed?" Chicky said. "I doubt it."

"Family probably didn't like the christening outfit Kosta bought for the kid," said Teddy the Horse. "They all come over here and want the same things we been working years to get. The big house. The car. All the stuff. Wanna go right to the top."

"Could be," Lefty said. "But I don't think so. Something's wrong there. If Naum ain't saying . . ."

"What?" Teddy said.

"That's gotta tell ya something," Lefty said.

"I didn't always tell my kids everything," Nicky said. "Not even when they got older. Some things priests can't say."

"I wouldn't wanna be the priest," Sharky said. "People tell you stuff. Or you see things. You tell one, you tell *anybody*, you're violating somebody else's private business. I bet ya sometimes ya gotta even lie, even to your own wife, say you don't know when ya do. Or say nothing, and get beat up for it."

"Hell of a position to have to be in," Chicky said.

"Money, sex, and power. Three things'll trip ya up. Ya remember Naum talking about it?" Lefty said. He unfolded the crumpled paper Kosta had crushed in his hand. It was a quote from *Unseen Warfare*:

> *Once the eyes become accustomed to looking passionately upon the mature beauty of living bodies, once the sense of smell is delighted by the fragrance of myrrh and aromatic things, once the tongue and the mouth taste or rather become accustomed to the rich and tasty foods, and finally, once the sense of touch is accustomed to fine and soft clothing—who will be able after that to convince people that what they have up to now enjoyed is not a true and rational pleasure, but on the contrary an irrational and temporal one?*

At the bottom of the quote, Naum had signed a handwritten note:

Kosta. We should talk about your destruction of your relatives, of Pia and Gregory and their daughters, Angeline and Melia, and the hellish cell you've prepared for your soul.

But Kosta never saw the quote.

He never saw the note.

Naum, weeks before, had gone to the liquor store offices and told Kosta privately, "No, given what you've done, you cannot be godfather to the new family you've sponsored. I didn't tell them why you couldn't be godfather, but I've arranged for someone else to be their sponsor in Christ."

Kosta Koli never lost his composure. You could tell by his smile. Kosta Koli came to church anyway that day. Who or what was going to stop him?

It was while Kosta was joking with the boys by the candle stand that Naum took the call.

Little Harry came to the altar. "Father, ya got a call. Sounds serious."

And when the old priest returned to the narthex, he whispered to poor Kosta Koli, "You have to go, Kosta. It's your daughter, Ekaterina."

That's all Naum would say.

The parish family found out later the same day.

How or why Ekaterina had come to suspect?

We never knew.

Effervescent Ekaterina. The same age as cousin Melia. Nineteen and her father's daughter to a tee.

"You ain't payin' the freight, Melia . . ."

Coerced her weeping college roommate, backed her into a corner, forced her cousin Melia to tell.

"Details, I want all the details."

Hauled that junk right out into the sunlight and made Melia tell what Kosta Koli, Ekaterina's father, had done to Melia, to her sister, and to their mother.

Ekaterina Koli.

Her father's heart.

His only child

Bright with every gift of life

Had taken her own.

The Escalator

W E HAD THE CITY'S LAST horse-drawn milk wagon in our neighborhood.

Bill the milkman?

Boy, we loved that guy, him and his horse, Leche, coming down Norris Street leaving cartons of fresh eggs, loaves of crusty bread, boxes of doughnuts, jelly and custard-filled, cream-top glass bottles of ice-cold milk, and magic chocolate straws. Put one in your glass of plain old vitamin D and the twizzle-striped straw made it come out chocolate in your mouth, upside-down the bottle a coupla times, mix the cream in outta the bottleneck.

Back then, the two-story milk-bottle-shaped water tower on the roof of Harbison's Dairy—platformed up there over the three-story hard-fired brick dairy?—that shiny white bottle with the bright red script lettering made you want to get a warm bakery bag of chocolate-chip cookies from the Cookie Ranch out at the mall and dunk right in.

People said *that*—that up there? Was the same as having the Eiffel Tower in the neighborhood.

Better.

When we were kids, Milkman Bill would lift us up in the wagon and damn if we didn't take those reins and yell "Giddy-up!" thinking we were Hopalong Cassidy or the Cisco Kid piloting a buckboard over the plains.

Didn't matter. Not to Leche. A stocky well-muscled gray mare, imperturbably oblivious to our stagecoach antics. A Belgian dapple draft horse with more poise than a Tennessee thoroughbred. Leche made each long-established stop in front of the exact same brick. Dignified in the quiet certainty of her ancestral equine gait. The Belgian gray mare never went further or faster than a row house at a time.

Bill walked the pavement. Same as he'd done for years. Same measured-out stops along the block.

Same penciled note from the same lady of the house stuck in the neck of the same empty glass bottle set out on the same rail-sided landing at the top of the same scrubbed marble steps.

With the same decorative foot-scraper just to the left of the polished bottom step. Only the old people who were used to dancing around horses remembered what a foot-scraper was for. Poor old scraper, standing there elegant as a lattice-work wrought-iron bridge.

Years rolled by with the wheels on their wagon while Bill pulled pretty much the same two-handed order from the open-sided shelves of Leche's lazy rolling caravan. Their familiar pattern cast comforting shadows of habit over the ornamental grates on our coal-chute ground-level cellar windows.

Summers, Leche and old Bill, steady on, meandering past kids skipping barefoot under fireplug spray, sledding winters down the ruts of ice-packed tracks, ducking neighbors through the middle of friendly-fire snowball fights, delivering what each household believed to be its own unique daily bread.

Same as same had always been.

———•———

NOWADAYS, I REMIND MYSELF of Leche when I follow my wife through the mall.

I know my Judy's every stop down the arcade in the Promenade Mall. I know every bench. But unlike Leche, who knew the length of every stop, including Bill's conversations with yacky old Mrs. July—unlike old Leche, I never got the knack of knowing exactly how long my Judy would stay in any given shop. Remains a mystery to me to this day.

Like the thing in church the other day.

Father Naum was talking about something he called *synergy*.

If you ask Naum why he became a priest, he says he did it 'causa he liked the uniforms. He said, "Who else gets to wear a cape to work? Fifty dollars a month and all the meshe I can eat?"

So when I see Naum, I ask him, and he breaks it down, the synergy thing.

He said, "It takes two. You and God, working together to cooperate. God won't force you. You got to want to sync your way of doing things, what you want, what you think, what *you* think is good for you, with what God *knows* is good for you."

Now I'm just a civilian works the loading dock at the putty factory, and I'm looking at him thinking, *Yeah, but what I think is good for me on Monday changes before Tuesday turns to payday.*

Naum said, "Trust is a big part of it. My confessor told me,

'So, Naum, until you get to trust God, you go ahead and do your own thing and let me know how that works out for you.'"

I'm saying to myself, *And how's that working out for me? I mean, look at me. If it wasn't for my Judy . . .*

"'Specially," Naum said, "when it's getting near the end. Really got to pay attention how going independent is gonna work out when our time comes. And who the hell knows when that's gonna be, right?"

Then Naum said, "Tell ya the truth, I had to tell my confessor it *ain't* workin' out all that good where I'm concerned. I mean, look at me. If it wasn't for my Greta . . ."

Both of us standing there thinking, *That wife of mine must be from God.* Girl's way out of our league.

He went in his cassock and unfolded a note from a bishop called Metropolitan Anthony Bloom.

In the Church we are imperfect in two different ways: imperfect while striving towards God or imperfect when we turn away from Him. It is not a matter of success; it is a matter of direction.

Naum said, "So, I'll tell ya what, cuz? Why don't we give it a shot, the two of us together, me and you, try and get it going in the right direction, the synergy thing? We'll cooperate, like we're supposed to do in church."

Now, I'm sitting there on the bench in the mall waiting to move to my next stop, watching the girls go by. Happy I don't have a daughter. I'd be worried all the time.

And I'm thinking about cooperating with God, and at the same time trying to think if I could ever get myself to cooperate with a daughter, or her to cooperate with me . . .

And finally out comes Judy from the Cookie Ranch and moves

me to one of my favorite benches across from the escalator and leaves the whole bakery-warm chocolate-chip package in my lap.

Warm cookies? And me? Alone?

Talk about synergy.

I was thinking how sweet it'd be if only I had a cream-topped ice-cold bottle of Harbison's milk when I see this little black kid in the middle of the down escalator, trying to run up.

And up at the top is his father, calling out, "C'mon, Mikey, you can make it."

And tireless little Mikey, you know how you are when you're seven or eight, even nine or ten, never out of gas. He's running up that damn down escalator, and every time he gets near the top, his little legs just give out, and down with the moving steps Mikey goes gliding.

And then his father starts up again. "C'mon, Mikey."

And darn if that father didn't sound like he really believed the kid could do it. And that jazzes up Mikey. He pushes his glasses up on his nose, and up he goes again. And all the while, relentless, that escalator, it just keeps rolling down, down, down.

And then there goes Mikey, looking up at his dad and seeing his father's face, and they got their arms outstretched ready to catch each other, wearing matching plaid flannel shirts and brand new dungarees and sneakers, and I notice I'm the only one noticing. So I don't wanna be like, "Hey Mike-kay!!!" and all cheering and stuff, like some sad lonely weirdo on a bench with nothing better to do than scope out happy strangers in a mall. But there I was. And it took my mind offa Judy taking so long and offa Naum's theoretical hoohah.

Well, I was eating cookies like the Cookie Ranch was never

gonna make no more and all the time hoping for a resolution for Mikey and his pop before Judy got back and moved me along to another bench, when down from right near the top glides little Mikey, the kid a little lower than the angels, who did his best but just couldn't keep up the fight.

I mean, after a while, who could blame the kid. Down he goes. Standing on that mechanical descending step, looking up at Pop. And it's not like the kid wasn't giving it his best.

Shoulda seen the look on that boy's face. I can't say for certain what it meant, but I don't think he wanted to fail his father.

And I don't think the kid wanted his father to think he couldn't count on him.

And I don't think he wanted his father to think he wasn't strong enough or didn't love him enough to come up and be with him where he was.

He just couldn't do it on his own. Who can?

So when Mikey's father ran down that escalator smiling and grabbed Mikey up in his arms and kissed him all the way to the top, telling the kid how great he was and them telling each other how much they loved one another, I mean, you would've thought they were going together right up that escalator to God's own heaven.

It took another twenty minutes before Judy came out. "You left some for us, I hope."

I lied and said, "Yeah, I only had one or two."

After Mikey got up to his pop and before Judy got back I had to quick sneak down to the Cookie Ranch and buy a whole new batch.

The next bench stop was the last one before we went together to the men's work clothes department in Sears. I needed a couple of work shirts and some new bib overalls.

I *was* planning to sit there on the last bench and think some more about cooperation, synergy, and which direction I was going in, and then try to talk it over with Judy.

Instead, I told her the story of Mikey on the escalator.

Judy said she thought it was cute, and told me, "Next time, try to do a better job hiding the empty bag. Now give me the Cookie Ranch receipt for the replacement bag. And wipe the crumbs off your beard."

Suckers

——⊰◆⊱——

Then the LORD said to Cain, "Where is Abel your brother?" And he said, "I do not know. Am I my brother's keeper?"

—GENESIS 4:9

PEOPLE WERE AFRAID of Leo Ray Miller. It was years ago when he killed that man at the Marco wedding reception, the reception where someone from the church was captured on video stealing the wedding money.

All these years later, people in the neighborhood were still afraid. They said Leo had a look about him. And he did. The lack of anything in his eyes when he sized you up. Like nobody and nothing meant nothing. Like he was wearing a rigor mortis mask. People in the neighborhood crossed the street.

When he was in prison somebody gave him two books, a Bible and something called an *apophthegmata*, a book of sayings by Orthodox Church Fathers on radical self-honesty and living without hypocrisy.

None of the priests would admit to it, but we had our ideas

about which one'd put up with a full-body cavity strip search and go into that particular prison.

The Sunday after he got his release, Leo had his wife Aida iron him a new-out-of-the-package white shirt. He put it on and buttoned it to the collar. He hated ties. Black pants. His black Doc Martens laced halfway up his calves. His old black leather jacket. Slicked back his hair. Grabbed his two books and headed straight to church.

He was so early he was waiting outside when Father Naum showed up with the key. The Bible and the book of patristic sayings left him with nothing but questions he didn't like not being able to answer.

Naum handed Leo the key. "I have things back at my car. It's too cold to be standing around outside. Here, take the keys. In case the people start to come. Open up and set the thermostat. Seventy. It's on the right behind the candle stand."

Leo Ray claimed he had never met Naum.

Naum never said one way or another. If you asked him, he'd only say, "God knows the truth."

Leo didn't like it, being alone in the cold, dark church. Something in there spooked him. He propped the front door open in case he decided he couldn't stay.

The furnace made a creaking noise when he set the thermostat. Sitting liquid in the radiators started flowing. Coagulated cast-iron rust gurgled in the pipes like a hoarse voice whispering lost words in a language Leo Ray had never heard.

A bus pulled up out front. It kneeled.

Buses that kneeled. Something new since his release.

A heavy woman was helped out by the driver. She was wearing

a long double-breasted coat with a fur collar. Her thick gray hair showed from beneath her rabbit-fur *ushanka* cap. She wore mittens. Her shoulder bag could've been prison issue, like her boots.

They had their usual exchange, Fedya and the dark-skinned driver with the sunny disposition. "Whaddaya do in there every week, Miss Fedya?"

"Be wit' da Got, Mister," she said.

"You make sure now you talk with Him about me, you hear?"

"Always lighting candle for you, Mister Harold," Fedya told the driver.

Big Harold the driver came off the bus and unfolded her walker. She pitched it ahead with every step. Her legs looked so stout and strong, it seemed to Leo Ray like the walker needed her.

He couldn't take his eyes off the bag on her shoulder.

She'd been sized up before. She smiled to let him know.

"Thank you," she said to Leo. Her accent was robust. She handed him ten dollars from her bag and took two thick, dark beeswax candles.

He stood there behind the candle stand, not knowing what to do. Leo wasn't used to people not being afraid. But this one?

She had no regard for him. She played it right down the middle. He was just the man behind the counter.

He figured she was faking it.

She looked at the ten and said to him, "Enough?"

He pushed a handful of honey-fragrant candles across the counter, the thin ones, and just stared at her. Then folded her ten and put it in a circular gold plate padded in the center with red-purple velvet.

"I light two for you," she told him, and went about her ritual.

Lighting a candle. Standing it upright in the sandbox on stilts. Making the cross. Kissing the icons. Saying prayers. Bowing, and doing it all again.

Leo's belligerence when he was inside had racked him up so much time in solitary with his two books that he found it difficult to be around people, even though he knew in his head that the books advised otherwise.

He asked her name.

She said, "Fedya."

He said, "Leo Ray."

She went back to her prayers.

He looked at her row of candles and said, "Light is good."

She smiled and lit another candle. Her column of living light illumined the narthex alcove.

Leo shivered when she said his name, "Leo Ray." She kissed the icon of Christ.

Ink shapes, theory, things he'd encountered on Bible pages were taking life in the woman, Fedya, and in the little things she was doing.

Teddy the Horse came in with Nicky Zeo. They were carrying boxes of doughnuts and talking about people they knew who were at D-Day, Omaha Beach, and Normandy.

"I can't believe they made it," Teddy said. "I still think about the ones who didn't."

Nicky saw Leo behind the counter. "Hey, Leo." Nicky knew enough to keep it simple with Leo.

Teddy said, "Good to see ya here, kid." But he wasn't so sure.

Leo didn't answer. He knew what they were thinking. The old blood was heating his brain. Lucky for them, he thought, when they had enough sense not to say any more and went upstairs to the hall. *No way,* Leo almost spat, *I'm staying around here.*

Through the glass doors of the narthex he could see the silhouette of the iconostasis and the outline of the curtain covering the Royal Doors. It had been a long time since he'd considered his crime, his sin, considered it in the light of Christ.

It was an argument that got out of hand. It got loud. It was the intention of both men to go home to their beds that night.

Before, Leo hadn't known.

He thought he did. He'd heard things. He was solid in his opinions.

But being in prison and reading his two books over and over again, and having no chance for meaningful communication other than with his own thoughts, made him more and more aware of the juxtaposition of light and darkness in the thread of his being, and of what he described to Naum as "the potency of my violent ignorance."

What Leo did that night in front of the open bar at the wedding reception bricked him up in the other man the same way people brick up broken-out windows in abandoned houses on dead-end streets.

A dead end for the other man.

A dead end for that man's family.

A dead end for Leo's family too.

An abandoned dead end, bricked up against any chance of anyone ever living there again. His walking-around body had morphed into a coffin for his atrophy-sick soul.

When he confessed all this to Naum, he told him, "There is nothing, Father, nothing this side of the grave to help me."

Leo thought of that night.

He thought of that night every night.

Things in his life couldn't stay like they were. Who wants to be around a walking coffin with a dead soul in it?

One man committed murder, and two men died.

Leo told his wife, Aida, "I ain't alive." He told her, "Why you staying? Ya like being around a talking corpse, don'tcha? Ya weirdo."

He'd tried everything. Nothing offered hope. There was no making it right. No way back.

The life of self-offering, of giving back, making up for your crime by doing good deeds, all that clichéd closure shit suggested by so-called well-intentioned halfwits only made it worse for Leo Ray Miller.

In his despair he told Naum, "I'm tired of hearing all that closure bullshit. I'd rather live with it than pretend there was something I could do about it. Not even your God's got anything for this."

Naum told Leo, "I can make an idol out of my sin and end up thinking there's nothing greater than my idol."

Leo Ray didn't like being challenged. He said, "Sin *is* your idol. It's your living."

The Leo Ray Miller he had sown that night at the reception sprouted and spread like an ugly weed. It grew up through the cracks of whatever lies he told himself. It choked every intention, it poisoned every relationship and turned every so-called good deed into a self-serving con.

He wanted to believe.

There had to be some relief beyond his short-term capacity to fool himself. He wanted hope. Even if relief had to wait till what was left of his amputated life was over.

There were days when Leo just hoped there was *something*, some damn thing. Something he didn't even know he didn't know.

And there were other days when he doubted if there was anything he hadn't already figured out. There were days when he thought, *Why not just do everybody a favor and hang myself and get it over with?*

One thing, though, if he was going to do anything, it had to be started here and now. This side of the grave. He could feel it. That's why he brought his books to church. He didn't have time to waste.

Naum said to him, "Thank you for opening the church."

Leo left the candle stand and followed Naum inside. He stood with Naum in front of the Royal Doors. Naum handed him an open book and ran his finger down the paragraphs he wanted Leo to read.

Leo Ray stood there thinking, "Great, another book."

Naum said, "Blessed is our God, now and ever, and unto ages of ages."

When Naum touched the word, Leo Ray said, "Amen."

Leo read the words of the Entrance Prayers assigned to him by Naum.

It was just the two of them to begin with. Then Deacon Dionysios arrived, and the three of them took turns. Then Deacon Donat came and joined the prayers.

Deacon Dionysios said, "Let us pray to the Lord."

The rest sang, "Lord, have mercy."

Naum said, "Lord, stretch forth Thy hand from Thy holy

dwelling place on high, and strengthen me for this Thy appointed service that is about to begin."

The deacons said, "Amen."

Naum asked forgiveness of the deacons and Leo. They did the same with one another. They turned and bowed to the people who were beginning to come in, asking forgiveness. Each one said, "God forgives all."

To Leo, the whole thing was nothing more than a staged psychological operation that made him nervous.

Naum took Leo aside. He said to him, "Wait here, Leonida. I won't be long."

Naum and the deacon entered the sanctuary, Naum through the north door and the deacon through the south door.

Leo Ray heard every word Deacon Dionysios said. He watched through the open door.

Leo saw them bow three times before the altar table. Naum kissed the book of the Holy Gospel, the altar table, and the cross. The deacons kissed the altar table.

Naum came out. He took Leo to the place of confession. He showed Leo how to kiss the cross and the Gospel on the stand and how to place his forehead on the Gospel book. He placed the stole over Leo's head.

He whispered to him, "Leonida, three things. From what you tell me, it seems that night, at the reception, you tried to justify yourself with contentious words. From now on, your only hope is in silent repentance.

"You're a strong man, Leo. You used your physical strength in actions of anger. Your armor-plated ego got the best of you. The one antidote at your disposal is to become weak in the strength of peace. Like our Master Jesus, open arms, defenseless on the Cross.

"A moment of willful epilepsy blinded you, and you destroyed what we are not capable of creating, life. So now, having died with Christ in baptism, death of self in our Lord Christ is our only hope beyond the grave, and this resurrection can begin for you here and now if, seeing the icon of Christ in all people, you will put others first, starting with those closest to you, and die to self. If there is anything left of your heart, Leonida, you can be saved.

"God has planted His garden, the Church, and in it you will find all that is necessary for union with Christ and for your salvation. Especially other people. The temptation to self-reliance is an existential lie. We are saved in the other. Especially those closest to you, like your wife and family. People will help you to see God and know His forgiveness, and you will help others in the same way.

"We have all sinned, Leo. We're all in it together. Now, do you have the courage to find out—was that man that night, who like Cain slew his brother, was that really the true you?"

Ink shapes Leo had encountered on a Bible page in prison were taking life in Fedya, in the deacons, in Naum, in Teddy the Horse and Nicky carrying doughnuts upstairs to the church hall, in the little things they did, in the people of the parish struggling to find forgiveness and life in Jesus Christ.

It weirded Leo out. He didn't like all the people stuff. The man was happy carrying his cross by himself.

Gauged the grave he was digging for himself according to the depth of exile he was feeling that day, according to the measure of life from which he chose to exclude himself.

Leo Ray *I'll be damned alone or saved alone* Miller. Self-sentenced slayer of his brother. Only happy when he was brooding in the morbid incarceration of his solitary cell.

Leo Ray didn't like what Naum had to say. He was an independent operator. He wanted to go home and tell Aida church was okay, but putting up with everybody's idiosyncrasies, feta-cheese breath, attitudes, and opinions, when they hadn't gone through half as much as he'd gone through, was nothing but aggravation in the flesh.

When Naum removed the stole, he bowed to Leonida and said, "Please forgive me."

Leo Ray said, "Don't push your luck, Padre."

He stood there looking at Naum like he was a cockroach in his kitchen. He said, "You want radical honesty, Father? Here's radical honesty. If you think you can live without hypocrisy, then you really are a hypocrite. And you are, ain'tcha? That's your scam, sayin' you're a hypocrite out loud, but really not caring one way or the other on the inside as long as these dummies keep buyin' the humility act and givin' ya the priest-bit payoff."

Naum was afraid of Leo Ray.

He had that look about him, standing there in front of the confession stand. Sizing up Naum, nothing in his eyes.

Nothing and nobody except Leo Ray meant nothing to Leo Ray.

He told Naum, "Forgive yourself, old man. You think *your* way back is the only way, you and your church? I'll take my chances on my own. Ya ever hearda Pascal's wager?"

"I am a hypocrite," Naum said. "Who isn't? But you know, for us, from the beginning, it hasn't been *our* way. He's the Way, and the Truth, and the Life. Put aside your own will and live. His will is for you to return and live."

Leo said, "I'm dead already anyway."

"Better dead with Christ, Leo," Naum said, "than alive with the devil."

Leo said, "Don't worry, old man, you may be dead, but I ain't."

Naum said, "God protect and save you in the end."

Naum started to tell Leo, "The fathers say just because a man commits one murder, he doesn't have to be marked forever a murderer."

But Leo Ray didn't hear. He cut him off. "Whadda you know?"

Leo took his time leaving. He hardened his face into that rigor mortis mask.

In the narthex, Teddy and Nicky watched as Leo blew out all the candles in the sandbox on stilts. Then snapped each candle in two, one at a time. He stared them in the face, took Fedya's folded ten out of the circular gold dish, and put it in his pocket.

He came out the door of Saint Alexander's onto the cold pavement and laughed at the people waiting for the bus. "Buncha halfwits. What was I thinking putting that asshole on my visitor's list?"

They coiled around the far side of the wooden pole like a clowder of cats drunk on a primal fear of snakes.

"Here's some books for ya, suckers." He dumped the Bible and the apophthegmata in the wire trash basket chained to the telephone pole.

The people waiting for the bus knew better than to meet him stare for stare.

Leo Ray Miller marched down the pavement goose-stepping

his boots and swinging his arms. People in the neighborhood saw him coming and crossed the street.

Pretty self-satisfied when he told Aida, "Kicked the old man's philosophical ass. Suddenly had nothing ta say when I told him, I have my reasons, O great bearded one, and my heart's got reasons my reason don't know nothing about."

Naum would have liked to give Leo the full quote from Pascal, but he knew better, at least this time.

The heart has its reasons, which reason does not know.
We feel it in a thousand things.
It is the heart that feels God, not the reason.
This, then, is faith: God felt by the heart, not by the reason.

Aida said, "Wow, Leo. Where'd you get that?"

Suddenly Aida was afraid.

Leo didn't think she knew the reason he took her last name, Miller, when they married. But Aida did. Girl found out what she didn't wanna know . . .

And there stood Leonida Rezart Marku, wound like a dagger with a corkscrew blade.

But she knew how to untwist it too, how to survive when Leo Ray Miller got himself all tightened up.

For a spring-loaded second he just stared at her. She could feel the coiled tension in his stance.

Then he said, "Whaddaya saying, Aida, I ain't smart enough to think that up?"

Aida said, "Leo, I ain't saying nothing. I just never heard it before. You know I'm not smart like you."

"Well, I did make it up. Made it up when I was locked up."
Leo didn't tell her it was Pascal.

The heart has its reasons, which reason does not know.

There was a time when Naum would have spoken the truth in love and said, "Yeah, but, Leo, if our heart hasn't been broken by suffering, by love and longing for the other, by knowing how much God loves us and how far we are from Him, then what reason can the heart know beyond its own appetites?"

Leo would've told Naum, "You don't sound no different than those faggoty mandatory group sessions in the prison detox unit."

Naum was pretty sure he would've had Leo's spit dripping off his nose like early winter rain.

Bow your head, Naum, in front of Leonidas. Be still. Make the cross without moving your arm and call God to remembrance.

Be patient . . . until the coming of the Lord . . . Behold, the husbandman waiteth . . . being patient over it, until it receive the early and the latter rain . . .

After she retrieved them from the bus stop wire trash basket and asked Naum's blessing, Fedya gave the books to Mister Harold, her friend, who helped her with her walker and drove the kneeling bus.

Mister Harold told her, "Well, thank you, sister. Maybe someday I'm gonna have to come and see just what it is you doing in there every week, Miss Fedya?"

And Fedya said, "Okay."

The Book

‒‒‒∋‹∙›⊱‒‒‒

I WAS MINDING MY OWN BUSINESS, resting in the sun on a window ledge outside the putty factory loading dock next to some poor soul's set of false teeth . . .

And along comes Bobby Majewski, picks me up, sits down with his Thermos, opens a box of Oh Ryan's Irish Potatoes, plops me in his lap, puts on his bifocals, takes his little yellow pencil nub from behind his ear in case he has to make a memory mark, like an asterisk or an exclamation point, or do a little underlining.

(Now understand, if you weren't from the neighborhood, you probably might not know they're not Irish and they're not potatoes, and that Oh Ryan's only makes 'em once a year around Saint Patty's Day.)

But darn if Bobby didn't sit there and pop all fifteen of the creamy little cinnamon-rolled coconut spheroids in his mouth like miniature footballs, and damn if he didn't splatter the crumbs and coconut all over me.

Now the Bobby they knew? In the neighborhood? Never had no use for nothing to do with religion and even less for books on the subject.

But that's not the point.

The point is, at the end of every coffee break, Bobby threaded a shoestring through me like an aglet through a lace-hole and set me right back where he found me, on the putty factory loading dock windowsill next to that set of false teeth.

And wasn't nobody more surprised than me when after only a few days Bobby almost made it to my last couple of pages.

Then came that sunny Friday morning Bobby never figured on coming, and I was gone.

He was a tough guy, Bobby.

Came to work at the putty factory in our neighborhood right out of the Navy. Could fix anything. Rode an old-school chopper with chrome Z-bar handlebars that curved out and back.

Wore short-shorts, even in the winter, and red ankle socks with cut-off T-shirts, biceps like boulders, jump-boots, and a Marine Corps cap.

Bobby was not happy. Picked up the false teeth and said, "What're you smiling about?"

Can you believe it?

Bobby Majewski, who had no use for anything to do with religion and even less for books on the subject, unless, like he said, "It gives me ammunition to provoke religious nuts."

Bobby, who had no doubt the world revolved around Bobby, stood there staring at the window ledge, just starting to wake up to what it meant to take a good thing for granted.

In the past, taking things for granted had never resulted in Bobby questioning his own life, questioning things he'd done, or maybe thinking about things he regretted doing, or should have regretted doing or not doing.

In the past, if a book started doing that, making him feel

bad, or making him stop and think, or provoking a bit of self-reflection, even a little bit, if it started to feel like somebody was boxing him in or trying to impose some kind of law on him living his life, that's when he'd close the cover.

People with any sense knew better than to go near Bobby during those couple of days when he was sitting on the loading dock with me in his lap staring out over the railroad tracks, sweat—or was it tears—running down his face, looking out over the railroad tracks like something in the sky was blinking a sign.

On my inside back cover he penciled lines from my pages that jumped out or had a relevance to something he couldn't stop thinking about. Things he'd seen. Deeds he never talked about, deeds done in the war. Or something he was dealing with in the here and now. One-line quotes, maybe a sentence from my pages that made sense to probably only him, like cipher codes speaking Bobby lingo.

"Damn," he said, after he lost me. "Wish I woulda made a copy of those sentences."

If he could've kicked himself, he would've. Bobby said, "Should've kept that book someplace safe, not leave it on the windowsill."

Carla, the waitress over at Betty's, Bobby had a crush on her. She said to him, "Why don't you ask around at the factory? See if anybody . . ."

He put up his hand before she could finish.

Carla knew Bobby. Never had to hand the man a menu.

Knew what he would order even when *he* hemmed and hawed. Girl knew how much he'd leave on his plate. Never wanted a doggy-bag, not her Bobby, like some of the geezers who left a ten-cent tip, stuffed their pockets with napkins and jelly packets, and perp-walked out the door.

Carla knew Bobby better than Bobby knew Bobby.

Carla knew he loved her, and he knew she knew it.

She also knew men were a little thicker in that particular area, the area having to do with love.

She figured he probably couldn't tell, and she knew big tough Bobby was afraid to ask if she did, but Carla loved him too.

She said, "Bobby, I would've loved us to sit and talk about that book sometime. Why didn't you ever bring it in here? You think I'd get jealous?"

Carla asked, not to get an answer. She asked just to introduce the notion, to get Bobby to think.

She knew what he was signing when he put up his hand. She knew it was a shield to deflect the thoughts she was thinking his way, deflect them back her way.

Bobby wasn't a manipulator. What you saw was what you got. Putting up his hand as a shield was his way of admitting he wasn't strong enough to let just anybody get on the back of his bike, hold him around the waist, and whisper in his ear.

"I should've just done it. Done what she said. It's just that I didn't want anybody knowing I was interested in getting into a book like that."

Carla told him, "Bobby, if you wanna make a book like that come alive, you got to connect it with life, and the only way to do that is to connect it with other people, or let it connect you—to like a church, or me, or us, or something."

Carla had a waitress kind of wisdom when it came to timing.

She said to herself, "Man just needs a little more time with the menu. He'll come ask me when he's ready."

Bobby developed a theory about books after Carla told him he had to connect what he read, not with concepts, but with real people and with life to make it come alive.

But he kept his theory to himself.

He told me, before he lost me. He'd hold me in his big hand, turning me around, giving me the eye from every angle.

"Book, you're a pot. Your letters are seeds. Your pages are flowers. Your words are stems. Your ideas are leaves. The more I read you, the more I aerate your soil, the more you aerate some part of me.

"And the more I aerate your soil, the more you give up your fruit. And the more I share your fruit, the more fruit I have to share.

"Now, book, where's the garden you came from? And what's the soil?" Bobby spoke what he was thinking instead of the other way around.

After Bobby, there was tall, skinny Uncle Frank Ledger, who everybody in the neighborhood called Uncle Bucket Head.

He's the one used to air out his teeth on the window ledge. Came in one Thursday afternoon pulling a double, four to midnight, midnight to eight in the morning, sees me there next to his teeth and likes my cover, little worn, but something attracts him to me. So Uncle looks around, figuring nobody in this joint's likely to be reading a book with such a fancy cover, the man puts in his teeth, shakes off the overnight, and takes me home.

Frank never knew about Bobby.

Bobby never knew Frank took me home.

When Frank showed me to his wife, Kitty, he said, "I think you *can* judge a book by its cover."

She said, "Want me to read it to ya, don'tcha?"

Kind of sheepish, Uncle Bucket Head said, "Yeah."

Nobody outside the family knew Uncle Bucket Head couldn't read, but everybody in the neighborhood knew there was nobody kinder than Uncle Bucket Head, and nobody more full of fight than Aunt Kitty.

At home Aunt Kitty and Uncle Frank sat on the sofa after supper. He rested his big head on her shoulder.

Stout Aunt Kitty.

Comfortable Aunt Kitty.

Claimed it wasn't her fault. The two left-hand missing fingertips? It was their fault. They weren't paying attention when she was promising to make Jenny across the bench two shiny new black eyes and rolled that razor-crescent Chaveta knife without looking over at Bayuk Cigar factory.

Aunt Kitty, cushy as a broke-in pillow.

After a few days, Kitty got out her mechanical pencil, the one she used for crosswords. Put on her Ben Franklin specs, and they began to scratch notes in me.

Put stars next to sentences.

Underline stuff.

Put paragraphs in parentheses and add stuff to the list of phrases Bobby started, things that caught 'em by the heart or got into their head and messed with their ego.

Somehow or another, something in me was changing something in them, something in the way they looked at life and each other. Changing one one way and one another.

It really got to Uncle Frank, who couldn't've read a thousand-million-dollar check made out in his name in neon.

And Frank, getting all affected and wanting them to drop some of their lazy self-indulgent habits, stop drinking so much, and maybe get up off the couch and go to church and maybe spend some time and money helping others?

That really got to Kitty.

Every time he asked for a sit and read, she said, "Maybe later. I'm relaxin'," or "I gotta go da bathroom."

One city-summer Friday after work, Uncle and Aunt Kitty got it in their heads to take a ride down the Shore, rent a place for Saturday and Sunday night. Leave the Shore early Monday morning before light, beat the traffic on the AC Expressway. Back to Philly before the rush and be on time for work.

They both knew two nights wasn't a real vacation.

The putty factory closed the same two weeks every year. Everybody who worked there got the same two weeks' vacation, and half the neighborhood spent it down the Shore.

But they wanted to get away anyway. They needed to.

Probably had to do with the extra overtime lump in Uncle's pay envelope, or the bonus Kitty got when they claimed it had nothing to do with the out-of-court fingertip settlement when she took off a tip on the right hand and they laid her off at the cigar factory. Or maybe it was the weather got them thinking about the Shore.

And Uncle, for some reason, decided he was gonna stash me in his back pocket and have Auntie read to him on the beach.

They got down the Shore so early, the only thing open near their rooming house was a bike rental and gas station.

Held up her fingers. "Two bikes," Aunt Kitty said to the guy in the straw hat and the shades.

He took off his sunglasses to get a good look at her fingers. "All I got ready's a two-seat tandem."

So they took it.

"Stay on the Boardwalk in the designated lanes," the man said. "You got three hours. Late, and I gotta double the fee."

"Where's that doughnut place?" Uncle said.

The man pointed south with his hat. "All the way at the other end of the Boards."

Uncle'd heard about the place with the hot-oil rectangular reservoir with the metal screen hand-shaped flipper that flipped the cake doughnuts halfway through their swim. He couldn't wait to see it.

"Mmm, hot doughnuts." Uncle loved 'em with powdered sugar.

No way she was sitting in back. Aunt Kitty won rock, paper, scissors. She always did. Uncle couldn't bring himself to look at her fingers.

Uncle pouted, but he got on back.

Upset him pretty good when they finally got seats at the counter and he found out I was gone.

Aunt Kitty said, "I ain't gone looking."

But Uncle pulled such a face she went anyway.

They unlocked the two-seat tandem bike from the Boardwalk rail outside the doughnut joint and retraced their entire thirty-block route, her pedaling up front and cursing all the way.

No luck, up and down, back and forth on the Boards.

Looked and looked, and looked again.

Even on the side streets they'd traversed.

Even pedaled the alleys they'd pedaled before.

And even some they didn't.

That right there only made sense to Uncle Bucket Head.

What it did to Aunty Kitty, looking in places they'd never been, it made her poke a finger nub in each of his ears and tell him she could feel 'em touching 'cause there was nothing in between.

He hated when she did that. But he always laughed anyway.

But there was no way they were gonna find me.

Somebody else'd picked me up.

When they got back to the doughnut place, Aunt Kitty got lucky and found two seats at the overcrowded counter. She was talking to Eddie Gjarper from the neighborhood.

Eddie was part of a crowd three people deep, standing at the counter waiting for a stool to open.

Kitty was sitting there nursing her third cup of coffee and doughnut number six by the time Uncle Frank got back from figuring out the combination so he could lock the bike to the Boardwalk rail.

It was one of those locks that you spun to make a word. Uncle's word was DALE.

And being he couldn't read, he was having a hell of a time remembering, till something made him think of that song they used to sing when he was in the army about hills and dales and dusty trails . . . And he asked some old timer in a VFW hat to help him.

"Hey!" Uncle said when he finally sat down on the stool Aunt Kitty'd been saving for him.

He didn't even look at the paper plate with the three dough-nuts—chocolate, plain, and cinnamon-sugar—she'd ordered for him.

He couldn't believe it. "Hey!" was all he kept stuttering.

There I was, flat on the counter.

Eddie standing there with a beach towel around his neck, still waiting for a stool to open.

He told Uncle, "Yep. I was telling Kitty, I found the book back at Twenty-Ninth Street on the Boards."

Uncle Bucket Head couldn't believe it.

Coarse, five-foot, loaf-round, shiny-headed Eddie was one of the most religious guys over at our little Saint Alexander the Whirling Dervish Orthodox Church. Taking up all the oxygen at study groups, never missing a chance to quote some Greek term he had trouble pronouncing from a theology book he claimed he was reading. Always lighting candles. Making big bows. Prostra-tions to beat the band, and crossing himself so grand you could practically feel the waves snuffing out your candle.

Yep, there he was, Eddie. Our Eddie.

Rushing the end of summer in his down-the-Shore get-up. Over-the-knee surfer shorts. Hawaiian shirt. Sunglasses stuck in his straw hat. Flip-flops, one orange, one blue. The whole bit.

Licking his fingers. Dabbing at frosting and squeegeeing cir-cles of powdered sugar offa Uncle's paper doughnut plate.

If the stools at the counter'd had 'em, they woulda held hands and cried. They were wincing at the thought of the loud guy in the Hawaiian shirt crunching one of their heads, closing their eyes and hoping the kid dropping batter circles in the grease would make the announcement they made most days around this time, "Sorry folks, no more doughnuts, that's it . . . Ran out of dough."

Eddie finally gave up waiting for a stool, licked the chocolate off his fingers, and got the last dozen to go.

He said to Uncle, "Mind if I take this, I mean, if you're done reading it?" Eddie was a wise guy, a mean one.

What was he gonna do, Uncle? Admit he couldn't read?

Uncle said, "Sure, Eddie, just I'd like to have it back."

Eddie said, "Yeah." And winked at Kitty. "It don't got a lotta nice pictures, do it?"

Eddie said to the kid behind the counter, "Ya got a waterproof ziplock bag back there I can have?"

The kid held up the gallon-sized bag, a new one.

Eddie dusted me off and dropped me in.

When Eddie left, Uncle said, "Why'd you tell him?"

Kitty looked at the half-eaten cinnamon-sugar doughnut left on Uncle's paper plate and said, "You gonna eat that?"

On the ride home, there wasn't much talking.

Kitty tried to make conversation, and Uncle Bucket did his best to be polite, but the whole time he was wanting to say, "Maybe I can't read it, but I try and do my best to live it."

Meanwhile, Eddie was coasting down the Boards on his rental bike, steering with one hand, me dangling by two fat fingers from the grip. Him eating a doughnut with the other hand, singing some hymn Eddie thought needed theological correcting and thinking to himself, *I can't wait to pull out this little book at the next study group and show up old Naum . . . Point out the lack of logic, the impossibility of the physics . . . The Church has no rational sense of reality.*

And here comes a seagull, decorates Eddie's sunglasses, and right before he goes over the handlebars, a sister gull swoops in for the bag.

Eddie spun down the Boards like a pinwheel in the wind.

I took a downward trajectory between the Boards and javelined upright, ziplock bag and all, buried in the sand right up to my title.

Eddie never bothered looking for me.

High tide was a trip.

The island was a year and a day away.

The man in the boat was so dark he seemed like a purple shadow against the bright blue sky.

His face wore a peaceful smile. He was beautiful. Long dreads. Slender fingers taking me carefully from his net, slowly releasing my ziplock cocoon.

The air felt so good. I wasn't soggy at all.

The man had tears in his eyes when he kissed me. Apparently, I was precious to him.

He said, "I cannot bear this blessing alone." And he took me to church.

His wife, with the golden eyes and the gap in the upper middle of her fine white teeth, cleaned and straightened my pages, made a new jacket of fine gold fabric, tailored just for me. She embroidered a cross on my new garment.

On Sunday the man carried me. This beautiful man was a priest. Of course I recognized him. He wept when he saw me in my new jacket.

All the people gathered around. I was covered with kisses. People were touching me.

The priest was blessing them. With me.

He raised me above his head and said, "Wisdom, O believers!"

The priest said, "I, your cousin, Athanasios, was out fishing on the sea. And bobbing on the water . . ."

Father Athanasios, the beautiful man with the slender fingers, stood with Miriam, his wife, who had made my fine cover, and the two of them held hands and stood facing the people in the little homemade church.

The Father said, "A book is like a pot filled with very rich soil. A good book is not so different from a good heart. Inside it has many seeds. It has many flowers on its many stems. It bears much fruit.

"If we live with it, it will live in us. If we cultivate its words, it will cultivate our soul.

"If we care for it, tend its flowers, and share its fruit, if we ask God to help us so that we are not selfish with it, and if we can avoid the pride of reading it merely for knowledge, but are blessed instead to read it for salvation in communion with God and others in His Holy Eucharistic House, it will take root, send out many deep shoots, and blossom in many hearts."

The priest was quiet for a moment. He stood holding me on his shoulder. The people did not take their eyes off him, or me.

"But if we are selfish," the priest said, "and it remains in our pot alone, it will die. The sower must go forth and sow its seeds. It is intended by God to be offered to all mankind. It is the recording of the heartbeat of the faithful family in which it was given birth. It is the icon of His garden, meant to call and unite all the faithful known to God, God who gave it to the faithful family to share with all His creation.

"And if we do His will in this, His fields will be white with grain, and we, blessed by His Holy Spirit to be laborers in His field, servants to each other and all mankind, we will be blessed to share in the great work of His great harvest, when He gathers into His house those for whom He has sent His Only Son, our Master Jesus, sent to save from death those whom He loves and those who love Him, by the grace of His Holy Spirit."

The priest held me in his hands and chanted the Word from my pages from the royal doors of the altar.

The people sang "Alleluia."

The incense rose up over the icons out of the heaven-colored homemade church and spread above the island and the ocean, and the sweet prayer of all the people rose with it.

I like my new home on the altar.

I like my new jacket.

The people love me.

I love them too.

Philoxenia Means Hospitality

———>•<———

O F ALL THE PEOPLE in our little parish, the one who con-
tributed the most was also the one who detracted the most.
Philoxenia.

No one spent more time in church. She had a key and knew
the code.

"What does she do in there?" people would ask.

No one knew, but they were certain it must be something
important. After all, she'd been doing it for years. She'd grown
old in the community, gone from schoolbags to handbags to
back-bending oversized canvas bags of things even her husband
was not permitted to touch. A mysterious collection of churchy
things that smelled like incense and oil.

Father Sophonismos—his name means "a sound mind,
self-control"—he always came to her defense. "She irons the candle wax out of the rug with brown paper bags, on her knees."

But he knew she was merciless in her scolding of those who
tilted a drop of beeswax. Even he was afraid and would rather the
hot wax drip on him or the page of his *Sluzhebnik*. Service books,
after all, a new one he could buy.

"Look how organized she's made our library," he would say.

But heaven help the person who disturbed or disrespected the order of the shelves. Dewey himself would have received a parcel of Philoxenia's disciplinary demerits right down to the last decimal. His system indeed!

"And flowers, see how she decorates the temple," Father would say.

He knew the canons regarding flowers in certain places, but she worked so ardently. Well, it gave her such satisfaction . . . *I should say something to ruin her joy, over such a little thing?*

And at the same time he knew that at the sight of the first stranger or visitor or inquirer, there she would go, skirts billowing, speeding over before he could button the collar of his cassock.

And by the time he arrived, every negative rule and discipline, from fasting to burial rituals, would be presented as gospel, along with a preemptive penance of one hundred prostrations.

The wilting and withering of potential catechumens, choir members, children for the church school, and candidates for the clergy made Philoxenia a coffee-hour Calamity Jane. As good as she was with flowers and things . . . Indulgent Father Sophonismos kindly called it the "paradox of our little Philly."

One day a priest called. He was in need of help. His name was Father Mathetes—his name means "a student or disciple." He was a long-time friend of the community who had stepped in to rescue the parish many times, serving funerals, weddings, baptisms, and liturgies, when there was no priest at the little parish.

Now he had fallen on hard times. His wife had died. He was raising the children on his own. He had received a blessing from the bishop to start a business writing icons and had done well.

But now his health was not so good. The quality of his icons had diminished, and the family was in danger of losing their home.

Ninety-year-old Mary made the best *fasule*, some said, in the history of the little parish. How she got the beans so tender, no one knew. Father Sophonismos, during the Great Fast, had to restrain himself from eating bowl after bowl. After all, what kind of a fast is it if one floats with fasule? But with a good loaf of bread and a few tablespoons of heat from the juice of a pepperoncini, ah . . . there was nothing better.

And when Mary died, her daughter, knowing Father's predilection for the Lenten soup, gave Father Sophonismos Mary's secret recipe along with three thousand dollars to spend however he saw fit.

"Father Mathetes, don't worry, I have a project for your iconographic talents in the little parish. We need an icon of the Hospitality of Abraham. I've spoken to the board and they agree. Let's do it," Sophonismos said.

How perfect, Father Sophonismos thought. To show our gratitude for all the years Father Mathetes served our people . . . To depict in color and egg tempera on a specially prepared board requiring ten or twelve precise applications of warmed natural gesso, a liquid concoction of chalk dust, marble dust, and animal-skin glue, smoothed carefully as it dries to remove bubbles, and sanded between coats for an even surface—a long-learned discipline to marry all these diverse elements together to show the unity of love in God's Kingdom.

And wasn't this also the goal of the little parish? Wasn't this the difficult calling of the priest, to harmonize the many different people and personalities, even the irascible ones, even Philoxenia?

And weren't the people called to cooperate with and support the priest in what is called *synergia*, a cooperation of human will and God's grace, not for individual salvation but for the blessing of all?

Of course everyone would get behind Father in his attempt to help old Father Mathetes. With a little effort, self-sacrifice, and prayer, the little parish could be an icon of relationship and hospitality.

The relationship of the Persons of the Holy Trinity needs no preparation, no discipline, no gesso, no glue, it just *is* . . .

But this icon that Father Mathetes would make, and the process of making it, thought Father Sophonismos, will show our community the model, the *typos* of kindness, of loving one another. "We love because He first loved us."

This was hospitality and relationship in action.

But not everyone was navigating by the same Bright Morning Star.

Along with all the elders of the parish, Philoxenia had been consulted beforehand. The reasons had been explained. She had given her approval. Her assent was recorded right there in the board minutes. But for some reason it was not in her to follow the compass heading set by the priest and the parish elders for what they saw to be the good of the little parish as a whole, for Father Mathetes, or for all the people and their diverse needs.

Philoxenia had her own compass heading and no doubt about who it was in the parish who was veering off course.

Saint John Chrysostom says, "It is like a captain having pirates sailing with him on board ship and continually plotting hour by hour against him and the sailors and crew."

So what was the splinter that irritated her eye where Father Mathetes the iconographer was concerned?

He picked bad times to come into her church.

It interfered with her nocturnal sojourns.

He had bad breath and talked too much.

His nervous laugh was too loud and his joking out of place.

His children scuffed the floor and drank the last of the juice.

Cookie crumbs were everywhere in the church hall. The mice would complain when those children finally departed.

Moreover, he did not match her understanding of the temperament of an iconographer nor the iconographic standard or process she knew to be authentic. Why, he didn't even have a psalti reading while he worked—the man used a CD player, for goodness' sake. And the way he dressed! This is how a priest and an iconographer dresses?

But at the same time she prepared little meals for him, followed the children with her broom, and offered to read if he would prefer a real singer, one who'd been in the choir many years. After all, many people, she recalled, said the singing of the choir was actually the only reason anyone came to the little parish anyway.

But after a short time her tolerance grew thin. She said the parish priest, Father Sophonismos, had not received proper authorization to spend this money. He had been bribed with fasule money. She questioned his choice of iconographic subjects: the parish wasn't called Holy Trinity or the Hospitality of Abraham, was it?

In the end, the iconographer, Father Mathetes, was accused of using certain rags stored in Philoxenia's bags for paint clean-up, and this violation of the *paradox of our little Philly* sent him and his unfinished icon out the door of the little parish.

"He touched her rags!" People winced.

Who wanted to argue? What if *she* walks out? Who would fill her place? She does everything!

After this incident, Father Sophonismos thought perhaps the community would join him in finding a way to widen the community's concept of welcoming and hospitality. And so, by way of example, he paid his exiled brother priest out of his own pocket.

But people would just tilt their heads and smile. "Well, that's our Philly." Whatever it is that she's doing alone there in the little parish all these years, and even overnight, let her keep the key. If her husband doesn't complain, why should we?

She's there. She obviously loves the work. It gives her something to do. She has the original key. She knows the code. For goodness' sake, she devised the burglar alarm code!

And it saves others from—well, us, I guess, from—I mean, understand, hospitality, relationship, love, these things require sacrifice, and discipline, and time. I mean, we have families, jobs, responsibilities.

Philoxenia, she does so much. Granted, everyone who sees her coming runs the other way. Okay, so she has all these rules. Maybe they're there for her benefit. Who knows? Maybe she was injured somewhere along the way. Maybe she just needs a little compassion, a little time, someone to sit with her, to put her at ease with herself, to make her feel welcome, someone to love her and someone for her to love. After all, her name does mean "hospitality," doesn't it?

Thirteen Camels

———⟾•⟽———

T HEY WERE AT SHOOKY'S TAPROOM having a game of after-
work shuffleboard, the Black Bridge Gang—Lefty, Chicky,
and Two-Beer Eddie Flynn—when in walked Sharky and Teddy
the Horse.

They called him that for short. Used to be Teddy the Horse
Trader, a diminutive natty dresser who sold cars for a living over
at Auto Heaven on the Avenue under the Tunnel. The only one
of them always in a jacket and tie. Salesman of the year, twice.
Won a four-hundred-dollar pen each time. Smiled when he got
the second gold-plated Montblanc and told the boss, "Would've
preferred the cash."

As kids they camped together, hot summer nights, three stories up on the wide riveted beams under the Black Bridge, the
iron-bound railroad trestle that spanned American Street right
off the North Pennsylvania main tracks. Tracks so close to the
second-story windows of their railside shanties, they could pick-
pocket the slow-moving coal cars as the rounded mounds rolled
by in the dark.

The Black Bridge Gang trusted old Naum. He baptized the
kids and buried the elders.

When it was time for military service, he got the Black Bridge Gang together before they were deployed, blessed them, gave each one a pocket prayer book, and said, "You're men now. Killing is never just. Not for us. Others? They have such a thing. A just war, they call it. A justified killing. For us, my friends, it's always the lesser of two evils. And you? You will all travel home safely."

And whatever he meant by that, the Black Bridge Gang made it back, to a man.

Sharky drove a truck. His own truck. Hauling product for the putty factory.

Chicky Cilligan and Two-Beer Eddie Flynn worked right there in the neighborhood at Stetson Hats, blocking every cowboy's favorite, the Boss of the Plains.

Lefty cut hair. He'd gone to barber school on the GI Bill. Told Jimmy the kid to do the same when he got back from the Army. Now Jimmy and Lefty worked together in the barber shop off Second and Diamond.

The church was neighborhood walking distance or maybe a trolley ride, like most things in those days.

The old-time fathers and mothers, the ones who came over on the SS Leviathan and swore they saw Humphrey Bogart working with the deck crew, most were long buried, and yearly memorials on the anniversary of their death packed our little Orthodox church of Saint Alexander the Whirling Dervish.

"You can't bury love," the priest would say. "To be out of the body is to be with Christ. And the Body of Christ is not divided. Death has no dominion over the believer. We pray for them and they pray for us, as with all the saints. We are all alive in our Master, Christ Jesus. May their memory be eternal in God."

Something inside them wouldn't allow most of the Black Bridge generation to miss a memorial prayer for their grandparents or parents. Their mothers had knit whatever it was into the fabric of their being. They were connected in love by a mystical fiber.

Lefty said to Teddy, "Ya think anybody'll be doing the prayers for us when we're gone? Any a our kids?"

"Don't even wanna think about it," was all Teddy would say.

———

IT WAS GETTING NEAR SUPPERTIME when Sharky and Teddy the Horse walked in. Everyone at Shooky's had to be getting home.

Old man Shook gave the boys the high-sign and nodded at the clock—*Ortleib's—Philly's Famous Beer*—the red hand sweeping the seconds off the black face up over the bar.

Back then men stopped off for a beer after work, then went home, washed their hands at the kitchen sink, dried them on the towel hanging through the handle of what people still called the icebox, and asked the wife, "I have time to peruse the *Evening Bulletin?*"

She always factored that in. If you think it's easy keeping a household and a family harmonized like an Orthodox a capella choir, try it sometime.

Getting the holy bread rising before dawn

Getting *him* off to work

Breakfast for the kids before school

Putting the house in order

Getting the meshe in the oven

Mother just about had time to look in the mirror before putting supper on the table.

There was a family life, all rooted in Sunday.

Skipping church? Something about that set the rest of the week spinning off kilter. And if Nunna found out you didn't prepare, fast, and all the rest of it, and receive Holy Communion at least a coupla times a year?

Lefty said, "Teddy, you took Holy Communion Sunday."

Teddy said, "I did."

The boys knew Teddy hadn't received for a long time. Lately he'd been avoiding liturgy altogether. Not seeing his mom, one-hundred-and-five-year-old Olga . . . "Kills me," he said. "Not being with her on Sunday."

Teddy, who always had a line, didn't have one this time. No excuse. Didn't, just didn't.

His friends knew enough to drop it.

But this time, beer glasses empty and all parties ready to depart for home, Teddy, not sure why, just wanted to tell his friends.

"So, I'm out in the lot at Auto Heaven and up comes Father Naum from behind, grabs me, gives me a kiss and tells me he's happy to see me. Wearing his worn-out dungaree bib overalls with the beat-up straw Stetson, pulling his wire basket, going shopping on the Avenue."

"How old is Naum, anyway?" Sharky said.

"Older than he acts," Lefty said.

Two-Beer Eddie said, "Yeah, and younger than he seems."

"So he says to me, 'Theodri, the church is much better when

you're there. It's not the whole family when we don't see you. You know God misses his children, and Nunna Olga misses her son.'

"I told him, Father, look . . . I can't, not right now . . . I was at work. I was embarrassed to tell him, but at the same time, I had to tell him. So I says, Father, I smoke fourteen Camels every morning. I been doing it since I was a kid in the army and I can't stop. Now how can I smoke fourteen cigarettes and come to Holy Communion? I don't even want to come in the building. I just can't."

The men knew how seriously our people regarded being received into the life of Communion with Lord Jesus.

"It's not water," the old folks used to say.

It was hard enough for Naum to convince our people they could take their heart meds with a sip of water on Sunday morning.

Saint Paul said in our villages: *Many of you are sick, and some have died by receiving unworthily.*

Chicky said, "So what'd he say? 'Bout the fourteen Camels?"

Teddy said, "He asked me could I smoke thirteen. I said, I think I can. And then he says to me, 'So, this Sunday, smoke thirteen Camels, and come. And next month, we go down the steps on the Black Bridge, one at a time, and we smoke twelve, and the next month eleven, and down and down and down.'"

Teddy said, "Naum told me, Krishti comes down to us a step at a time, and we follow Him home a step at a time, patient, slow. He knows we're weak, so He walks with us, helps us back up the steps."

"Thirteen Camels," Lefty said.

Lefty stood up from the stool and put two ones and four

quarters on the bar. He said, "I bet that old fox offered to buy you a pack of Camels, didn't he?"

"More'n that," Teddy said. "He drags me into Honest John's. Hands John the money, holds out the pack to me and says, 'Take out seven Camels and hand them back to me.' So I do. I take out seven and hand them back to him. That way I have my thirteen Camels, right here in this pack."

Teddy slipped it from his pocket and flipped the Sunday morning pack over Shook's bar, making each cigarette jump up. "And this—" He took one from behind his ear and said, "This here is Camel Thirteen. Look, Naum borrowed my Salesman of the Year pen and wrote '13' on it."

"Camel Thirteen," Eddie said.

"Yeah. I tried to get Naum to keep the pen, I could tell he liked it," Teddy said. "But he wouldn't."

Chicky said, "So what you tell him?"

"I told him, Naum, you should be the one selling cars."

The City Monk

———❖———

YOU MIGHT THINK it was a sad life.

It wasn't.

At liturgy the last Sunday of every month and at coffee hour afterwards, Walter was the happiest damn guy you ever met.

Yep.

Walter.

Our Walter.

Walter from the payroll office over at the putty factory. In that same windowless room nine am to six pm for almost forty years.

What the hell does he do in there?

Never came out. Not even for lunch.

Never missed a day.

They say Walter never took a vacation except for the whole of Holy Week and the first three days of Bright Week.

You know Walter was in the navy?

Yep. The *Enterprise*. Big aircraft carrier. Got to be a chief warrant officer.

Some said Walter was a spy. Collected intelligence. Evaluated signals he intercepted about surface, air, and antisubmarine warfare outfits. Operational stuff.

What the old-timers say.

Misto and the other old-timers were the only ones ever saw Walter drunk. Talking on the steps outside Shooky's after midnight the summer he got home.

Walter was crying.

He'd been downtown. Again.

Things he'd seen. Things he'd done. On deployment over there, and downtown.

Stains he was washing out of his uniform with Shooky's beer.

"I was there. In person. Me. Participated in reconnaissance missions. Interrogated prisoners. The shit we did to those people. But what about the shit they did to us?"

Walter was waking up the neighbors. "What about what they did to me? In that camp? You think I told them? Order of battle? Plots? Estimates?"

Misto had his arm around the younger man, sick on the steps, rubbing Walter's back.

When Walter stood up, he said, "I did. Finally I did. And I hate myself for doing it, more than for what I do in those backstreet bars."

Walter said, "They knew. They knew about me in that camp. They could tell. And how to exploit it."

Misto said, "Don't worry, it's gonna be okay."

Walter kissed Misto's hand. He said, "Will it, Babagjysh?"

"Sure, my boy. You don't be afraid. It's gonna be okay. We gonna talk to the priest," Misto said. "Maybe the priest got a way."

After his parents died, Walter sold the house on Bodine Street near Laurel, not far from Kaplan's Jewish Bakery where the whole neighborhood used to get the Russian black bread.

He gave half the money from the sale to his sister, Ruth, the other half to the church, and found a first-floor two-roomer with its own front door next to a garage on Frankford Avenue somewhere near Montgomery, and that was Walter's second cell.

The payroll office at work. That was his first cell.

Desk with a phone. Pretty good old wood swivel-seat side-arm chair. Filing cabinets, two. Gunmetal gray. A computer came along eventually.

Didn't take Walter long to master the software. He said, "Why wouldn't I make things better for the people and easier for me?"

Hated the overhead fluorescents. Never used them. Got himself two desk lamps, dark-shaded, three bulbs each. Brought his lunch in the same stainless steel Stanley Hammertone lunch bucket his father'd used all his years on the putty factory loading dock. Thing was still brand-new solid, bracket inside the curved barn-top lid for stashing his sixteen-ounce coffee Thermos.

And his two-room home. Cell number two.

A comfortable bed. Single. Been his bed since his mother, Cecilia, put away the crib and ordered the Roy Rogers Cowboy Camp blanket. Red, cream, and pony-brown woolen panels with the cactus and steer-horn heads, six-shooters, and the horse Trigger up on his hind legs. In the wringer washer once a month. His mother loved that thing, and still in good shape. "Better'n me," Walter used to say.

Two chrome kitchen chairs upholstered gold. A fair-sized wooden table. Sturdy. Square, solid legs. Plank-top slats he scavenged on the American Street railroad tracks. Bolts from the same pallet crates. Built it himself, our boy. Only thing he kept of Valerian's, his father, the old man's lunch bucket and his tools.

Simple pink-shaded brass floor lamp next to the icon corner above his bed. Used to be Mom's.

No newspapers. No magazines. Didn't need no TV.

A toilet. Sink to spit in, and a tub. Mirror to trim. All a man needs.

And you better bet Walter's whole joint was spit-shine clean.

Compact refrigerator. A 1951 gray-tone Gibson with a pitted aluminum handle in the shape of a downward-pointing arrow with a body shape like Walter's head, wide at the top and narrow at the bottom.

Walter cooked on a three-ring 1950s New World Thirty-Three gas cooker.

The one trash can outside his front door was the easiest throw on Gary the trash guy's route.

There were times when the loneliness had Walter walking his cell talking to himself. Times when being alone took him by the arm to his icon corner or interrupted his weariness and fear when he stopped to consider the black-and-white family memories framed on the wall in the shadows by the bathroom in the hall.

Times when the organic closeness of his loneliness became so comfortably familiar . . . *his loneliness* got lonely at being ignored and murmured to the man, "Damn you, Walter, if I were a person you'd miss me."

Like a hermit crab in his shell, Walter inhabited his loneliness and carried it with him wherever he went.

"I'm shy. I used to run from my father and hide. Do you know I was married? For three years." Walter couldn't open his eyes when he said, "So shy she went with another man and got pregnant."

In Walter's world, it was Lent all the time.

We'd see him. Great head of hair on our Walter. Always in what looked like navy-issue khaki trousers. Crease pressed sharp and new-belt neat. Shine on Walter's shoes? Like butter. Button-down white Oxford short-sleeve dress shirt, even in the winter, ironed crisp, with what we figured was a warrant officer tie. Could be. Had a flight jacket when the wind-sock stiffened.

And the covert beard? Made Walter the paymaster look like a bushwhacker businessman from the Australian outback. Just enough gray in the length to cover the knot in the tie that made us sure he was a spy.

Something about Walter made you think he was tall. He wasn't. The man was trim as a sloop in a sea of thieves.

He had a regular meet with the priest.

None of us ever knew about it. But we found out later it was anchored on Walter's calendar like a feast day or a funeral.

Apparently, in the way of an ascetic, when you're battling your appetites, it ain't good to self-diagnose or write your own prescription.

"First rule of the unseen warfare," Naum the priest told Walter. *Never believe in oneself or trust oneself . . .*

So when they met, they both knew the process wasn't gonna conclude in hours, or days, or weeks even, or months.

It was a long time, because it takes time.

Naum said, "Ya gotta know somebody ta help 'em."

So if God gives the time, take it. Be a good steward of the time.

Daily reading was part of the cell rule Walter received from his confessor, Naum. Walter knew the Scripture.

Our Master said, *While it is daytime, we must do the works of Him who sent Me. Night is coming, when no one can work. While I am in the world, I am the light of the world.*

Walter got used to segmented sleep keeping watch with the Marines, sailing on board his carrier. Keeping vigil was easy.

The vigil kept Walter.

He was at his table, glasses on, fingering his way in the dark across the light on the pages.

One chapter a day from the Gospels till he got 'em all done. Two chapters from the Epistles. Two in the Acts of the Holy Apostles.

Wrap it up with two in the Apocalypse of Saint John the Theologian, who leaned on the breast of the Master and took the Virgin with him to live in Ephesus, where he worked in a bath-house as a janitor, where his amazon boss beat him every day. That John. The fast-running beloved disciple.

The last seven chapters of the Apocalypse, one a day. Naum wouldn't say why—one a day.

The priest told Walter, "Saint John Chrysostom says, *The one who does not read the Scripture daily betrays his baptism.*"

And by that, Walter knew the reason had to do with time.

It hit him different each year, Walter. Like unrolling a scroll he'd never known existed in a whole new language he was just starting to learn.

So when Walter finished the yearly scriptural rotation Naum had prescribed, starting all over again at the beginning was like encountering the living word in the first pink dawn of a brand new creation in a newly revealed and more revelatory language for the first time there were ever people speaking or daylight, or clocks or calendars or customs or feasts or fasts to measure time.

The Fathers advised, *Don't read for knowledge. Read for salvation.*

Said to himself, "Walter, that's what I'm talking about."

So. Daily reading fulfilled. It was lights off.

Time to fulfill in action.

Breakfast after morning wash-up. Oatmeal on fast days. Dry toast. Water. Or nothing.

Non-fast, a boiled egg. Toast with butter. V8 with lemon and pepper. A big glass. Cheez-Its for a treat.

Pack a lunch. Brew coffee, Walter. Thermos. Don't forget.

Saved a fortune on meat. Some dairy. A little fish here and there.

Check the weather on KYW News Radio. Then turn it off. Don't dreck your decks with the rest.

And walking, Walter was trolley-bound out the door to the putty factory he'd come to love, thanks to Saint Abramios the Lover of Labor. Walter was grateful for his job.

No murmuring in the Desert of Sin between Elim and Sinai.

Walter's first confession was the hardest. Not that different from the dentist when you haven't been there in years. But the more regularly you address it, the fewer cavities you find.

Walter learned how to discern and confess the inner cause and not be tricked into treating the outward symptoms.

Amartia = off the mark = sin = disconnected.

Disconnected from God, who is life, and so from life in communion with all creation, no longer able to recognize your fellow pilgrims as brothers and sisters.

Lying? Cheating? Stealing? Sexual sin? Jealousy? Anger? All outward symptoms of sin.

The cure? Christ Jesus—medicine for the inside. A reconnect to *the* Life, to the One who is life.

And connected to Him, the outward symptoms over time resolve themselves.

Walter figured all that didn't mean he could just go ahead and keep picking the scab and aggravating the symptom, the outward wound.

It didn't mean that. It wasn't some kind of license.

Walter said, "If ya got poison ivy and ya scratch it 'cause it's itching and it keeps spreading and getting worse 'cause you're scratching it, and no matter how much you scratch you just ain't getting any satisfaction or relief but you're spreading it and making it worse, then stop scratching."

Be a shame if after all those years Walter hadn't figured out something so simple and be good at it.

But he was getting better, a little at a time.

Eight hours of account-ledger spadework took Walter a little more than four and change.

And if he ate as he worked at his desk, Walter *Bob Cratchit* had time enough to intersperse prayers in his payroll-office cell.

It was his custom to begin with three prostrations in front of the folding diptych icon he kept on a shelf above his desk.

The Mother and Child on one panel of the diptych, and Saint Basil the Great on the other. Walter's baptismal name was Vasil.

Make the cross.

In the Name of the Father, and of the Son, and of the Holy Spirit.

Come Holy Spirit, pray Thou, Thyself in me

I got no prayer on my own
I know not how to pray as I ought
Giver of life, Source of prayer
If you don't give me prayer . . .
I got nothing
Turn off the twin lamps, Walter.
Tell the darkness, "It's me, Vasil."
And all through the day
As the Holy Spirit wove
The prayer of the heart
Into the fabric of his being
Tungsten filaments
Stretched across
The interior vacuum
Of the clear glass bulbs
In the switched-off lamps
Radiated an incandescent afterglow
And illumined the darkness
Before the diptych
On Walter's desk
But Naum said it wasn't enough—to merely abide alone in the desert of urban solitude.

Summertime Walter worked a plot at a community garden on Frankford Avenue not far from his place, and taught beginners how to get a plot going and how a garden could be a prayer book if you let it.

Wintertime Walter traveled the neighborhood, knocking on the doors of old folks after he'd shoveled their pavements and telling them he'd seen a band of angels clearing their walk.

Year-round, Dottie and Denise had a volunteer they could count on two days a week to help with whatever needed doing at their Honor Thy Father and Mother Adult Day Care Center.

Turns out Walter was a hell of a cook and didn't mind doing a dish, and nobody at the adult day care was the wiser that Walter was scrubbing his soul while he was scrubbing their pots.

O Lord Jesus Christ, Son of God, be merciful to me, a sinner.

A city monk

A self-exiled habituate of ritual prayer

Anonymous

Austere

Isolated

Invisible

But in no way marooned

You might think it was a sad life

Most of the time

It wasn't

For our Walter

Being a city monk

The Letter

———◦———

IN THE SEVENTEENTH YEAR, they stopped having sex and moved to separate bedrooms. The daily stare-down was withering their marriage.

And finally on their twentieth anniversary, after midnight, he went down the hallway where she lay sleeping and rifled her handbag for money and the car keys, determined to break his sobriety, his three-year stint of celibacy, and his loneliness.

He hadn't signed on to be a monk. He was tired of being rejected, neglected, and unappreciated.

Okay, sometimes when he was alone he had to admit, maybe he was being eaten by his own appetites, maybe he had a part in their marriage rotting on the vine.

But damn, girl, take a look around. Ask your sisters. You should have some husbands. You should've had my father. My poor mother.

I'm a good provider. I put up with a lot. You just never listen to me.

The kids seemed alienated.

Especially so with his twenty-one-year-old daughter. Shouting matches all the time.

And the man couldn't understand why.

Tempers . . . father and daughter? Two of a kind, his wife said.

But he did know one thing. It wasn't his fault. He knew he deserved better, and he was going out to find it.

In her handbag he found a legal envelope and in it, a letter torn to shreds. Blue ink. In her handwriting, crumpled down inside her bag.

He took it to his room and smoothed it out on the floor like a jigsaw puzzle, determined to put it together, bit by bitter bit.

Three looseleaf pages. Covered on both sides. Six pages in all. Twenty twisted years of accusations against him.

And as he tagged the jagged pieces of their marriage into a sad mosaic, every line reduced him further to the floor.

The corpse at every funeral—the bride at every wedding
Never wrong
Has all the answers
The expert final word on everything
Thinks he's so funny
His own kids despise him and can't wait to get away
I'm so smothered, I can't breathe
Dominates everybody's time and business like a needy baby
There's nowhere to hide from his brilliance
Dr. Jekyll—plays the religion card in public
Mr. Hyde—the pervert in the bedroom
Cannot bear to be in the same room with him or hear his voice
I avoid his calls
His touch
Being with him
I've had to deal with this since I married
I am only patronizing him till I don't have to

He is a mendacious creep
I'm no longer emotionally invested
I will never feel the same again
I've squandered all those years
Our love is over
He has a hero complex
A rescue fantasy
He is a religious devil
I do not love him
Dead and past
Looks like a stranger
My life is wasted
I creep when he touches me
There is no us
Go away
You no longer have a woman
Get out
He is a very tiring individual
I hate the weekends because I have to spend them with him
Wants to be venerated as a saint
Perverse mixture of sex and religion
My marriage never existed
I am a deceived spouse
He is a boring cliché
I live around him
I feel like a fly born trapped
Between the window and the screen
And he's a relentless snoop
He'll even find this note, I just know it

But he'll never find my escape stash
Till it's too damn late

At every line he denied, denied, denied.

Railed against her.

Blamed the universe, cursed the black sky outside his bedroom window for being black.

"Let them all go to hell." He wept frustrated tears of resentment . . . "And what does she mean?"

I may not be much but I'm all I think about

He was a regular at liturgy. Of course. How could the priest miss the man center aisle making the overexaggerated sign of the cross with the big prostrations, even after his wife stopped attending?

When he confessed, he told Naum, "When I finally put it all together, I was already on my knees, alone in my room, in front of my icons, and something made me pray."

He said that as it got light, God spoke to him, there in his room, on his knees. Told him to copy the letter for himself and return the original pieces to her handbag, and work on the list as if it were true, whether he agreed or understood or not.

It wasn't easy.

———

FIVE YEARS LATER, in bed together, she asked her husband what had happened to him.

He told her, his *Gift* . . .

He knew now she was his sanity, his sanctity, and his salvation. He said he finally realized the gift God had given them in each other. The gift he had overlooked, taken for granted, and neglected in his selfishness.

He said, "Someone who loved me let me get a look at myself."

She had tried to tell him many times.

She never knew he went in her handbag and found the letter.

Well . . . If she did, would she have said so?

The Bishop

I. Dreamers and Their Dreams

NAUM DROVE PESHKOPI to the bus station. Two-Beer Eddie sat in front next to Naum. Deacon Dionysios and Peshkopi, that's what we called the bishop, sat in the back of Naum's old junker.

Two-Beer Eddie turned around and leaned over the seat, swapping stories with the white-haired bishop.

Two-Beer Eddie addressed the bishop by his first name: "Skendi, ya ain't gonna believe this one." And it made the deacon cringe every time.

The streetlights were coming on . . . Got dark around six that time of October, and Naum was taking the block-at-a-time cobblestone trolley route over the tracks west on Girard Avenue down past the Marlborough, what some people in the neighborhood call the Green Tree Tavern, winding his way over to Second Street, then heading south, catching every light.

Ramona and Madeline were already there at the bus station, trying to look inconspicuous, peeking out from the coffee shop inside the Greyhound Terminal, Tenth and Filbert. Twilight, and both of 'em wearing sunglasses. Damn cold night too for that early in the fall. The girls had been assigned by our Teuta Ladies Baking Society to meet the bishop, ask his blessing, and leave him with a box lunch for his bus ride.

When the bishop was a young man, he found an empty pistachio shell and it changed his life. He kept it in his pocket. He was never without it. Damn thing had more than fifty years' wortha smooth on it from his praying with it in his hand. Same with the hat he called his skufia, it never left his head.

Two-Beer Eddie Flynn knew the pistachio nut story. He'd heard it from his father when he was a boy.

Eddie's father had been a priest, old Father Andon. Eddie's son too, when the kid grew up, became a priest, Father Andon the Second.

"Yo', Skend," Eddie said, "you still carrying around that damn pistachio shell?"

The bishop sat back in his new coat. Darn nice coat too. Our Teuta Ladies Baking Society bought it for him special, up at Chelten Avenue Robert Hall, not on sale either. Black, real cashmere and episcopal-looking. Long, but not as long as the ratty old cassock the old guy wore everywhere. They tried to give him a new cassock and hat, but he insisted on that ratty patched cassock and his faded-out skufia sewn years ago by the woman he loved.

If the bishop coulda stretched out his legs in Naum's beater, that '66 two-door lemon-cream Impala, ya woulda seen the new shoes we got 'im too . . . Thom McAn's . . . Well, they mighta been Florsheims. Leather-soled oxblood wingtips, real rubber heels, things glowed in the dark.

"Scratch the sole," Lefty told the bishop. "Go ahead, stuff's real leather. Put 'em on, see if they fit ya. Give 'em a walk across the carpet."

We tried to get his old shoes and coat ta throw 'em in the trash. Carol said not even the rummage sale at Front and Girard would take his worn-down shoes and his screen-thin over-coat. The bishop stuffed 'em in a pillowcase in his brown paper shopping-bag suitcase, the one he carted all his bishop stuff around in, and said he knew somebody who needed 'em.

Sitting like a silhouette in the shadows backa Naum's car, the bishop took out the pistachio shell and started rolling it in his hand. He said, "After what happened, I wasn't sure there was a God. But I wanted something to take my mind off things, some philosophy or political cause, and maybe a platform, a pulpit, somewhere I could make known my views on life."

As a kid Skender was the kind who couldn't get enough of church. When he was twelve years old, he told his father, "Pop, I wanna be a priest."

His father, Lefter, gave him a thump and said, "You want a life of misery, a life full of other people's problems?"

"But Pop . . ."

Most times all it took was a look from his father.

"Boy, don't make me take off my belt," his father said.

Skender knew his father rarely hit him.

Lefter knew the kid was always with his nose in a book, always lighting candles in front of the icons at home, wanting to talk philosophy and religion all the time with anyone who would listen.

Lefter said to Besime, his wife, "Where did we go wrong?"

There was a factory in the neighborhood, a nineteenth-century brick behemoth that manufactured snow sleds. Lefter said to the boy, "You come to work with me. Mister Samuel Leeds Allen, he invented the Flexible Flyer. I'm'a teach you how to make the most important part of the sled, not the steel runners, anybody can run a machine can do that. The wood, my son, the beauty in the wood God made. From a tree, a simple piece of wood, to such a piece of art. It's an art your soul gonna love."

And it was true. The wood was good, but by the time he was sixteen, Skender had quit school and given up on beauty, goodness, art, and truth.

Every time the old dreams popped up somewhere in his body, beauty, goodness, truth . . . he squashed them back down. Crushed them. Useless things. Crushed them along with the strange calling he'd sensed from boyhood.

Every fool knew. Any grown person. Any person with sense. Any person who knew the real world would have outright discouraged such stupid dreaming . . . had they not felt sorry for the stupid dreamers and their stupid dreams.

Skendi was damned if he would end up a dreamer living in an imaginary world of promised dreams.

But each time he spat it up in the daylight, by night there was nothing left in his mouth but the bitter taste of nothingness.

The elemental spirit of angry spite regurgitated through the fissures in his soul, darker than the purple skin off the eggplant his mother stuffed and baked, the eggplant he said he loved but hated.

"Ta hell with it all," Skendi told his friends.

Every day before dawn he walked to the factory with his father over the Sedgley Avenue Bridge at Fifth Street and joined the crew in the break room, drinking dark brewed coffee that smelled better than it tasted.

"Drini Thike," his father told him one dull winter morning as they crossed over the unlit bridge. "You remember Drini. He followed the boss from the sweater factory who molested his daughter . . ." Lefter spoke so softly in Albanian, even though there was no one else on the bridge, his words hardly entered the ears of his son before the frightening images evaporated in the steam and fell like iced drizzle to the rail tracks two stories below.

Skender knew *gjakmarrja*, the code of vengeance.

It made him shiver in the frigid predawn. Our code of revenge. A literal blood-taking. An unquestioning obligation to take the life of another in order to salvage family honor.

There was no final page in our canon of brutal murder for murder. There was no other way to assuage a generational moral humiliation than through blood.

"The last time anyone saw that man," his father said, "was when he walked onto this bridge." Lefter stopped at the spot and peered down over the rail.

Skender said, "Pop, but didn't Drini go to church?"

"What if he did, Iskender?" Lefter said to his son. "You know I always tell you from when you're a boy, don't be afraid to turn and look behind you in the night, and better to keep your faith in your church and your knife in your belt." Then Lefter spat over the side and walked away from his son.

Iskender Dhenes knew the blood-oath. He'd been steeped in vengeance, and as he stood in the middle of the bridge, Skender said to himself, "They don't want me to be a priest, so be it. I'll take my own vengeance. I'll pilot my own ship wherever it takes me and to hell with everything, and I'll take what I want."

Not long after, he started hanging after work with guys his age who said they were hell-bent on living fast, dying young, and making a good-looking corpse.

II. Two Choices

MIKIE KERSHAW, his friend from the factory, told Skender, "Time to set it off, baby! I got a great spot for a cheap dance from some decent-looking females. Five-dollar dances at the bar. Drinks are cheap and the booty-shaking is priceless, man.

"Oh, and don't bring your gun, or in youse Albanians' case, your knife, causa they pat you down at the door. Otherwise, man, come on after work and enjoy a couple dances. Got lap dances too, twenty and a tip? In the back room. Can't beat it."

Out front the sign read:

World Famous Sugar House Go-Go Bar
Girls Dancing 24/7—Blacks—Ricans—Asian & White
Food—Fun—Girls
Dancers Wanted—Make at Least a Thousand a Week
Auditions 9 am–2am—7 Days a Week
No Experience Necessary—We Will Train

Skender went hard for a year before it started wearing on him, on what you might call his conscience.

Something about the darkness of the bar and the dimness of

the lighting mimicked the liturgical portal he'd known as a boy, in a perverse inversion of ecclesial time, space, and vibration.

Even in its distorted form, with the primal elements proportionately combined in a certain incendiary setting—men, women, liquor, and drugs—how could there not be a fire?

There was no doubt for Skender. The fabric of his existence was being torn all over again with the same microscopic fissures. He could feel the interior door of his being opening on a beastly conflagration . . .

Angels, of one kind only, were seeking entrance to his soul, and what Skender knew?

It was he who was giving them admittance.

No resistance. No patdown at the gateway of his senses.

It was a simple script.

1. They knock with no need to say "legion"
Skender knew
2. He opened the door anyway
3. Solicit his permission—they did
Invite them in, Iskender
3. Anything—to eat—they're not asking a question
4. Bread was broken—a cup too
A life knowing good and evil—that was their promise
5. So let's get naked
With no need for the first robe—the whole armor of God
No belt of truth
No breastplate of righteousness
No feet fitted in readiness to serve
No shield of faith or helmet of salvation

No sword of the Spirit or word of God

6. Divest yourself—free yourself, Skender

Why even bother trying to preserve your baptismal garment and the earnest of the Spirit pure and undefiled unto the dread Day of Christ our God?

If that promised day hasn't come by now
You believe—don't you—it never will
Intercourse—with us—set it off
Conceive and give birth
To our child
Your destruction

This simple script transpired so quickly in the eye of Skender's heart, there was hardly time to drop the cup, abort the thing, and blink.

Sitting at the bar in the dark, one too many of those blue flaming drinks they set on fire in your glass, Skender started talking to himself: "There's only two choices, a good one and a bad one."

"Who you talking to, brother?" Mikey asked.

Skender looked up over the people crowding for drinks and the dancers on the bar and said, "I'm talking to me, the horse's ass in the mirror."

The night of the fight, Skender found out some things he didn't want to know.

Summer, the dancer he'd been enthralled with, was his cousin. The truth came out when he got in a fight with Karim, another man obsessed with the same rounded-out dancer.

Skender found out he was physically stronger than he thought and narrowly escaped arrest when the police discovered that it was Karim who had a folding nine-inch dragon street knife, a blade he turned on the cops in a cocaine rage.

And Skender, who had acted in self-defense and was unarmed, according to the eyewitness testimony of every topless bartender, the fight-inciting patrons, and the dancers on the bar, was told by the detectives to go home.

It was that night that Skender found out the hard way . . . Summer, the girl who got the best of his every paycheck, the cousin he never knew was his cousin, was pregnant.

A week later he went to see her at Kensington Hospital—his cousin, Summer—her real name was Vere . . . Complications with the pregnancy, she lost the baby.

He tried to get on Karim's visitors list up at CFC prison, but Karim turned him down.

Skender quit the factory, packed a bag, and set off walking downtown to the Filbert Street bus station. He told his parents he'd be in touch and kissed their hands.

"Where are you going, my love?" his mother asked.

"To find an indication of the way to heaven, Mommy."

Maybe it had taken time and circumstance, but somehow the good work begun by the Holy Spirit in the baptismal font had come to the fruition of light, dissolving from his being the generational wound of the blood-oath and the egomaniacal code of vengeance, allowing the true image of humanity given in Christ to say *yes* to the Father and be born again in Skender's soul.

And a year later, he did get in touch with his parents, because the year before, on the day of his departure, something as simple as choosing a seat on a bus led to an encounter with a stranger in the next seat that changed his spiritual trajectory.

An encounter with a woman called Artesia, which caused him to leave one path and choose another.

III. The Empty Boat

IT WAS DURING A RETURN VISIT to his parents' house that a second thing happened by way of a habit he'd developed as a regular guest at the monastery.

Skender had acquired the habit of getting up in the night and praying all through the early morning hours.

The elder at the monastery told him prayers before dawn were most effective because they were most broken-hearted, and when Skender found the pale brown pistachio half-shell as he knelt in the dark on the floor of his childhood bedroom at his parents' house, he found the words of the elder to be true.

It was the empty boat.

The vacant vessel that had managed to catch nothing in the night. The one Lord Jesus sat in as He taught the crowds who had been pressing against Him. The one He asked Simon Peter to put out a little from the land.

The boat and all that went with it were left behind after Lord Jesus had filled it, left behind by Saint Peter, left on the shore, even filled to overflowing as it was . . .

Skender made the cross.

And everyone who has left houses or brothers or sisters or father or mother or wife or children or fields for the sake of My name will receive a hundredfold and will inherit eternal life.

His father's words—"Don't be afraid to turn around and look behind you in the night"—might have been good in the world, but not if Skender was to become a fisher of men. Young Skender knew, once he set his hand to the plow, there was no looking back.

It was as if the pistachio shell was the sign Skender had been praying for, the empty shell, to put out a little from the safety of solid ground, to offer his empty boat willingly, with every fiber of his being, to present it back again to its Maker.

In the room, where as a boy he had called out to . . .

He did not know a name to call . . . Maker of the Universe . . .

The restorative reciprocity he received on his knees that night took him and his pistachio shell back to the elder and the monastery in the mountains by the lake.

When Skender's elder, Joseph, was a toddler, he had fallen into a scalding pot of boiling water. His frantic mother rushed him to the village church. The priest held the baby Joseph by his elbow and dipped him three times in a font of holy water.

His elbow was the only place on Elder Joseph where his skin had the appearance of—as he put it when he pulled up his sleeve and bowed his head—*dru i vjetër*. Old wood.

Father Joseph, the priest-elder.

In food and drink, austere.

Moderate in prayer. "In mercy, Lord Jesus, make me, a sinner to be love."

Always asking "Lord, help my unbelief."

Quoting Chrysostom: Hard on himself. Easy on others.

One beggar telling another beggar where to find bread.

Knowing there was only One Teacher who did not have to learn what He taught.

The elder who rode his bike for miles over hills and snow-packed country roads to buy chocolate for the children held up four fingers and told Skender, "Three things. Love God. Love people. Repent and become prayer."

One day, on a frozen lake at the monastery, they built a hut and cut a hole in the ice to fish.

Skender was shivering when the elder broke a long silence and said, "Holy Paphnutios said, 'If any one shall maintain, concerning the married presbyter, that it is not lawful to partake of the oblation when he offers it, let him be anathema, for marriage itself is worthy and without blemish—it is chaste, for it has been sanctified in the mystery of Holy Matrimony."

Skender had a soul to listen. He tried to let things sink in before opening his mouth.

The elder always reminded him, "The steam bath loses its efficacy when you open the doors."

As they were returning to the skete, Skender said, "Master, I don't understand what you said. Or why you said it."

The elder did not answer.

It made Skender worry.

He saw the long black veil in the wind, the whiteness of the elder's beard folding back over his shoulders, the movement of the old monk floating over the ice of the lake and gliding onto solid ground as they entered the gray wood of the monastery grounds.

Skender was always afraid to mention, when he and the elder walked together through the fields, there were never any footprints in the snow except his own.

When the elder looked at him, he said, "You are not married and you are not a monk, but you will be."

Skender did not sleep that night. He held the shell, and in the morning the elder was found stiff in his cell. A letter he left for

Skender said, "I pray that you will trust that all is sent down from God and leave the monastery."

IV. *Embelsi* Means Sweetness

THREE YEARS WENT BY.

Things had changed since Skender, in obedience, left the monastery.

"Embelsi!" Skender called his bride-to-be. "Where are you, girl, it's time."

In two weeks Skender and Embelsi were to be married, and in two weeks more, Skender was to be ordained deacon, and a month later, priest.

His Embelsi had hand-sewn his cassock and skufia. "I'll never get a new one," he told her.

They were in upstate New York, staying with her relatives on a tree-lined avenue paved with bricks. The bishop had sent them to visit the small parish community they would be serving.

The roads were icy. The bride-to-be was twenty-three. Two years is not a long time to be engaged. Sometimes two years is forever. Sometimes it will just have to do, forever.

The truck slid sideways on the ice. Their car was totaled, but Skender and Embelsi were unhurt. It made Skender worry.

After they got home, Embelsi just didn't feel herself. Then the cancer diagnosis came.

Skender would not sit.

Skender, in his wedding garment.

Perhaps he couldn't.

Standing by his *nuse*.

Standing, the bridegroom, by his bride.

The incense rose around her like accompanying clouds.

The priestly vestments, next to her, were shadows waiting to be renewed in the Paschal light of Bright Week.

Her mother stood by the coffin and cried, "Here am I, O Lord, with the child whom Thou hast given me."

The bridegroom stood and wept.

And all of us with him.

Skender Dhenes refused to sit.

He stood by the coffin of his Embelsi, squeezing the shell till his hand bled, too dead to cry, but not yet dead enough to be buried with her.

Not long after her funeral, he was ordained. Father Skender took monastic vows.

He served for a time, a time long before Naum, at our Fishtown parish, Saint Alexander the Whirling Dervish.

V. Just Passing Through

THERE WAS NO ONE in the neighborhood who didn't love him, Orthodox, atheists, Jewish folks, Protestants, Catholics, and our Albanian Muslims alike.

His pockets were always filled with chocolate and candy for the neighborhood kids who greeted him as he shopped along Kensington Avenue, doing his daily marketing, pulling his wire-wheeled cart under the Tunnel.

Many a Monday the Teuta Ladies would come in to clean and find the church already sparkling, the church hall, the bathrooms, the trash put out, the sweeper run over the rugs, and the morning Nicky Zeo and Teddy the Horse caught the priest, Father Skender, cleaning, the young monastic priest swore them to secrecy about what he called his "external cleaning." When they tried to take the broom from him, he said, "My key to the Kingdom, why are you trying to take it from me?"

He'd sworn Konstandin Kendros to silence. "Please, Kenny, not till I'm gone."

Kenny, we called him. Cancer like you wouldn't believe. The doctors at Fox Chase Oncologic gave him six months. At the Monday check-up after the Sunday Father Skender anointed him . . .

The next Sunday, Konstandin Kendros came to Skender. "Nothing. It's all gone." Kenny lived another twelve years.

And there were others with similar stories to tell.

If you pressed him, Father Skendi would smile at you for a long minute and say, "These are stories we tell ourselves. Only God is good." And that was all he would say.

After a time, Skender was consecrated bishop. He lived in a single room at the back of our cathedral in University City on the other side of the Schuylkill.

He never varied from living the life of a monk. Him and his pistachio shell, somehow staying faithful to the apostolic calling. Steeped in the ancient ways. He knew how to overcome the temptations that stood in his way.

No episcopal palaces or stately homes on this earth. He had other conceptions of life. There was a cross over Bishop Skender's bed. He had a floor lamp, a stiff-backed chair, a writing table, a few books, one icon, and a small chest of drawers.

Once when Nicky Zeo went to visit at the bishop's tiny

rooms behind the cathedral, he asked, "Hierasi, where's all your furniture?"

"Where's yours?" Peshkopi said to Nicky.

Nicky said, "Hierasi, I'm just passing through."

Hierasi said, "Me too."

When he was our priest, Father Skender didn't come right out and punish the disobedient or the unruly.

"Or so it seems," said Rabbi Aaron.

The rabbi said, "Yes. No. Maybe. Okay, so no *overt* discipline, or defrocking, or excommunicating the unruly, but boy, when I was a young rabbi and new here in Fishtown, old Father Skendi, across the street there from the temple, took me as a friend . . .

"All he had to do was look at you that way, broken heart in his eyes . . . And you're the one depriving *him* and suddenly you're standing there awakened to the fact that you've defrocked yourself and cut yourself off from God's love."

As he was as a priest, Skender was the same as a father bishop.

When Bishop Skender came to visit a parish community, he never stayed less than a week. He stayed in the home of the parish priest or with one of the faithful, never in the same home twice and never at a hotel.

During the week of his annual visit, the bishop spent individual time with the elders, the ladies' group, the lay leaders. "Come and have breakfast" was his favorite quote from Lord Jesus. And the bishop would add, "My treat."

Weekdays, we'd see him walking the neighborhood during his episcopal visits. Talking to people at the bus stop in front of the church. Sitting on the front steps having a beer with the old folks after putting their trash on the curb or helping to sweep their pavement in the spring or shovel the sidewalk when it snowed. He loved shopping on the Avenue and trading stories with the merchants.

It wasn't unusual for him to visit the children at their schools, from kindergarten to high school. It was almost as if they loved presenting him to their classmates in his cassock, white beard, and skufia at Show and Tell.

"This is my bishop."

And he'd stand there smiling while the class applauded and cheered.

He used to visit the sick at Kensington Hospital or take the bus up to CFC prison.

"How are you making it?" he would ask everyone privately. "Is there anything I can do to help?" Then before leaving he would say to each and every person he met, "Please remember me in your prayers." And he meant it.

The bishop would ask the priest and the parish leadership, the choir, and the church school people the same questions: What are you reading for your soul? How is it for you, your prayer life? Are you going to confession when your heart hurts? Marriage okay? How are the kids, your parents?

"Not easy being a widow." Sipping tea with someone who'd been left alone, he'd say, "I know it myself."

"You are God's people," he would say. "Take care of each other. Be kind to one another. You are God's people. Be easy on God's people."

Once when Naum and his family got a call on vacation from the parish president telling them to return because the priest who was covering got sick . . . Naum got a call from the bishop. We don't know how it happened. "Father, please, it's your vacation. Stay with your family. I am covering. I will serve as a priest."

Walking around the church building and grounds, he would remark on the condition of the building. He would look at the furnace, the windows, and the ceiling, ask about the roof and the plumbing, telling the people, "Amazing job. How old is this building?" or "Do we know anyone who does carpentry?" Never overtly criticizing, but there was nothing that missed his eye.

And in the altar, "Come, Father, show me the antimension. Oh, the chalice and the spoons are so clean. Hmm . . . What do you do with the communion cloth when it comes to this condition?" Never chastising but never tolerating sloth.

"And Father," he would ask the priest, "has God shown you any vocations among our faithful? Do any of our men have a calling to serve God's people? Pray, and God will show you who has a heart to suffer with our Lord Christ for the sake of those He loves. Someone prayed for you, and for me. A healthy body replicates its cells," the bishop always said. "There are vocations out there. The laborers are few."

He would sit with the priest, Naum, alone in the altar for an hour or more, looking deeply, face to face, with the man he had blessed to attend seminary all those years ago.

"Father Naum," the bishop would tell him, "it's not wrong to follow the example of our Master, for us to have disciples. There is only one priest, Lord Jesus, and we, all of us, have a different obedience in His one priesthood. Call out to God and ask him to show you the next generation of servants, and the Holy Spirit will do the rest."

The choir and the church school staff, he spent much time with them, asking everyone, "Is the liturgy so beautiful that heaven shows through?" He wanted to make sure the ancient fires were kept alive as they *were once delivered* and always full of life.

VI. Three Questions

Bishop Skender would ask the parish leadership, "Is there anything I can do to help with the finances?" It always took them by surprise.

When Carol, our parish president, asked, "What can we do for you, Hierasi?"

He said, "A bus ticket to my next visitation, and a box lunch would be nice."

People would ask him, "Hierasi, why the bus?"

Teddy the Horse, who was top salesman at Auto Heaven on the Avenue, said, "Hierasi, I'll *give* you a car."

Bishop Skender traveled everywhere and visited all of his parish communities by bus. Many of them he had planted as missions, the little white-bearded old man in the black dress with the paper-bag suitcase. He traveled to the parishes in his care, coast to coast.

The bishop was self-sufficient, thick-headed, what we call *koka dru* in his desire to be independent, not a burden to anyone, and yet he was able to maintain a balance of give-and-take in relationships throughout his life, a reciprocal existence as befits a monk.

Perhaps the only indulgence he left himself was the memory of his Embelsi. Once when Naum asked him, "Hierasi, what do you do after the services are all over, when liturgy is finished for the day?"

He said, "When the parade is over? Father, I go home and I sit on the edge of my bed and I cry for my *Sweetness*."

Naum knew her name, Embelsi, meant "Sweetness."

He was our first and earliest bishop in America. He was from among us. He walked the bridge from the factory in the cold before light. Those who came after? They were from the seminary, or somewhere . . .

For a short time, Bishop Skender had been one of Naum's professors at seminary. He lived with the other monastics, across the road from the seminary student housing.

A monk called Vasily, who'd known Skender for a long time, told Naum, "Besides his love and prayer, the main characteristic of his life is his pastoral devotion. No matter the situation, wherever God places him, he prays to see God's purpose and to be a responsive icon of God's love."

When Captain Stefani's wife died, the retired cop offered, "The kids are raised and off on their own. I got nowhere to go, Hierasi, and all day ta get there . . . Pay my own freight, got a good pension . . . Teddy'd give us the car, let me be your driver. It'd be an honor, please."

Bishop Skender told Stefani the retired cop, "I very much appreciate your offer to drive. But one of the ways I manage to keep a balance of interior life, of prayer, and of pastoral service is, in fact, by taking the bus everywhere. I encounter so many people of such diverse backgrounds and needs . . .

"Sometimes, because of how weird I look to the American eye, I am a witness for Christ just by my presence and strange appearance amongst so many who otherwise would never have contact with Christ or the Orthodox Church. I don't even have to tell them . . . They seem to know.

"At the same time, Stefani," the bishop said, "such trips allow for large portions of time in which I am able to pray in silence."

He took a worn journal from his bag and showed Stefani.

Young Skender took a bus from Tenth and Filbert that long-ago day when he quit the factory and first left the home of his father and mother. Skender the civilian took the only seat remaining on the bus going south, determined to join the Marine Corps at Beaufort, South Carolina.

The stranger who sat next to him on the bus was a small, dark woman called Artesia. She was writing in a journal.

They didn't speak.

Somewhere in rural Maryland the woman, Artesia, got off the bus and walked into a field. Skender watched her as the bus pulled away. For some reason he couldn't take his eyes off her. When she turned and stopped, Skender felt she was looking directly at him.

As the bus pulled away, he turned in his seat and watched till the woman in the field was out of sight. He never saw her again.

On the seat was the book, *Artesia's Journal* . . .

And in her own hand:

Three Parables—Three Questions:

Parable 1
The devil went forth to sow his seed
Some of the devil's seed fell on rocky ground where it did not have much

soil. It sprang up quickly because the soil was shallow. But when the sun rose, the devil's seedlings were scorched, and they withered because they had no root, because Christ Jesus was there.

Question 1: How deep is the soil within me? What have I cultivated to grow in the soil of my heart? Is the rock in my rocky ground the Lord Jesus? Is my soil for rooting evil appetites shallow or deep? What is it within my heart that will wither at the appearing of God's risen Son?

Parable 2

Other of the seed sown by the devil fell among thorns, which grew up and choked the devil's seedlings.

Question 2: His crown of thorns, is it not enough for me, to choke the seedlings sown by the enemy?

Parable 3

Still other evil seed fell on ground ripe for rebellion, pride, self-direction, self-esteem, and produced a crop a hundredfold, sixtyfold, or thirtyfold.

Question 3: When the seeds of rebellion tempt me in pride, self-direction, and self-esteem to turn from love of God and neighbor, when the seed of death is sown by these things in my heart, does it find fertile ground for producing a crop of dead-end egocentric individuality, of evil?

When the bishop showed the journal to Stefani, the retired cop who had offered to be his driver, Bishop Skender said, "I'm hoping to one day return this book to its author."

And that's all he would say.

VII. A Servant of Salvation

PSFS.

Neon letters twenty-seven feet high
Visible twenty miles out and all around Philadelphia
Letters precise and slender as a mechanical pencil
Flexible-Flyer-Christmas-Sled Red
High atop the T-shaped skyscraping tower of
The Philadelphia Savings Fund Society

It drew them like a beacon to an empty meter at Twelfth and Market. Naum parked his Impala just across from the polished marble façade of the PSFS lobby, fished around, and found in the ashtray and down between the seats just enough quarters for an hour.

Deacon Dionysios opened the trunk and handed a soft caramel-colored leather satchel to the bishop.

The bishop held it up. "What's this?"

"Your paper-bag suitcase and all your episcopal paraphernalia are inside, Hierasi. We wanted you to have a sturdy bag with a good shoulder strap," the Deacon said.

His mitre and staff, all his vestments and books, he carried wrapped in old pillowcases inside his travel-worn paper bag.

"Thank you, Father Deacon," said Bishop Skender.

In the terminal, the bishop sat himself on one of the hard plastic seats bolted to the floor. He told Naum and the men, "I am grateful. Thank you."

Two-Beer Eddie asked, "If ya could wave your bishop's candles over all these homeless slumping around the walls and change 'em ta citizens, would ya?"

The old bishop was tired. He said, "God has given freedom, who am I to take it away? I might wave it over me and join them."

"Would ya at least try an' counsel 'em?" Eddie said.

The bishop said, "Edon, I'm a servant of the salvation of God's people, not a counselor."

No one noticed our Teuta Ladies, Ramona and Madeline, wearing their sunglasses in the coffee shop.

The bishop pulled Naum close. "Father, I'd like to wait for the bus alone."

He thanked the men again, and they left with his blessing.

Half an hour later, Ramona nudged Madeline, both watching through tears. "We can't tell about this. Never."

The bishop stood, opened his new leather satchel on the seat, and removed his old paper-bag suitcase.

He took off his new shoes and put on his old ones.

Shed his new scarf and coat, smiled like he'd seen an old friend in an unexpected place, and slipped into the familiar comfort of his thread-thin brown Chesterfield with the mismatched buttons.

He went among the men huddled along the wall and found one with no shoes and another without a coat.

He recognized the one woman against the wall who carried all her things in a black plastic trash bag. They called her Carnation Betty because she always wore a rose.

Bishop Skendi said, "Hi, Betty, remember me?"

She looked up and said, "Sure, Iskender. I remember you, and your mother and father too. They were always nice to me."

Bishop Skendi handed Betty the caramel-colored leather satchel. "Look, Bet," he said, "it has an adjustable shoulder strap."

She gave it the eye and told him, "I never cared for that

color," and stuffed the leather satchel in her 42-gallon contractor trash bag.

He noticed her rose. But everybody in the neighborhood knew how she reacted if you called her carnation a rose.

The bishop gave out chocolate and candy and went back to his seat.

He took his glasses and Artesia's journal from his paper bag.

The old man with the white beard, a sight in his cassock and skufia. Not hearing the announcer. Not smelling the smells. Blind to the stage decoration designed to deceive people by obscuring *the fashion of this world which passeth away.*

Reading with his fingertips. Running the flat of his hand in swirls over the feel of each familiar page. Wondering what would have happened had he found a seat in the front of the bus.

Ramona and Madeline swore each other to secrecy and left the Tenth and Filbert bus station, agreeing that if the time ever came, hypothetically speaking, when they just couldn't resist, one of them would have to confess to Naum and tell the girls in the Teuta Ladies Baking Society about the bishop giving away his new leather bag, his leather-soled oxblood Thom McAns, the scarf and the beautiful coat, and confess they'd gotten so hungry waiting all that time in the bus station coffee shop that they'd eaten the bishop's box lunch.

Jenny's Sow Shad Soup

—⊱•⊰—

8 ounces fresh mushrooms, sliced
4 slices bacon
1 cup red wine
2 quarts water
1 large onion, chopped
1 rib celery, chopped
1 tbsp. chopped fresh parsley
2 tbsp. flour
2 bay leaves
1/2 tsp thyme
4 peppercorns
Salt—she didn't say how much
Ground black pepper—same deal

Instructions (in Jenny's words):

Ya heat the water in a pot, even you can do that, right? Then ya add the fish head, the backbone, the tail, the fins. Throw in the onions and celery, the bay leaves, parsley, the wine, the peppercorns, the salt, and thyme.

Ya simmer the whole thing for an hour or so, very low heat, don't boil it, ya listening?

Strain the liquid, then measure it, then reduce it, boil it down to four cups or so.

Then ya separate out the head and the backbone from the rest of the pot, the solids . . . Ya following?

Then, ya take with a fork and ya pull the meat from the head and backbone. Don't toss it. Just set it aside on a saucer or something.

Fry the bacon in one a them big cast-iron skillets. Ya got one, right? Yeah, who don't? Then ya drain the bacon, okay?

Measure out two tablespoons of bacon grease. Sauté the mushrooms in the bacon grease for a few, add the flour, and ya make a roux, three or four minutes. Ya know what that is, right? Ya gotta be stirring constantly.

Slowly add the fish broth, all of it, then ya simmer for six, seven minutes, stirring as you go. Poach the roe in a little water, but don't boil it, ten minutes, maybe, or until ya see it's cooked through, depending on the size.

Cut the roe sacs in half, that's how ya check for doneness. Remove the roe outta the sacs, put it directly in the broth. Add your sautéed mushrooms, your flaked fish, and a little pepper. Heat it all up again, then ya serve it with the strips of bacon and plenty of bread on the side, like I did for you.

Ya got that?

F ATHER STEPHEN N. SINIARI is a priest of the OCA Diocese of the South. During almost forty years in ministry, Fr. Stephen served parishes in New England and the Philadelphia/South Jersey area while working full time for an international agency as a street outreach worker, serving homeless, at-risk, and trafficked teens. Born and raised in Philadelphia, Fr. Stephen currently lives on the Florida Gulf Coast with Margot, his wife of more than forty years.

We hope you have enjoyed and benefited from this book. Your financial support makes it possible to continue our nonprofit ministry both in print and online. Because the proceeds from our book sales only partially cover the costs of operating **Ancient Faith Publishing** and **Ancient Faith Radio**, we greatly appreciate the generosity of our readers and listeners. Donations are tax deductible and can be made at **www.ancientfaith.com.**

To view our other publications,
please visit our website: **store.ancientfaith.com**

 **ANCIENT FAITH RADIO**

Bringing you Orthodox Christian music, readings, prayers, teaching, and podcasts 24 hours a day since 2004 at
www.ancientfaith.com

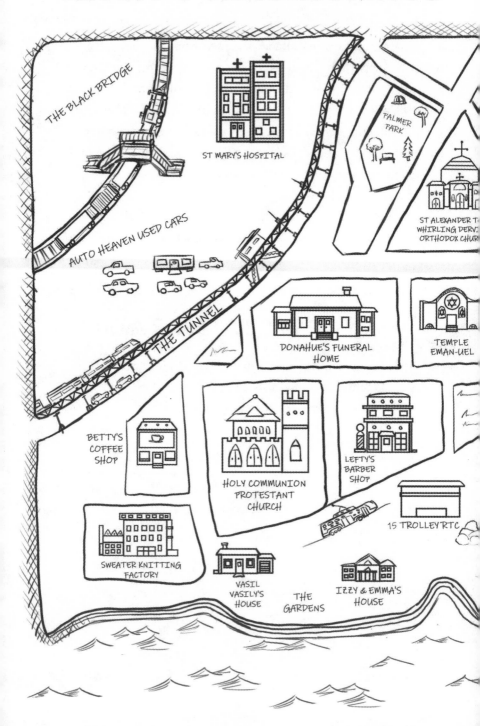